Nothing Natural

JENNY DISKI

SIMON AND SCHUSTER

NEW YORK

The author gratefully acknowledges permission to reprint lyrics
from "As Long as He Needs Me," by Lionel Bart, from the
Columbia Pictures-Romulus film *Oliver!* Copyright © 1960
Lakeview Music Co., Ltd., London, England. All U.S. and Cana-
dian publication rights controlled by TRO—Hollis Music, Inc.,
New York. Used by permission.

Quality Printing and Binding by:
Orange Graphics
P.O. Box 791
Orange, VA 22960 U.S.A.

For Roger, with love

Let nothing be called natural
In an age of bloody confusion,
Ordered disorder, planned caprice,
And dehumanized humanity, lest all things
Be held unalterable.

BERTOLT BRECHT

ONE

Morning. Rachel woke with the late summer sunshine breaking through a crack in the curtains. A warm day with blue skies. Morning seemed more hopeful in the summer; it was possible to open her eyes and get out of bed without a struggle, without fighting that weight lying on her chest and the powerful need to return to oblivion. Warm days, light clothing, and a sense of well-being went together. Perhaps if she lived in a country where the sun was guaranteed, where, even before she opened her eyes, she would know that the sun was streaming into her room; perhaps then she would be certain too of her mood. But then, perhaps, a life without shadows and dull grey skies would become tedious. One-dimensional. Change was change, even if it was only out there, beyond her window.

She got out of bed and pulled a tee shirt over her head, made for the kitchen and turned on the electric kettle. Down to the bathroom, had a pee, brushed her teeth and splashed water over her face, then collected *The Times* from where it had been pushed halfway through the letterbox. The air felt fresh and warm around her naked legs as she poured the boiling water into the teapot and then stood by the open kitchen window inspecting the plants while she waited for the tea to brew. She gazed out of the window. There was a hole in the road where some gas pipes were being laid. At least they had finished drilling; her peaceful holiday mornings had been shattered for the past couple of days by the sound of the road being torn up, and it had taken her some moments before she had understood that the disruption was external. This morning had been blissfully silent, the hole deserted and festooned with a safety barrier of coloured ribbon; a chasm outside her front door.

Now pouring the tea and straightening out the paper she was conscious of the calm, and swilled the peace and solitude around like a meditative mouthwash, storing it in her memory for the days when work and childcare made mornings hectic and noisy. Sometimes she could charge herself with quiet, good times, like a battery, for use later when things became dismal.

She scanned the front page and saw that the news was as yesterday. Summer news: a strike, politicians on holiday, an earthquake somewhere hot. She sipped her tea and thought of Carrie in Italy with Michael. Carrie, eight and worried about earthquakes in West Hampstead, was far enough away from the epicentre in Sicily not really to concern Rachel. She hoped Michael had the sense not to let her see the news; as far as Carrie was concerned an earthquake in the same hemisphere was worth trembling over. Little shoulders shaking, thrilling with the thrill of fear, wide-eyed, mouthing, "Nooo . . . an EARTHQUAKE! Help!"

Rachel smiled at the image and turned the page. Home news. She put her cup down slowly and blinked at the picture at the bottom of the page. Two drawings, of a man and a woman. Artist's impressions. The man in the top drawing was instantly recognizable as Joshua. Her immediate reaction was pleasure at seeing his face, and amusement that this stereotype, who would look like any man with a three-day growth of bristles, steely brush of cropped hair and broad, deeply lined face, should be for her Joshua. She had time before reading the paragraph above to imagine thousands of people recognizing friends and lovers in this photofit image. She remained amused as she read the headline: COUPLE SOUGHT IN SEX ATTACK. Well, that's appropriate, she thought as she started to read the story. A girl aged sixteen had been lured by the couple into their car, a blue Fiesta, and raped. Afterwards she had been "forced to take part in other sexual acts with the couple. Police in Inverness have set up a hotline, witnesses or anyone having any information should ring the following number . . ."

Rachel felt the heartbeat following the final sentence thud like a jackhammer against her ribs. She looked again at the picture as she reached automatically for a cigarette. The hair and beard were exactly right, the mouth not quite, but then she always saw him in her mind as smiling, grinning, his perfect white teeth bared. The dark eyes were fixed and staring, looking like a scared sixteen-year-old's image of a mad rapist. But they also, didn't they, looked like Joshua's eyes when he fucked her: glaring, cold and angry. Didn't they? Was she imagining that? The more she looked the more she didn't know if she was seeing what was there; and at the same time she became certain that she was staring at a remarkable likeness of Joshua Abelman, her lover for the past three years. She felt panic rising from deep in her abdomen, all the objective amusement of a moment before driven away by the phrase: "Police in Inverness . . ."

She had last seen him three weeks ago, just before she went to Cornwall.

"Are you going away?" she had asked him.

"Yes, I'm spending a week in Scotland in late August."

Naturally she didn't ask where exactly, or who with.

It was now the last week in August, Rachel having returned home three days before. Joshua would be in Scotland. Late August; the first of September was three days from now. The girl had been attacked the day before, Monday, near Drumnadrochit on Loch Ness. She breathed long slow breaths and sat quite still as she stared first at the picture and then at the words above. He wouldn't, she thought, he wouldn't be so stupid. And then she noticed that she had thought *wouldn't*, not *couldn't*. Most people would be able to think *couldn't* of their lovers. *Wouldn't* related to intelligence and foresight, not to capacity or desire. She put the thought aside for the time being and looked at the picture of the woman. An intelligent, middle-class face, with cropped boyish hair and wide dark eyes. She didn't recognize anyone she knew in the drawing, but it was the face of someone she might have known, someone she could imagine Joshua with. She was a woman in her thirties who looked ten years younger, who might look childlike sometimes. Like Rachel could look. What had Joshua said? "You've got the body of an eighteen-year-old and the mind of a wise old woman. A perfect combination."

Little girls with a wealth of experience, who knew how to play the game. Rachel sipped her tea and smoked, but her eyes kept returning to the drawing. This is silly, she thought, absurd. You're playing games with yourself. There is only the coincidence of Scotland, nothing real. The photofit looks like a million men and you just happen to know one of the type. The car is wrong, anyway: Joshua drives a Saab not a Fiesta. And people don't do that; not people you know. But people *do* do that, have done it, and worse. And of course *somebody* knows them.

She debated for some time but there was really no conclusion to arrive at. The point was that she knew him to be capable of exactly that sort of thing, that was what she had learned in the last three years. She had come to understand that, given the chance, people could live out their fantasies, and that, given their head, the fantasies could grow and seep into real life until sometimes it was hard to tell the difference. She had understood, not intellectually, but really come to know through Joshua and her relationship with him, that the dark, passing fantasies of rape and violence which she had once noticed and dismissed from her mind were the overflow from a stream within herself that was as real and as much a part of her as, say, her love for Carrie. She knew that he was capable of anything and she had learned from him that that was also true of her. But the point was that, once known, one was in a position to deal with it. What she had always felt about Joshua was that he intelligently sublimated his more dangerous needs with willing victims like herself. And vice versa. He was clever, he understood what was going on. So did she; surely that was what their relationship was about.

Damn, she thought, if only it hadn't been in Scotland. Without that the passing resemblance would have meant nothing, would have been grounds for a wry smile, a nod to the possibilities. But Scotland plus her memory of all the conversations they had had about finding a second woman . . . Not that he ever called women women, they were always "girls."

"You must know someone, a girl you could get to come round, Rachel?"

"I don't. You don't understand: there are some women I know who are lesbians who might make love to me but wouldn't touch you with a bargepole. And there are some women I know who might make love to you but being of a more or less feminist persuasion wouldn't consider a threesome for your entertainment. And the other women I know just . . . wouldn't. Anyway I'm amazed you haven't long since acted that one out."

"Yes, it surprises me too," he smiled, "but none of the girls I know would wear it. You *must* know someone."

"Well I don't. If you care that much about it you'll have to organize it yourself."

"It's not desperate, just something I'd like to try."

Nothing had ever come of it beyond talk, but she was surprised to learn that she was the only woman he had found even to consider the proposal. What about the other things they did together? She had always supposed that Joshua had several women who were prepared to indulge his fantasies (and theirs) just as she did, only more so. She felt herself to be something of a novice in the field.

When she had mentioned the idea of a threesome to Michael and other men friends, just to see their reaction, it turned out to be a pet fantasy of theirs too. It seemed something of a universal of the male psyche. They all wanted it but no one she knew had achieved it. Which meant, getting back to the newspaper, that it could have been anyone. She took her cup to the sink and washed it up, then she went back to the bedroom to get dressed. She chose another tee shirt from her wardrobe and a pair of light, baggy jeans. She stripped off the tee shirt she had on and stood naked while she pulled out a pair of pants from the drawer. She was brown from the Cornish sun, except for a small triangle around her pubic hair which stood out blackly from the band of pale flesh around it. Rachel liked to be naked, liked her body, which was small, compact and effortlessly thin. She looked at herself in the mirror as she pulled on her pants and was consciously satisfied with what she saw. She was in good shape, supple and firm, it *was* the body of a young woman, but then she didn't feel it ought to be anything else. It didn't seem to her that at thirty-four her flesh should be sagging or her muscles flabby. She was lucky in her body, but somehow she

suspected that bodies lived up to the assumptions of their own-
ers. It hadn't crossed her mind that she ought to be getting
middle-aged and crêpey. But it did strike her as surprising that
she, whose mind felt so elderly and constantly dissatisfied with
itself, with who she was, should be so easy about herself physically. To be psychologically consistent she ought she supposed
to loathe her body, to see it as too fat, or too thin, to wish her
breasts bigger, her nose smaller, her hair straighter. In fact, as
she got older she enjoyed how she looked more and more. She
liked her wild curly hair, and her long thin face. She was pleased
by the Jewishness of it, the Semitic nose, small black eyes and
full mouth. She liked the contours of her ribs and shoulder blade
which stood out as she turned sideways to the mirror, and the
jutting curve of her sharp hipbone above the neat brown thigh.
She looked pretty much the way she wanted herself to look and
didn't hanker after straight blonde hair and all the other things
she wasn't. Which was extraordinary; something not to have to
angst about. She looked at herself in the mirror with relief at
finding pleasure in it.

Rachel pulled on her clothes and turned back to the mirror.
Joshua would like the tee shirt, not the baggy trousers. She
could wear the tee shirt with shorts if he came, he'd like that.

Christ, I wish I could stop it, she muttered to herself, I can't
even get dressed without thinking about him.

There probably wasn't an hour in a day when she didn't think
of Joshua who, she reminded herself fiercely time and again,
almost certainly thought of her only minutes before he called.
How many times in three years can you consider the nature of
your feelings for someone? Countless, countless times, it appeared. No matter that there was never any satisfactory conclusion, or even much point in the query. She was clearly obsessed
but that, she supposed, was what other people called love. She
couldn't call it that; if it was then the world had got it wrong. No
one in their right mind would sing hymns of praise for what she
felt about Joshua. No one would extol it, write songs, make misty
movies. Joshua was a catastrophe that had happened to her; a
growing tumour she had most uneasily learned to live with.
Joshua was a disaster and didn't feel like anything else. She
couldn't pretend any pleasure in her need, or any level of emo-

tion higher than mud. She wanted him, needed him to talk with, to fuck, to beat her, to be amused by her, but she was damned if she loved him. And she didn't want to wash his socks, cook for him, or wake in the morning beside him, did she? Did she? How could she, he really wasn't there. He was all hollowed out, an emptied man.

"What you see is what there is," he had said once, warning her against what she had carefully expressed no need for.

That was true. He was a shell who provided for her needs because they were his needs too. There wasn't anything beyond that. But what if this cipher turned out to be a rapist, a real force of destruction out there in the world, what did that mean for her, about her? What did it mean that she thought it even possible? She wasn't sure if it made any difference if he had really done it or not.

The phone rang. She knew it wouldn't be Joshua.

"Just checking to see you're still with us, Mrs Kee. Not pregnant or rushing off on a second honeymoon?"

It was Donald Soames, head of the local Home Tutoring centre. Rachel was employed by the Education Authority as a tutor to kids who were not in school. Usually they were adolescents who had been suspended for being disruptive, sometimes they were waiting for places in special schools for mental or physical disabilities. Rachel usually got the disruptive ones. Donald Soames thought she was good with the difficult kids and often passed on the ones that other tutors had refused to teach. Sometimes it worked out, sometimes it didn't. She was, in any case, getting tired of problem kids; the energy had gone, it was more or less a way of earning money while still being available to pick Carrie up from school.

She felt her back teeth clamp together.

"Hello, Donald, no, no changes."

"Jolly good. One never knows after the long summer break. So you can get back to young Michelle and her ghastly problems, can you?"

"Yes. I'll go round in a couple of days and arrange this year's timetable with her." Rachel was always brisk with Donald who, given half a chance, would witter on for hours about "the bods up in County Hall" knowing nothing of life down among the "face-workers" of the education system. Donald actually spent his entire working life knee-deep in files and on the phone, and only rarely actually saw a real life pupil.

"Good. Jolly good. Do come down to the Centre if you need anything in the way of books. Bye-bye for now."

When she put the phone down she felt something like relief. A kind of structure loomed; Carrie would be home and back at school in a few days and she would be back tutoring for two hours a day. Mixed feelings. Initial commitment to anything was a barrier she had to overcome, a sense of acute unease about any kind of regularity, especially when it was people she had to commit herself to. But she knew that she had to go through that. Empty, aimless days were, in the long run, dangerous. In Cornwall where the official title "holiday" permitted it, she had lain for long days on Laura's unmown grass, soaking up the sun, taking in the scent and sounds of rural life. Like a stone. Usually she had a book with her, and even got through two novels while she was there, but the real pleasure was just holding still, doing absolutely nothing. Even thoughts of Joshua faded slightly. She had had a powerful need to stay there. A slow, easy life. Talking with Laura, feeling easy about being there, accepted. The rhythm of lying fallow suited her. But there was Carrie and also the knowledge that eventually indolence would go sour on her. There wasn't ever any doubt that she would have to go back and get on with it, as much as she dreaded it. And now, seeing how in a few days life would start to have a pattern to it she felt, amidst the anxiety, some energy waiting to be used and some pleasure at the forthcoming order.

But the lurking anxiety was mixed with concern about the newspaper item. She spent the rest of the morning pottering around the flat, dusting, polishing things in a haphazard way, returning half a dozen times to the paper on the table to stare at the picture. Finally she took some scissors from the drawer in the kitchen table and clipped the report. She slipped it into her diary in her bag, and turned to look vaguely out of the window. The hole in the road remained unattended. She wondered how to spend the rest of the day, her earlier sense of optimism having dissipated. I could use the time productively, she thought, and go to the Centre to sort out some books. This she rejected even as she considered it. Or go on a spending spree in Hampstead. Or stay at home and masturbate. Very funny. Though if I don't go out, she mused, that's just what I will end up doing. Why? Need or comfort? Both.

Joshua hovered around the edges of her thoughts like a flashing red light just on the periphery of her vision.

"I don't want to think about . . . anything," she whispered to the street outside. Joshua, sex, her need, the newscuttings were off limits for the afternoon. Hampstead, clothes, spending money. No work, no brooding, she decided. And then I get the chance to wallow in guilt about spending money. I can make myself feel good and bad all at one go and without owing it to anyone but me.

Go on, kid, she told herself, spend, spend, spend.

TWO

Three years before, just after Michael had moved out, Rachel met Joshua at a dinner party. They had been invited so that they could meet. Molly Cassel, an old school friend of Rachel's, liked throwing people together and when she heard that Rachel and Michael had separated she had immediately got on the phone.

"Rachel," Molly had enthused on the phone. "You must come and meet my friend Joshua."

"Why? I'm not really in the mood for meeting men. What's so special?"

"Well, he's a strange bloke. Very clever, but a bit odd. Not someone to get involved with, but interesting."

"So far it sounds like I could live without him. Why isn't he someone to get involved with? Not," she added hurriedly, "that I'm a candidate for involvement."

"Oh, he screws around a lot, but never more than once with any one woman. He really messes people up. He's got two kids from an ex-marriage he sees all the time, but he's a bit weird about women."

"Molly, you're doing a lousy selling job. I don't need a one-night stand; I don't need anything actually. Anyway, what's his problem with women?" This wasn't genuine curiosity, just conversation.

"I don't know. He's really a friend of Tom's. I suppose he gets bored easily."

"Very easily. This is the least enticing invitation I've had in weeks. Thanks all the same but I'll skip it. He probably can't get it up more than once. Low sex drive type. Woman hater."

"Mm . . . I gather that's pretty much it, about not getting it up, I mean. But he's terribly clever, you'd enjoy talking to him."

"No!"

Three weeks later, the telephone conversation forgotten, Molly had invited her to dinner. Rachel, having just seen off her current lover and thereby what remained of her social life, went with a minimum of enthusiasm. She arrived late to find Molly, Tom and Joshua already seated at the refectory table dipping into the houmous. She glared briefly at Molly as she was introduced to Joshua, and sitting at the table prepared to jolly her way through another pointless evening. She recollected what a waste of time socializing was and how much she liked spending the evenings alone in her flat. She longed to be there.

Joshua smiled at her. He directed a beam of gleaming white teeth and knowing amusement straight towards her; he shone himself at her.

Oh shit, she thought, I've seen this one before. The Charmer.

Joshua gave her his full and undivided attention, smiling all the while. The questions came thick and fast, impudently personal while the shining white grin rubbed the edge of rudeness off them. The act was excellent, but it *was* one she had seen before, and she found herself watching his technique with some admiration. She answered his questions as frankly as he put them as if she were being interviewed. So she had split up with her husband? Yes, well they'd never found a way of introducing each other at parties—my husband, my wife, never slipped comfortably from their lips, so they had decided that my ex-husband etc. came much more easily. Relations were cordial, she added. But why had they broken up? Well, they'd been leading separate lives sexually for some time and it had got harder and harder to organize what with living in the same place, so Michael had bought a flat just round the corner. Hadn't they been jealous of each other's affairs? Yes and no, but mostly no.

And so on. All the time smiling and polite. Her life history was requested and given with some major omissions. She had been adopted? And had she known Molly for long? A teacher? And what did she enjoy doing?

"Dancing, reading and fucking," Rachel replied with a polite social smile on her face.

Molly choked on her fruit salad while Tom, a dour individual, examined his spoon carefully to check he had eaten everything on it with the last mouthful. Joshua's grin, improbably, doubled. There had been all along a collusion between himself and Rachel; they looked each other squarely in the eyes as they spoke, each knowing that the other knew precisely what the game was. The act was good, total attention with just a touch of superiority; enough to flatter Rachel while at the same time making her feel uneasy, slightly attacked. She was to be hypnotized by his dark, intent eyes and the paradoxically enchanting, easy smile. She was to be thrown off balance but feel that somehow he was really interested in her, just her. A fascinated rabbit dying to be gobbled up.

Except, she though, that I see through you, sunshine. You're just a little too calculating, or I'm a little too smart.

At the end of the evening he stood up and offered her a lift home. She looked at him in his tweed suit: the clothes were good, not too smart. He was a large man, plump actually, but tall enough not to look absurd. She like large—fat—men; small thin ones left her cold, literally. He looked grown up, confident, his wide fleshy face made massive by the deep furrows that outlined his mouth and ran seriously across his spacious brow; his beard was one of those carefully contrived to seem no more than a reluctance to shave but was in fact a permanent face-altering feature, his short grey hair was shot through with its original black. He didn't look like a sexual incompetent, but you never could tell. More often than not the confidence was all exterior and once the clothes were off it broke apart to reveal, yet again, a little boy. But it might be interesting to see what was what. She wasn't committed one way or another and at worst she was in for a single boring night, if Molly was right. She didn't feel in any way threatened by this man, on the contrary, she felt that she controlled the situation. She had loaned her car to Michael who had Carrie for the night, so she accepted the lift.

She was relieved to be back in her own territory, as she

turned on the living room lights. Joshua prowled around reading book titles on her shelves, investigating the kitchen which opened out from the living room. It was a good, comfortable place; an old sofa covered with a North African rug, an armchair, stripped wooden chests acting as surfaces for rocks and shells gathered from various seashores, and bookshelves filling the alcoves. Rachel's small rural longings were catered for by masses of plants which flourished wherever light and available space permitted. She turned on the kitchen light to make coffee; Joshua turned it off.

"I don't want anything. Put on some music."

Oh dear, Rachel thought, and began to feel a little gloomy. When it came to it even one boring night seemed too much. She imagined herself, as she put on a tape of vintage Fred Astaire, lying awake beside a sleeping post-coital man, the hours dragging slowly by. He would certainly snore, and she would lie gazing into the darkness wishing him away, wishing him never there in the first place, wanting her bed to herself, remembering that mediocre sex wasn't better than none at all.

Maybe, she mused, I'd better send him home now, he's not even all that attractive. There certainly wasn't that ache deep in her abdomen that made him necessary to her. But he held her now and moved slowly to the music with her in his arms. He had turned off all the other lights so that the room was in darkness and as they rocked softly together she knew it was too late to tell him to go. She decided that she'd just have to put up with the night ahead; she didn't want a scene, and in any case, it wasn't unpleasant, swaying in the darkness. Joshua kissed her slowly and then led her by the hand next door into the unlit bedroom. He undressed her efficiently while she stood passive, watching his face as his fingers undid the buttons of the tee shirt she normally just pulled over her head. When she was naked he ran his hands down her back and slowly over her buttocks, then lay her on the bed while he took off his own clothes carefully, unhurriedly. She lay watching him, and sensing his extraordinary confidence began to feel what she had been supposed to feel at dinner—impressed, excited, uncertain. Now she wanted him.

Joshua got on to the bed beside her, on his side, resting on his elbow. His hand moved across her belly and up to stroke each breast, then, as his hand moved down towards her vulva he ducked his head and sucked for a moment at each nipple. Lifting his head he looked carefully at her face, watching; a long, cold stare. He kept his eyes on her all the time, his face impassive, observing, as his fingers found her vulva. He parted the labia and began expertly to massage her clitoris, all the time keeping his eyes on her face, observing her reactions, like a technician working on a new model of a machine he had spent a lifetime servicing. The long, slow strokes gave way, as she got wetter, to a circular motion, and she began to breathe deeper and faster as he increased the pressure and speed. Her eyes became vague and distant, focusing on the waves rising from her wet, excited cunt and the sudden overwhelming need to be penetrated, filled. He slipped a finger deep inside her and she gasped, breathing heavier, beginning to moan softly as thumb rubbed clitoris and finger moved slowly inside. Joshua watched unblinking as she started to move her pelvis rhythmically up and down against the movement of his hand to increase the pressure and dropped her knees against the bed and his thigh so that she was wide open. She came with small sharp cries, lifting her hips off the bed, arching her back and grasping the arm that still worked on her between her thighs, pressing hard against the heel of his hand to the rhythm of the contractions pulsing inside her.

"Please . . . please . . ." she sobbed, then holding her breath for a long moment relaxed down beside him, releasing the air in her lungs and feeling her heart pounding. Joshua pulled her on top of him and she saw his face beneath her, the eyes still watching, cold, but glistening icily with excitement. He put her hand onto his penis so that she could guide it into her, and then with his hands on her hips moved her slowly up and down. As she began to come again she felt and heard him slapping her, quite gently, on the bottom, almost tentatively, and when he saw that she continued to move, a little harder, not so that it hurt but so that the sound of each slap rang around the room.

Christ, she thought, this is new. What is this?

Then the feeling of his penis inside her, the sound, and the smarting on her buttocks made her come with long deep moans and she heard and felt him coming in grunting spasms.

She lay sprawled on his chest for a long while, catching her breath and feeling her body gradually quieten. She wondered in the silence about the smacking. She had never been with anyone who was into spanking—she supposed that was what it was. She was curious and a little embarrassed, but also excited by it.

"Fancy a fuck?" Joshua spoke jauntily into her ear in his rich acquired Oxbridge tones.

"What did you say your name was? Never mind, let's do it!"

He rolled over so that she was underneath him and this time fucked her hard and fast, whispering, "Can you feel me deep inside you? Suck me into you."

His eyes remained open all the time still looking angrily at her and when they had both come he pulled out of her almost immediately so that Rachel had to catch her breath at the suddenness of his absence. Then he lay still with one arm around her, his eyes finally closed.

Rachel lay in the dark room next to the sleeping man who breathed heavily.

Well, that wasn't what I'd been led to expect, she thought. It was, on the whole, worth a sleepless night, she decided. She dozed off and on, waking often with sudden starts. Once Joshua woke as she jerked awake and whispered to her, "It's all right, darling, it's me, Joshua, don't be frightened."

They both woke early, she a little before him, and as he opened his eyes and oriented himself she saw him stare sharply at her before he realized that she was awake too. He was out of bed instantly.

"I've got to go. Taking the kids to the country today. No, I don't want tea. Thanks."

He was dressed within seconds, glanced at her briefly and nodded a curt, unsmiling " 'Bye" as he left barely five minutes after he had woken.

"Jesus," Rachel whispered to the icy cloud that hung heavily in her bedroom, "Jesus Christ."

After Joshua left Rachel felt nothing. She was tired and the day was taken up with Carrie. Michael returned her and the car and they all had lunch out. She took Carrie to her piano lesson and then whiled away the hours pleasantly enough before it was time for Carrie's bedtime story. Then Rachel sat in her living room, soaking up the silence, thinking of the night before. She didn't actually feel nothing; she felt numb, chilled by the way Joshua had exited. She had no expectations of seeing him again, it was the most clear-cut one-night stand she could remember. There was no need and no point in thinking about him.

But still, I would want more, because it was good, she thought; why wouldn't he want more? More didn't have to mean more intensity, she didn't want that anyway, it could just mean *more*. She didn't, on last night's showing, believe what Molly had told her. If he didn't see women a second time it was more likely a fear of intimacy than technical problems. She imagined sound waves pulsing around the planet, dissipating into space, carrying the message from male humanity, the inevitable male wail: "*I can't bear people making demands on me!*"

She pictured Man, lying on a sofa, the back of his hand to his forehead. She pictured Woman laughing helplessly at the absurdity of it.

How many men had uttered one or other version to her long before she had time to explain that she didn't want commitment, domesticity or a live-in companion? All of them one way or another. And when she had explained, they had all looked at her in disbelief: she's saying, but she doesn't really mean it, she's a woman after all, they all said with their eyes.

Somewhere, she thought, there must be a man who wouldn't mistake me for his mother. Damn the little boys, where are the grown-ups? It was true though that most women did seem to want to set up home, have kids with someone; most men too presumably, since they were marrying the women. Why didn't she? Well, she had of course, but not with conviction. She and Michael had contracted for Carrie's babyhood and left the rest open. She had never imagined herself living long-term with anyone, not even as an adolescent had she had fantasies of happily-ever-after. The unhappily-ever-after of her own family probably accounted for that, but still, all the agents of conditioning, the fairy stories, books, songs, education, seemed not to have left much mark. Was it really true? Was she lying to herself? You couldn't ever know finally if you were telling yourself the truth, but she really did seem more capable of and contented with living alone than anyone else she knew. I just slipped through the net, she decided. She wanted sex and friendship, they didn't have to go together.

But still, here she was after a satisfying night of sex, feeling wretched. She did feel miserable, low. One-night stands—she had heard talk of women who, having bedded a stranger the night before, never gave them another thought. It had never been like that for her, and she hadn't met any other women who could do it either—only heard tell of them. Sometimes, at worst, there was disgust, or regret; sometimes she wanted a man to ring her, make contact; or she fantasized, recollected. All sorts of reactions, but the experience, whatever it was like, good or bad, never just dropped away from her as if it had never happened once the man had walked out of the door.

She supposed men could do it. Men said they did and this fascinated her. She couldn't imagine not thinking about someone she had just fucked, however casually. If it were true that people did then she envied them enormously. Perhaps it was just bluster. But then again perhaps she needed not to believe it because otherwise she was so much more vulnerable than them. Nothing was more humiliating than thinking about someone you knew was not thinking of you.

She couldn't fit the two thoughts together. She she *she* blustered, gave the impression very effectively of being tough and independent. Did other people believe her? That *was* how she wanted to be. To service a need and then forget it. She didn't think about lunch once she'd eaten it. Was it like that for men? A pressing need in the testes which once relieved no longer concerned them. She had dark thoughts about biology. The amorphous need of women's sexuality: how many orgasms were enough? Men evacuate; women escalate. It was one thing not wanting to cook some man's dinner, another not wanting more of the same. And more. Greedy bitch. Doomed by greed and biology.

What she needed was a completely unemotional (ha!) sexual

affair. Fun and fucks. She could go to the movies with friends, she didn't need a social relationship, just two equal, adult people coming together (ho!) for friendly sex. Nothing heavy. Was she telling the truth? Yes, yes, she was. But there did seem to be a problem between body and mind. Not insuperable, she assured herself.

But, God, she did feel miserable.

Two weeks later Joshua called.

"Are you free this evening?"

"Sorry, no. Why don't you come for dinner tomorrow? Around eight."

She didn't have anything on that night but she wanted time to think about it.

"Right. See you then."

So. It wasn't exactly a speedy return of service, but it *was* more than once; Molly apparently had been misinformed and she, Rachel, had assessed their night together correctly. It had been good enough to warrant more. He wanted more of her, had enjoyed her enough to come back for a second helping. She was pleased with herself, though there was a small sneering voice in her head which told her not to be so bloody grateful. Don't be so pathetic, why are you always so astonished when a man wants to see you again?

Well, anyway, tomorrow night. She smiled to herself. Dinner. She pictured sitting at the living room table with him eating— what?—sipping wine, anticipating good sex later. She would make the Greek lamb and a fresh fruit salad. Nothing complicated, and she would buy a really nice bottle of wine. She feasted for the rest of the evening on the following night. Smug.

She remembered suddenly how he had smacked her and wondered how she would feel if it happened again. She couldn't figure it out: it was, she had to suppose, aggressive. You smack someone if you're angry with them, and she recalled his eyes as he made love to her. Well, if Joshua were a woman-hater he had certainly made a careful study of his enemy. Her image, if she had thought about it at all, of "spankers" was of ex-public-school Englishmen, men who were sexually inadequate, replacing the terror of real sex with a bottom fetish. Repressed homosexuals punishing Mummy for being a whore. Chinless wonders, thin,

pallid men who sometimes hit the headlines and made the
nation laugh. The English Disease. What went with it? Black
stockings and suspenders; little maids' outfits. Embarrassing.

None of this fitted her impression of Joshua. What she had
picked up from him was anger and authority, he was no chinless
wonder. Her mind wandered towards De Sade, *Justine*, *The
Story of O*. That began to fit the image better; but he had, after
all, only smacked her, and quite gently at that. Unless of course
he had been checking her out, testing her reaction before . . .
Before what? She stopped thinking in that direction. The spanking thing had been silly, a small quirk in an otherwise excellent
lover, no big deal. Forget it. They would have dinner tomorrow
and fuck, just like other times with other men. She'd found
herself a terrific lover who wasn't going to get too involved.
Well done, Rachel!

Joshua arrived with a very good bottle of wine. The corkscrew
lay on the ready-laid living room table and he opened the bottle, poured them each a glass and they sat sipping, Joshua on the
armchair, Rachel curled on the sofa, with the scent of thyme,
garlic and lamb wafting around the room.

"We can eat in a few minutes," she said.

"I'm not very hungry. It'll keep, won't it?"

She felt cross as she turned the oven down low. Her schedule
for the evening was being disrupted; were they then going to
fuck before dinner? She supposed they were; she would have
preferred later and she was obscurely thrown off balance and
irritated. It was her flat, her dinner, he was her guest; yet he just
dismissed it all and the good smells didn't interest him. Bloody
hell, when someone was invited to dinner they ate when they
were told to. She didn't want to fuck him now, she wanted to eat
and drink and play games with his eyes. She wasn't ready. She
returned to the sofa and drank some more wine. He didn't look
as though he were about to ravage her; he sat with his legs
crossed, holding his wine glass and looking at her with cool,
level eyes.

"Tell me your fantasy," he said, smiling a little through his
wine glass.

She couldn't, it was too difficult. If she were drunker or more aroused perhaps, but even then she would have found it hard.

"No. You tell me yours, perhaps it'll inspire me."

She was not going to play his game, at least not entirely on his terms. She still felt anxious about the food.

"It's no good if you manufacture it. I want to know what you think about in the dark in bed when you touch yourself. Well . . . mine is that I seduce a very young girl, an innocent, an adolescent. I'm the first man who has ever excited her and very slowly, gradually, she begins to come."

Rachel felt a little disappointed; it was hardly the most inspired or original fantasy she had heard.

"Well, that's a bit exclusive."

"Exclusive of what?" he asked, a little surprised.

"Me," smiled Rachel. "I'm thirty-one and no virgin."

Joshua laughed, a genuine laugh, his eyes narrowing with amusement.

"Your turn," he said.

"Oh, the usual rape and violence stuff."

Joshua's face switched immediately to impassive, his eyes serious again.

"That won't do. I want detail," he snapped.

Rachel found it hard to remember the thoughts she had, the scenes she invented; they seemed to drain out of her memory as she tried to think of them. Why, anyway, was she trying to give him her authentic fantasies, why not make something up? But she did feel impelled to tell him something like the truth.

"Um . . . someone, a man comes through my window while I'm asleep in bed. He, well, he ties me to the bed, he's very strong, and he rapes me. Oh, I don't know. Something like that."

She felt it was very lame. And why the hell, she reminded herself, should I tell him anything, let alone worry about the quality of it?

He looked at her quietly.

"Has anyone ever tied you up in real life?"

She laughed.

"Yes, actually someone did once. Only it seemed so ridiculous I started to laugh. Ruined it, naturally."

She recalled how contrived, how absurd it had been, the man looking so serious, concentrating hard on the task of trussing her up.

"He obviously didn't know what he was doing." Joshua didn't match her amusement at the memory, but looked very serious. *I* know, he was saying, if I had done it you wouldn't have laughed.

Rachel's smile faded and she returned his gaze for a moment before turning her head away sharply towards the kitchen. She blinked and stood up.

"Shall we eat? I'll make the dressing for the salad."

She went into the kitchen and got out a small bowl. The kitchen was separated from the living room by a half-wall which was loaded with plants. On the kitchen side against this wall was the table she used for preparing food and eating breakfast with Carrie. Now she beat oil and vinegar together to make the vinaigrette, the bowl on the table, looking at Joshua over the wall which was just above waist level. Joshua got up and moved towards the kitchen.

"I'm still not hungry."

"You mean you don't want to eat at all? I thought you came for dinner."

She wondered at the stupidity of that last statement even as she said it.

"No, I don't want to eat. Perhaps I'll get peckish later. What a conventional girl you are. I didn't come for dinner and I couldn't care less about eating."

As he came closer, his glass in his hand, Rachel felt nervous, like a schoolgirl who had no idea how to behave. She felt so silly standing there, bowl in one hand, fork in the other, whisking intently; so inept and foolish as she went on beating the mixture.

"Well, the food will spoil. I don't see having a meal in terms of convention. It's not a political act, just some food."

She was gabbling, panicking, sensing his approach, her eyes fixed on the busyness of her hands. He stood behind her and slipped his hand under her dress.

She was wearing what had once been an expensive and elegant silk chiffon tea dress, circa 1940. A previous man in her life had called it laughingly her Oxfam schmutter. It was now a faded pale blue, worn at some of the seams, with a full, floating skirt. On Rachel it was a witty dress, too pretty had it been new, but an amusing contrast since it was obviously second-hand, with her interesting but unpretty face and unkempt hair. It clashed pointedly with her matter-of-fact toughness; a flirtatious dress worn by an unflirtatious woman. She loved wearing it because the fabric felt wonderful against her skin.

Joshua's wrist lifted the weight of the skirt as his fingers stroked the inside of her bare thigh and moved up to feel her crotch. Rachel worked on at the already well-amalgamated dressing. Nothing was happening. A man was standing close behind her with his hand up her skirt but Rachel behaved as if nothing was happening. She was flustered and playing possum. Why, she wondered, am I like this? The initial stages of sex always were like this; she never acknowledged it, always behaved as if she and the man were there for some other purpose. Sex? The last thing on her mind. What the hell else were they there for? She wanted a purely sexual relationship, didn't she? Well then, cut the crap and behave like it. Stop fencing it around with social nonsense. She was ambivalent? Yes. She wanted to be taken by surprise? Yes. For God's sake, she told herself, you *are* thirty-one and by no means a virgin. But still she didn't react.

Joshua said, "Bend over the table."

His voice was calm but firm, he was giving an order. She turned to look at him, then slowly put the bowl and fork to one side and leant across the table, resting on her forearms. Joshua lifted the back of her skirt and laced it carefully on to her back so that her naked legs and knickers were exposed. He delicately edged her knickers down using the tips of his thumb and forefinger, and she lifted each foot as he slipped them off and stood for a moment looking at her. He stroked each buttock gently then slipped his finger between her legs and stroked her clitoris until it was wet. Suddenly he began to smack her, short, sharp slaps, pausing for a second between each. Six, eight smacks, hard enough to make her draw in her breath.

Rachel saw a vision of herself bent over the kitchen table, bare-arsed, being spanked by a fully clothed man. This was ridiculous, straight out of the pages of a smutty magazine. What am I doing, she thought, why am I letting this happen? But the part of her that wasn't watching was arching her back, lifting her buttocks to receive each smack as it came.

"That's right. That's a good girl," he told her soothingly, but the tone was harsh. "Now arch your back more. Lift your arse. Yes, that's it."

Another series of smacks, very hard, Rachel crying out a little with each one. Then he opened his zip and pushed his erect penis against the cleavage of her buttocks.

"Where do you want it?" he demanded.

Panic. Where do I want it. I know where he wants it. I don't want to say. I don't want to have to ask.

"Anywhere," she breathed.

"Where?" he repeated angrily.

"Do what you want." She wanted him to just take her. She wanted him.

"I said where? Do you want my cock in your cunt or your arse?"

Very angry, icy cold.

"Oh, please . . . in my arse . . . in my arse."

He stood behind her, holding her around the hips, pulling her towards him and gently, carefully, began to push into her. She cried out in pain, it hurt, really hurt as he probed deeper and deeper. She felt a sudden urge to shit and cried against it and then he was fully inside her and she felt her muscles relax, allowing him to move deep, deep into her. She groaned from somewhere in the back of her throat and heard him sigh.

"Is that good? Does it feel good?"

She said, "Yes," her voice low and deep, mingled with her groans, and she pushed herself back up against him, feeling his soft belly on her buttocks. He tightened his arms around her and moved inside her slowly, listening to the low, purring sounds she made. She felt everything: violated, released, hugely and darkly excited. She wanted him inside her totally. She was angry and rendered helpless, wanting this more than anything. She became aware of his excitement, his immense pleasure and strangely great relief; it was as though he had got home, was where, finally, he belonged. Her anger was muted by his plea-

sure and by the physical excitement she felt as he pushed further into her. As she started to breathe more heavily he touched
her clitoris and she came in long broken moans, on and on until
suddenly she hissed explosively through clenched teeth,

"Bastard!"

And again,

"Bastard!"

He came then, as though taken by surprise, heaving and
pressing against her as everything it seemed emptied from him.

For a moment he was still, then he pulled out of her and she
felt herself close tight as she lay against the table, her head
resting on her arms, breathing fast.

Joshua straightened his clothes and Rachel stood up, her skirt
falling back into place. She didn't know how to break the silence, and waited for him to say something. She wanted to be
comforted and held.

"Let's eat," Joshua said, quite composed, his voice cool and
amused, a small, ironic smile playing around his mouth.

She took the lamb out of the oven, drier than it should have
been but all right, and they ate it at the kitchen table from the
roasting dish, forks and knives spearing and tearing apart the
meat and vegetables which they put directly into their mouths.
Fuck the salad, Rachel thought as she eyed the dressing on the
table morosely.

Joshua ate noisily without speaking, he was hungry, enjoying
the food. Rachel picked. She felt damp and sore—and good. She
hadn't put her knickers back on, had stepped over them as she
took the food from the oven and they still lay on the floor. She
could feel her dress wet beneath her.

"More wine?" she asked.

"Mmm. This is good. You're a good cook, but I'm sure you
hate to be told that," he said, grinning between forkfuls.

"Right." She poured more wine into his glass and a little for
herself. They ate the fruit salad which was delicious, just right,
fresh tasting.

"I love grenadilla," Joshua cooed. "How did you know?"

"I didn't." Implying that had she known nothing would be
further from the salad bowl. "I always put them in fruit salad."

He looked at her and grinned hugely, white teeth bared. She grinned back. They were two grown-ups again.

Rachel wanted to be lying with Joshua, naked in bed. She was slow and sensual and moved lazily to put on a record. They sat again in their former positions, on chair and sofa.

"When I'm fifty-five I plan to retire. I'll live in Provence," Joshua drawled.

"Oh yes, dreamtime?" Rachel smiled.

"Not at all. It's a ten-year plan. And my plans always work. I will have made a lot of money from my stocks. That's the point of doing it, it's not a vocation."

Joshua had given up his job as an economist with the Home Office when he had received a legacy decent enough to launch himself into the stock market. At Molly's dinner party he and Rachel had each donned appropriate masks, he as liberal capitalist, she as moderate Marxist.

"There's no such thing as a good capitalist. By definition," she had intoned to irritate him.

"Nonsense, I'm one. You modern radicals can only think in stereotypes," he had responded to irritate her. The conversation continued, tongue in cheek, neither being really convinced of their position. Now Rachel stretched out her legs.

"So what are you going to do with your retirement, O Capitalist Pig?"

"I shall have a beautiful house in sunny Provence, read philosophy and enjoy my entourage of girls. Two exquisite young creatures who will adore me, and you. You provide the conversation and run the house, keep the girls in line and teach them a thing or two. I'll take care of the machines."

"*I'll* take care of the machines, you can run the bloody house. I think you've mistaken me for someone else, sunshine. I'm not the domestic type and I don't do well in groups."

Joshua laughed.

"Well, we'll see."

It was banter, but as Rachel looked at him she thought that he wasn't entirely joking. He really did have that fantasy in his head and seemed to be measuring her for the part of older woman in the ménage. She would be forty-one then, she calculated. He does see it as a possibility, she realized, feeling suddenly uneasy about him, as well as slightly pleased to be included.

"I've got to go. I'm expecting a call from the States at eleven," Joshua said suddenly, and got up. It was ten forty-five. He lived quite nearby.

"You are quite free to go whether or not you have a phone call," she replied tightly, furious at this nonsense and taken by surprise at the abrupt termination of the evening. Now she felt, or had been made to feel, that she had been fitted in between appointments. There was no call coming from the States. It insulted her that he had made such a feeble excuse for leaving and expected her to believe it. She was not some demanding woman who had to be managed.

"Thanks for dinner," he said, unconcerned by her frostiness.

"You're welcome," she told him coldly, and got up from the sofa.

He left, calling "Bye" at her as he let himself out of the front door.

She sat back on the sofa in the empty room.

"Bastard," she whispered softly.

She let her mind drift back over the evening and wondered first if she would see him again; she thought that probably she would, but wasn't quite sure. Then she thought about the way he had manipulated her, managed the whole evening as if in accordance with some plan he already had on arrival, a fantasy structured beforehand which he had set about making real. He had directed the evening as if he had had a script in his hand. There was about him generally a complete lack of spontaneity. Then the sex. Buggery. She explored the notion. All the received ideas on the subject told her it was an act of degradation. To fuck a woman in the arse was to show contempt; the imagery of shit, denial of femaleness—he didn't need what was essentially female, her cunt, settled happily for the hole that anyone possessed. It was male power and aggression, an attempt to humiliate. All true, probably, certainly, but there was more than that. There was, for instance, the fact that she had wanted it; that it hurt her and she had liked that; and that it had satisfied her sexually. Nobody talked about sodomy, not even in a world where people seemed to talk about little else but sex. Taboo. Maybe. Not many people did it? She didn't know, but some must. Shame. Dirty sex. It was still officially illegal between heterosexuals. What struck her as really strange, though, what prevented her from slapping on the obvious labels and leaving it at that, was the almost loving way in which he had done it. It made no sense, she knew, but there *had* been an extraordinary warmth in him when he smacked her and sodomized her which surely wasn't what she should have picked up from such acts of blatant aggression. She had felt something very like gratitude in him as he entered her. Crazy. But then if someone allows you to do something you really want to do is that really then an act of aggression?

And from her point of view there was something extraordinary about that kind of sex. It went beyond vaginal sex. She had felt during this last encounter infinitely more known, more penetrated, more possessed. It was the dark, secret route that took him truly inside her, a labyrinth without a boundary leading to the hidden place, the centre that she hardly knew herself. It was there that she wanted to know and be known.

There was an impossible mismatch between what she had felt and what she knew she was supposed to feel. A woman in her thirties at the end of two decades of the women's movement, who assumed equality and lived equally with men, was not supposed to admit to rape fantasies and submit herself to the power play of perverted male sexuality, let alone like it. That was it: she was appalled at how much she had enjoyed being ordered about, assaulted and degraded. She thought it wouldn't be possible to describe this to any of her women friends. Even if they could listen to it they would rage with disapproval. At him, of course, as she would have; but also implicitly at her. How could she have allowed him to behave like that, how could she have enjoyed it? *She* was shocked at herself, but couldn't forget that she had liked it. Beyond the politics she wanted to disown that pathetic creature who had followed instructions, obeyed orders, begged for it. She wasn't anyone she had ever met before—not, at any rate, in the real world of action, away from night dreams and dark thoughts. You are not supposed to enjoy that sort of thing, said the small harsh voice in her head. "Well, I did," she said aloud, and went to bed.

It was several weeks before she saw Joshua again, weeks spent in a dark sexual dream where it seemed to Rachel that she was wading ever deeper into territory which had previously been for her only symbols on a map. It was as if a key had been turned and she had, willy nilly, to explore the corridors and dingy places which had been revealed. She lived the public parts of her life, she thought, satisfactorily, but felt like a secret agent whose real business was merely concealed by the everyday matters that only seemed to be the substance of life. Carrie was fed, clothed and emotionally attended to, and appeared not to notice that her mother had her mind on other things. Rachel shopped, cooked, ironed and smiled at the other mothers at the school gate, where she hugged Carrie and wished her a good day. Then she was free until picking-up time to continue her seedy exploration. She drove home, put on the washing machine, and blessed the fact that she was between pupils. During that time her whole body was leaden, as if the blood had turned to some molten metal and lurched heavily through her veins. Sometimes her arms felt so heavy that she could hardly lift them and her eyelids pained her with the effort of keeping them open. She would, most mornings after dropping Carrie off at school, run a bath, telling herself that it would make her feel better and that afterwards she would go shopping, or cook something nice for Carrie's tea. It happened, invariably, that after the bath she was more exhausted than ever, had just enough energy to lie damply on the bed, the towel loosely draped around her. Even then, she told herself that once dry, she would get dressed and get on with things.

Lying there she began to play and replay the details of her two nights with Joshua, picking out themes. She would summon up most excitingly the confident tone of his voice, the authority of his fingers as they manipulated her to a climax, the sound and feel of his contempt, and she used these to go beyond what had actually happened, to develop full-scale dramas of violence and enforced submission. The hand that spanked her became a whip, a leather strap, first tied her then beat her; the voice, so sure of itself, gave orders to her to get in this or that position, on her knees, on all fours, to touch herself, where and how; began to pour abuse into her ear, whore, slut, filthy cow; the penis raped and ravaged her, made her cry out for more pain, made her beg for more, more, more.

She lay on the bed with her eyes shut allowing each drama its full extent so that it could summon up the next and the next. She had only to close her eyes for them to start. It seemed they had been waiting, simmering away somewhere inside her waiting for release. Now they came rushing at her, drowning her in their need for expression, pinning her to the bed. She touched herself and imagined everything, Joshua beating her, a woman beating her with Joshua looking on, Joshua bringing someone off the street to rape her while he watched. She went through all possible combinations, even once or twice herself as aggressor, repaying pain and humiliation, but that always ended like the rest with herself finally overcome and doubly punished. She would climax two, three, four times, and then lie exhausted on the bed, sick at herself. I won't do this again, I won't, she told herself. But she knew she would. She was hooked. It was a drug, she felt drugged, literally. She was compelled to parade the sickness and violence before her own eyes so that she should see what she contained. What she really was.

She got up after these sessions miserable and ashamed. Time was used up, nothing done. Well, she was learning something about herself; but she knew that wasn't true, or not true enough. She had no control over this process, she couldn't look at it, say, yes, this is part of me too and then see another side of herself, more positive, more connected to life. There was nothing, nothing good, worthwhile, only the dreams of punishment and pain.

She had, in the past, had fleeting fantasies like some of those she had now, so fleeting that she had barely noticed them, and they were always with a man without a face. Now Joshua's features had imprinted themselves on the anonymous protagonist and the dreams became real, tangible, part of herself rather than seeming to float by on the air. Her evenings were spent with Carrie asleep upstairs, on the alert, waiting for the phone to ring. She didn't go out; didn't even take a bath without

ensuring that the phone was first placed where she could hear
it. If she read or watched television it was always with one part
of her listening, waiting for a call. She began to feel that the
immense power of her fantasies, of her need, were enough to
summon Joshua, that he knew her condition, was allowing it to
develop.

This has got to stop, she told herself over and over. This
doesn't happen to me.

She had been sexually enchanted by other men, but not like
this. Not without regular contact and not for long. She usually
fed her need, saw the man often so that after the first few weeks
the excitement wore thin, and she began to perceive the details
which inevitably irritated her out of the obsession. It didn't take
much; the way he ate, or drank, the odd remark that damned
him forever as foolish, not bright enough. Anything was enough
to make her interest flag and quickly die. Then out. Finished.
That, previously, had been the pattern in all her affairs, so that
from the first she was waiting, dreading the moment when the
wrong thing was said or done. At first she would try not to
notice, but she knew it was a losing battle, the irritation would
develop into disdain, then contempt and embarrassment at his
mere presence. He had to go.

Now she was terrified that this process wouldn't happen, or
rather that Joshua's infrequent presence would keep it at bay.
"Just a few days of him, that's all I need." And she began to
suspect that that was precisely what she was not going to get, to
understand that Joshua was very like herself and could play her
as she had never been played before. She thought back to the
telephone conversation with Molly and the dinner party. She
had been so in control. What had happened? How had she
become such a victim? Divine retribution was probably over-
dramatizing, but nemesis sounded right. I'm in trouble, she
thought, I'm in deep shit. Where you belong, whispered her
small-voiced co-resident, just as the phone began to ring.

"Hello, Mrs Kee? I've got a likely lad for you if you're up to
it."

It was Donald Soames she realized, her heart racing with
disappointed hope. She took a deep breath.

"I think I've had my fill of likely lads, Donald. Couldn't you find me some nice, quiet, motivated lad for a change?"

"Sorry, the schools are hanging on to those for dear life. I'm afraid we're left with the dregs."

Donald's dismal contempt for his charges fired a little enthusiasm in Rachel, more in anger at him than from any real crusading energy in her.

"Well, who is he?"

"A sixteen-year-old in care. Deserted by mum at birth. He's been brought up, if you can call it that, in children's homes. Got some pretty dire problems that I'll let you find out for yourself. But he's quite bright. IQ of 120. That's not to be sneezed at in these times. Apparently he wants to take some CSEs before he goes out into the wide world. He hasn't had any regular schooling for years, but he can read and write. What do you think? I've visited. He seemed a nice enough lad."

"If he's so nice and so bright how come he's not in school? Never mind, what's the address? I'll visit this afternoon."

Thank God, she thought, work. It felt as if someone had handed her a rope just as she was slipping into a fathomless crack in the earth. Maybe she could haul herself out of it and get human again. Maybe the past few weeks were just a passing fever she could work her way through by getting on with life, like everyone else.

Wentworth House was in the heart of Hampstead, a small island of deprivation in a not very large sea of well-being. Its square, local-authority economic shape contrasted with opulent detached residences, still mostly occupied by single families. The opposing meanings of the term "residential" were standing side by side for those who cared to ponder. Enclosed on either side by "homes" was the "Home," perfectly pleasant actually, in a quiet leafy semi-suburban street. Probably the liberal planners of Camden Council thought it good for everybody to have to acknowledge the range of possibilities that life held. Probably they were right.

Rachel rang the bell, saw through the glass door that no one was coming and tried the handle. The door wasn't locked so she let herself in. A large kitchen and dining room stood empty, equipped for cooking for and for serving twenty or so people. A huge cooker, masses of cupboards and a serving-hatch opening out to a linoleum-floored space with six formica tables and plastic moulded chairs. Like a small school dining room. The glass doors leading to the garden were open, making the place light and airy, if not comfortable. A man in his early twenties came down the stairs and smiled at her. She introduced herself; he was clearly not one of the kids but nonetheless looked terribly young with longish blond hair, tight jeans and black short-sleeved tee shirt.

"Oh, right, Rachel Kee. We're expecting you. Mr Soames phoned to say you were coming. All the kids are at school at the moment, except Pete of course. He's up in the recreation room waiting for you. I think it'll be really good for him to be having lessons regularly. Come and meet him."

She followed him upstairs to the battered recreation room. Several padded plastic chairs were upturned while others were grouped in twos and threes around small tables. All the chairs had gashes through which poked wads of grey foam. Draughts, dominoes and chess pieces were scattered about, some on the floor, others on tables as if all games there were terminated by someone upending the board. In the centre of the room stood a half-sized billiard table and a boy, bent to a right angle, crouched over it, cue poised. There were no billiard balls in sight.

"This is Pete," the young man said, patting the boy gently on the back.

Pete was a phenomenon of the time: very tall, six feet or more, and thin as a stick, the head bullet-shaped, hair shaved to a scant quarter of an inch, making the nose, chin and Adam's apple seem to protrude excessively; the feet enclosed in enormous shiny-capped black boots which laced tightly up the ankles to emphasize the clumsy shape of the foot sticking out, it appeared, further than any foot ergonomically could. In between, skin-tight faded jeans with carefully placed rips were topped by tight tee shirt and a jeans jacket so small that the cuffs were almost at elbow level. A small swastika had been inked on to the back of one hand. He reminded Rachel of Olive Oyl from Popeye cartoons, all length and knobbly bits.

"Hello. Donald Soames tells me you want to take some CSEs next summer. I'm Rachel Kee."

Peter's indistinguishable skinhead face smiled a little shyly as he grunted assent and greetings. Rachel smiled back.

"Well, look, I live about fifteen minutes' walk from here. I'd like you to come to my flat for lessons. They'd be Monday to Friday for two hours a day, unless you want to do maths, which you should if possible. We'd have to find another tutor one day a week for that, I'm hopeless at maths. We can arrange the times on your first visit. What do you think?"

Pete grunted again. It seemed to mean that he didn't completely disagree so far.

It was immediately clear to Rachel that beneath the stereotype that had been worked so hard for was a sense of humour and an intelligence which made him an interesting prospect. She liked him and matched the friendly amusement that lurked behind his eyes with her own. There was enough recognition between them to make teaching him seem a possibility. It had often struck her how difficult it must be for the current subcultures to maintain themselves as they wanted to be seen. The punks of a few years before with their glorious multicoloured day-glo hair betrayed themselves with their glum, everyday, street faces. The hair, when they were just being themselves, looked like a leftover from happier moments. No one could live up to it all the time. In the end, in real life, the painted feathers became a burden. And the reverse was true of the skinheads. The shock-horror of shaven heads, swastikas, concentration camp looks that scared old ladies to death on the street were often, on contact, denied by the ordinary humanity of the kids who had donned the image. There was a boy she saw often on her street who, like Pete, was dressed to kill—literally. His darkish face—he was of mixed race—was covered with Nazi insignia, lightning flashes, National Front emblems. His clothes were ripped and hung about with chains and safety pins. He looked terrifying, like an awful portent of what was to come; and he walked daily along the street pushing a baby-buggy containing a bright, clean, smiling two-year-old. He came past her window laden with the day's shopping, sometimes with the baby's mother, sometimes alone, he and the child chattering and laughing together. A thoroughly modern father, this fiend. Rachel enjoyed the absurdity of it so much; she didn't like his taste, but loved his style.

She was aware, of course, of the other kids who looked just like her local skinhead and Pete, who did indeed live up to their reputation and roamed the streets terrorizing anyone who was the wrong age, colour or sex. There *were* kids who used those boots to kick heads and wreck lives and whose masklike faces got that way as their brain cells gave up and died from an overdose of glue fumes. Then again there were some very respectable-looking people who were adept at the destruction of others and those whose brain cells fared no better on a massive intake of alcohol. And so on. Liberal, she sneered at herself.

It did please her, though, when she found that image didn't have to conform to the automatic set of prejudices that went with it; when she had to stop and rethink the inconsidered phrases that bubbled up—from where? She liked to be surprised out of her laziness. Good/bad, black/white, love/hate, funny/sad, sick/healthy. Nothing, in the actual living, was so exclusive as its material image proclaimed. We choose to think so crudely; things were much more confused and fluid.

I'm one of nature's extreme relativists, she thought.

"Right. We'll start Wednesday. I'll pick you up for the first day or two so you can get used to the route. Let's make it ten o'clock."

As they went downstairs Pete asked her, "What kind of car you got?"

Rachel grinned at him. "It's a 2CV."

"One of them Citroens? Oh yeah," he smiled broadly, "same as my social worker's got."

Rachel pulled a rueful face.

"Seen one, seen 'em all. Never mind, it gets me around and it will get you to my flat on Wednesday. I'm looking forward to it."

They smiled at each other.

"See yer," said Pete, as he saw her to the car, banged the soft top and ambled back into Wentworth House.

The next evening Joshua phoned.

"Are you alone?" he asked. There was no greeting; he assumed she would recognize his voice.

"Oh, hello. Yes, I am." She surprised herself with her calm, level voice, pleasant, noncommittal.

"Good. I'll be there in about three-quarters of an hour."

She put the phone down and smiled. I knew he would turn up again. She checked around the flat—it was tidy enough—then stripped off the tracksuit she had on and went to the bathroom. She took down her diaphragm from the cabinet, squeezed jelly around its rim and inserted it into her vagina, wondering in passing if it would be needed. Then she washed in the bidet, brushed her teeth and fluffed up her tangled hair with her fingers. Back in the bedroom she stood in front of the mirror considering what to wear. Nothing special. No obvious effort to please. She put her black tracksuit back on; she felt good in it, it would do. She looked thin, athletic, relaxed. She looked like she looked before Joshua had phoned.

With half an hour to go Rachel was ready and sat cross-legged on the sofa smoking a cigarette. She put on some music, Mozart, a string quartet, then poured herself a Scotch. She drank very little usually, but wanted this one just to take the edge off her. Then she sat and listened to the music, sipping her drink and smoking. By the time the front door bell rang she was quite calm and unexcited. All the torment of the past few weeks, the sweaty fantasies, the hunger, had gone. She looked, and actually felt, cool and self-possessed. She had time to wonder that she could switch into that so easily, as she went downstairs to answer the door. She really did feel relaxed, like a woman about to greet a casual lover for a pleasant evening. Who the hell, then, had been lying on her bed anguishing for all those weeks? Where was she? She snapped on the hall light and opened the door.

Joshua stood in the open doorway smiling good-naturedly, plump and personable. This was not the Joshua of her dreams and nightmares. She realized that he had become a phantom, that in the past weeks of daydreaming she had stripped him of his flesh-and-blood reality and set in its place a mythological man. A creature of her imaginings, a dream-Joshua. The Joshua standing in front of her was all surface charm, pleasing, unthreatening, as he stood holding a Harrods bag, waiting to be greeted. There was no way of feeling other than genial towards him, an acquaintance, an uncomplicated lover. Two equals meeting again after a reasonable gap; people who had lots of things to do but who enjoyed each other's company when time and life's commitments permitted.

This was the reality as they both stood smiling in the doorway, the craziness of past weeks vanishing like a cloud. Rachel was a sleeper awakening from a nightmare which she remembered until the day's ordinariness made it fade from consciousness.

"Hello. Come in," she grinned, and led him upstairs.

She got two wine glasses from the cupboard as he pulled a bottle of wine from the carrier bag which he placed in a corner of the kitchen. They sat opposite each other at the table in the living room, sipping wine and chatting amiably. She realized after a while that she wasn't even feeling particularly aroused. There was none of that stomach-churning lust she felt with some men as she passed the time of day while waiting for the sex to start. This Joshua, this Rachel had nothing to do with the two people who had committed sodomy over the kitchen table.

The conversation was amusing. The experience of feeling "right" with someone was very rare for Rachel; now it was tangible, she revelled in it, lapping up the sense of well-being she felt from the humorous, slightly teasing, slightly testing banter that bounced back and forth across the table. They had a normal conversation, gave each other normal information. Rachel asked about his family, the wife, the children.

"Carol and I were together for fifteen years. I'm very involved with the kids, I'm usually around there in the early evenings and they stay with me once a week. My family takes up a lot of my time."

It sounded familiar enough to Rachel, not unlike her relationship with Michael, which she described to Joshua.

"What about your family?" she asked.

"I've got a Mother," he replied darkly, capitalizing it, "more ogress than mother, who will certainly outlive me. She's a sort of degenerative disease—a dependent, not a parent. I seem to have a lot of them—dependents I mean, not parents."

"Such a load. I presume you get a kick out of having people depend on you?" Rachel enquired sweetly.

"I'd be happy if they all disappeared in a puff of smoke—

except the kids. I do not enjoy my burdens, just suffer them complainingly."

She didn't believe him but let it pass.

"So I've noticed. But everyone's mother is awful. It goes without saying. Is yours really more awful?"

"You'd probably like her," he grinned, then looked serious again. "She's hard, grasping and vicious. There is nothing, absolutely nothing likeable about her. A mean, small-minded, stupid woman."

"What about your father?" Rachel asked, slightly thrown by the anger in his voice.

"Wasn't one. Just myself, the mother, and an aunt and uncle who lived with us while we lived on them. I left home when I was four."

"Very advanced. I'd have expected no less, you're not the type who sticks around," nodded Rachel.

"There was a family conference. By the time I was four I'd become so good at manipulating the adults they decided to get rid of me. I was very clever. They sent me off to prep school as a boarder."

"At four?" Rachel's jaw dropped. She felt she didn't really need any more information to understand what made Joshua tick. Banished from home at four because he was too clever. What else could he ever be but manipulative and angry?

"You poor thing. How awful." She was genuinely sad for the child she could picture so clearly.

"I survived," he replied tersely.

Yes, thought Rachel, but what was the price?

"I have a mother too," she said aloud.

"And?" Joshua enquired.

"She's a socialist saint. Academic. Very Hampstead, very worthy. Long since canonized."

"Ahh," said Joshua, "you have a degenerative disease too."

"Heavens no. She stamps out cancers as soon as they raise their ugly, unreasonable little heads. Splat! they go. You can't exist, she cries, you are unreasonable, illogical, therefore I abolish you. And off they go clutching their tails between their disordered chromosomes."

"Sounds terrifying," said Joshua, grimacing.

"Well, no, not actually, not once you're used to it. She's really very nice, but difficult. She's not my mother in fact. She adopted me when I was twelve. It makes a difference, you don't have all that infant backlog stuff."

"That sounds all right. Will she adopt me, do you think, if you ask her nicely?"

"Definitely not. She's had her fill of *enfants terribles*. You would be too much of a bad thing."

"You never know," smiled Joshua, his teeth sparkling. "I can be very charming."

"Yes, I've noticed," Rachel smiled back, "sometimes you almost creak with charm."

He looked at her sharply, and then inclined his head as if to acknowledge the barb. He changed the subject.

"Where's your little girl?"

"Upstairs, asleep."

"And do you get on?"

"Mm. Pretty well. She's very nice, very sensible. Look, we bought a fish today. Well, as a matter of fact we bought a fish tank, then we had to buy a fish to put in it."

She nodded her head towards the kitchen partition on which stood, amid the plants, a fish tank on a mirrored plinth. Inside, apart from the fish, were a perspex table and two chairs.

"A high-rise fish apartment. Carrier yearned for it so we're splitting the cost. Half each. She says she owns the top half, I get the plinth. The fish is called Rosemary—dignified isn't it? I wanted to call it Gefilte but Carrie said I don't take things seriously, so it's Rosemary. Still, when it dies, as fish inevitably do, it'll just be one dead fish. God, there is nothing more dead than a dead fish, is there?"

"I can think of a couple of people I know who might claim the prize. She sounds nice. Is she clever?"

"Enough. Who knows? There's more to life than being clever, I'm told, like having an innate capacity to name fish, for example. Or giving the impression of sanity when everyone else takes it in turn to fall to pieces. Do you have a woman in your life?" she asked suddenly.

"There's a woman I see occasionally, nothing serious. I don't go in for emotional entanglements."

He waited for her to ask more.

"And?" she obliged.

"She's the wife of my accountant." He smiled gently as he watched her cooly. "I go to her place and fuck her sometimes when he's at work. He's a very good accountant, a nice bloke. Likeable."

Rachel stared at him.

"Don't you worry that he'll find out? How he'll feel?"

"No. It's a very good marriage. There's no problem. I keep them both occupied. No harm done."

"You mean you're in control?" Rachel suggested levelly.

"Quite."

There was a short silence while Rachel took this information in. Not a man to have like you; this character would be safer as your enemy. But what was more curious was that he had told her this. Matter-of-factly. Perhaps with a hint of challenge: how would she react? What impression did he think it gave her? Did he think she would admire it? Surely not. Or did he not care one way or another what she thought? But then why tell her about it? She was mystified. It made him suddenly unattractive, this story. Didn't he realize that? She reflected that she had no idea of how he understood the world.

Joshua broke the silence.

"Come over here."

An order. As if a switch had been turned his manner changed, his voice became cold and compelling. And something switched in her too at the sound of his commanding voice. Whoever it was who felt such distaste at his story faded. Rachel did as she was told, perhaps a little reticently.

"Go and fetch me the carrier bag I brought with me. Then go into the bedroom and wait for me."

He arrived a few moments later holding a leather strap.

"I'm going to beat you," he told her quietly. "Bend over."

And there it was, the leather strap that she had thought existed only in her imagination.

He pulled down her tracksuit bottom and knickers and said in a gently explanatory tone, "I'm going to give you six strokes with the strap. It will hurt you and when you cry out in pain it will give me enormous pleasure."

Although the words detailed how she was expected to behave, they also aroused her. The pain did make her at first gasp,
then cry out. It did hurt, but the pain was controlled, he beat
her carefully, with a precise degree of force, not so painful as to
be unbearable. When he had finished she was crying, sobbing,
as much from humiliation as from the pain itself. He lifted her
up gently and said:

"What do you want me to do to you?"

"Fuck me," she whispered through her sobs.

"Ask nicely."

"Fuck me . . . please." And hold me, please, she whispered
to herself.

When they had finished they lay on her bed, close and silent.
He had made her come over and over, seeming to want her
orgasms as much as her pain. She lay exhausted and physically
satisfied, and a little scared that more of her solitary fantasies
should have come so real again with him. Being beaten, and the
way he had fucked her, had been exactly as she had imagined,
the very same words, the same cold, angry need in him, the
same disintegration of her self-possession.

After they had lain silently for a while Joshua spoke in his
conversational voice, the one he had used when they were
drinking wine at the table. Indeed he seemed to be continuing
the conversation.

"Children are a wonderful lesson in telling it like it is. The
other day my daughter told a friend that she loved me too
much. When he asked why, she said because her daddy was too
old and would die soon. It wasn't sensible to love someone who
was about to drop dead. Of course she's quite right."

Where was the man who had just beaten her and hissed "dirty
little bitch" in her ear as she came?

"Oh, and what are you going to die prematurely of?"

Where was the victim, the child who had cried and whimpered?

"Of irrelevance. I'm going to die of irrelevance," Joshua said
into the darkness, his voice humorous, ironical.

Rachel drew in her breath, then let it out in a short, harsh
laugh.

"Joshua, I suspect that both you and I have long since died of irrelevance. All that's left now is bodily corruption, and that's a doddle by comparison."

Joshua gave her one of his sharp, acknowledging glances which Rachel was coming to recognize as meaning "very true, but no more." Being dead already, being irrelevant, contained some hard nugget of truth which hung heavily in the air. She knew he knew it too. It was their secret, which explained and was kept at bay by their cynicism and sexuality. Rachel began to understand Joshua as a man who was deeply disappointed in himself and using his life to take revenge. A kind of nihilist in a world devoid of nineteenth-century romanticism. He was committed to destruction because he had evacuated himself at the age of four. No love, sent away, broken—but clever. And what can you do with clever all on its own? You can use it to hurt other people. And you can stop them from hurting you by feeling nothing. You can show other people that you are someone to be reckoned with. Clever little boy, full of promise, all empty inside. Got scholarships, went to Cambridge. Full of promise, but nothing came of it. Perhaps not clever enough. The prestigious jobs went elsewhere—perhaps to people less empty at the core. Clever little boy had a good position, but not brilliant, not enough to make the world (who really?) stare amazed, to make himself feel he was anything other than empty, irrelevant. So he chucks it in and makes money: there are other routes to power. He's still brighter than most people so he can feel superior; and he uses his talent for manipulation, learned as a child, to wreak havoc. He spins webs, this manipulative spider, and pulls the threads to make people jerk and trap themselves ever deeper. He oozes charm, enchants people, then leaves them dangling for just so long, or plays them off one against another. He has turned his intelligence and insight to the task of perceiving people's weaknesses, needs, and uses his insights to give pain. Rachel saw all this clearly and understood that he really had excised all feeling from himself. This particular frog was going to stay a frog, there was no inner prince waiting to be released. Neither she nor anyone else was going to breathe life into him; his degenerative disease had eaten away his insides.

She suddenly experienced an immense sorrow for him, and concern.

But that, said the voice in her head, is just the victim's way of getting her own back.

Maybe. But dammit, no! She *did* feel concern and sadness for him. To deny that made her identical with Joshua. She did feel it and she would acknowledge it at least to herself, there was that difference between them. She wanted to be tough and unfeeling but in fact wasn't entirely. She saw Joshua now as herself taken to a logical conclusion. He was what she might be; a mirror that reflected back a warning. The clearer she saw him, the more clearly she saw herself, and she knew that whatever else, she must not allow Joshua to stop her humanity, because that, tenuously, was all she had, and what irretrievably he lacked.

I am nicer than him, she thought, because I've hung on to my pain and he has abolished his. That's why I can feel pain for him, and why others' pain is his source of pleasure. He has excommunicated himself from the social world, life can't be anything more than a winning or losing strategy.

So why not get this fatally wounded man out of your life? said the voice.

I can't, not yet, she told herself; I have to go through it, there's something here I have to see through.

You're pretty good at understanding other people, said the voice, leaving the rest of the sentence in the air.

"I must go," said Joshua, getting out of bed.

After he left Rachel lay awake in bed recalling the evening; how harmless he had seemed when she opened the door; how he had suddenly become the dark, fantasy lover; the easy, flowing conversation in between. But now it was as if he had never actually been there; she could remember the events but they were no more or less real than her solitary fantasies. He left nothing of himself behind. She rolled onto the pillow still dented with the impression of his head, but he had not even left a scent. Maybe it never really happened, maybe I made it all up, she mused as she fell asleep.

When she woke the next morning she remembered first that she was picking up Pete for his lesson at ten. Only when she was getting out of bed and felt the ache in her muscles did she remember Joshua's visit. She turned to look at her bottom in the mirror and was shocked to see large blue bruises on her right buttock. So he had left something. The bruises excited her, and she stared at them for some moments until she realized that Carrie would be up soon, and hurriedly pulled on a pair of knickers.

So the man's left his mark, she thought, but that's all. Bloody Zorro. She couldn't make last night real in her mind. It dissolved like candyfloss. The memory of the events was there but not as lived experience, not as if they had actually happened, to her, last night. She might have read it, or seen a movie. It was a recollection of a drama, of a story she had heard, not part of the fabric of her life.

Well, so be it. If the movies were going to come to her instead of her having to go to them, why complain? Some people had videos, she had Joshua. She had a real live fantasy to play with from time to time. What harm? Lucky girl. The lady with the demon lover. No strings, no obligations. If you hang about waiting for long enough you get lucky.

She felt tough and jaunty this morning and pulled on a tight pair of jeans, a dramatically baggy sweat shirt and a pair of pseudo-riding boots fit for striding about the world in. The feel of the jeans close around her made her aware of her slim, energetic shape as she moved about the flat organizing Carrie for school, grilling bacon, pouring tea. In plenty of time they were in the car heading for Carrie's school. En route they duetted Carrie's current favourite song from *Oliver:*

> *As long as he needs me*
> *I know where I must be—*
> *I'll cling on steadfastly*
> *As long as he needs me*

"Why does Nancy love Bill Sykes when he's bad and does horrible things to people, Mum?" Carrie asked in the middle of the fourth reprise.

"Well, she can't help it. She loves him, it doesn't make any difference how he behaves," Rachel said doubtfully. It sounded like complete nonsense even to her ears. "People love people sometimes in spite of what they're like." Deeper and deeper in the mire. "Maybe she was just used to people behaving badly. Maybe she didn't think there was anything better, or didn't think she could get anything better."

"Why not," demanded Carrie, who at five expected proper answers to her questions and was at least as puzzled as Rachel by what she had heard.

"Because that's how life had always been for her. That was what she expected. People get into habits, even bad habits, and then that's what they want. Honestly Carrie, I don't know."

It was too early in the morning for this kind of conversation.

Carrie said, "I don't see how you can love someone who isn't kind to you. I wouldn't love you if you weren't kind to me. Sometimes you aren't, when you yell at me. But then I hate you —but I love you as well."

"Bloody complicated, isn't it?" Rachel smiled into the rear-view mirror.

"Yes, bloody," Carrie grinned back.

Rachel dropped Carrie off and went to the café in the High Street. It was a very self-conscious version of a Parisian café, the walls having been carefully rag-rolled in pollution-coloured paint to give the impression of decades of filth and tobacco smoke. She sat in a battered wicker chair and ordered a cappuccino, then got up and picked out a copy of *The Times* from the rack of newspapers. She reminded herself, as she did every morning, to cancel the paper delivery since she always read the paper here except during the school holidays. It was a good way to start the day, she liked the anonymity of café-sitting, but also the familiarity of being a regular and nodding pleasantly at the others who sat around breakfasting. Sometimes Becky came in on her way into town. Rachel and Becky had worked in the same East End comprehensive before Rachel had Carrie. Becky had since left and now worked as a freelance journalist, and they had kept in close touch over the years. Becky was one of Rachel's few women friends, one of her few close friends. If she wondered why quite often, it was because they seemed to have very little in common. It wasn't that they had come to different conclusions about life so much as that they had *always* concluded differently about it. And if she found she didn't *believe* in Becky, in her consistently different vision of life, she was nonetheless fascinated by her optimism and insistence on putting herself on the emotional line.

Becky came into the café this morning just as Rachel's coffee arrived, and she looked, as usual, immaculate. Her blonde streaked hair was cut to a knife-edged bob which fell straight and smooth to her jaw line, framing her startlingly pretty face. She had a high domed forehead and great pale blue eyes like a lady in a Flemish painting, her mouth small and delicate. Beyond the prettiness and careful make-up lay an intelligence which had decided to assert itself publicly after many years of hesitation. Becky's clothes were good; muted colours, classically well cut and evidently expensive; you knew immediately that the seams were double sewn and everything properly lined. Rachel's flagging hems, on the other hand, were stuck up with safety pins; if the effect was the same she didn't much care how it was achieved.

Looking at the two of them sitting together—Rachel dark, chaotically stylish; Becky blonde, neat, very *jolie madame*—it was hard not to feel one was being offered a choice, being shown a selection; and indeed the two women were very conscious of the contrast they presented and enjoyed the way each pointed up the qualities of the other, while still being perfectly at ease with one another.

"Hello," smiled Becky, "how's life? You're looking very strident this morning."

Rachel took her booted legs down from the chair opposite and pushed it towards her friend.

"OK. Late night last night. New pupil this morning. Busy, busy."

"The demon lover again? Well? How's it going?" Becky's big eyes widened with curiosity.

"All right. I think we're settling in for a perfect affair. He'll turn up every couple of weeks and a wonderful time will be had by all."

"What if you want to see him in between, though?" Becky queried.

"Not allowed. It's written into the contract that he calls and I wait." Rachel grimaced. "Well, it does go against the grain to have no control at all, but on the other hand I hate taking the initiative. I never call men anyway, so it suits my neurosis. This way I don't have to ask and no one will say no." Rachel heard herself sounding a little less than convincing.

"That doesn't sound like you at all."

"No, it doesn't, does it? Obviously I'll have to find myself another lover as well; that'll keep the whole thing light and I'll get to say yes or no after all. What I've got here is an ideal sexual affair. No one pretends heavy emotions, we enjoy each other's company, have a good time. It's the most honest affair I've ever had. It's such a relief."

"I don't believe a relationship can stay on that level. It must get more complicated as you get to know each other. Someone will start to want more."

"Or less," Rachel grinned.

Becky was Romantic to Rachel's Cynic. She had never believed Rachel's protestations that she *really* didn't want an intense relationship with anyone.

"I think," Rachel said thoughtfully as she sipped her coffee, "that the demon and I are very similar. If both of us want a relationship that separates sex from friendship then it might work, and we both want that. I know you're committed to the Great Love as the end point of relationships, but I'm not. Truly. At any rate this is more what I want than anything else. He's a fantastic lover. Some woman, somewhere, must have spent a great deal of time and energy on him. For which I thank her," Rachel raised her cup in salute. "But it *is* a bit on the strange side."

Rachel offered this to Becky, if she would pick it up. She wasn't sure she wanted to discuss it, but she was feeling so surprised at what she was finding in herself, at what she could allow and enjoy, that she wanted to bounce it off someone. To see how it sounded in the cold light of day.

"How—strange?" Becky's antennae quivered, eyes now large as dinner plates.

"The textbooks would call it sado-masochistic. He sado; me masochistic. Anyone would call it sado-masochistic. He—um—spanks me. Last night he used a leather strap." Rachel felt she had just lived into an unheated swimming pool; she waited breathless for the cold splash.

"What?" Becky mouthed. "You're joking. Rachel?"

"Oh, shit. No, I'm not joking. The funny thing is it doesn't feel violent really. It's very ceremonial, like a ritual. Cold anger, not hot fury. Nobody's going to get hurt, he's incredibly controlled. That's what's so weird—I feel absolutely safe with him. Anyway, feminist principles or not, it turns me on and there's no point in pretending that it doesn't. So why not play it through? I may learn something. Look, we all know I'm a psychological masochist, in search of daddy and all that. So here's Someone I can consciously act it out with. Why not?" Rachel was fidgeting with defensiveness. She went on: "Listen, I read the other day about a sado-masochistic lesbian commune in San Francisco. They've just put out a manifesto saying that it's all right for them to beat the shit out of each other because it doesn't involve the exploitation of women by men. Who, may I ask, is crazy? I'm fully aware of what I'm doing. And if he's using me, I'm using him. This may be the most mutual, equal relationship I've ever had. It's honest, Becky."

Becky shook her head slowly so that her fine curtain of hair swayed a little. "Rachel, you're mad, you can't play around with that kind of thing. I know you always think you're in control of your feelings, but how can you be sure you can control this? It's so dangerous. He might hurt you. And what about warmth, kindness?"

"Maybe allowing each other to act out our fantasies *is* being kind to each other. Anyway that's how it feels. Yes, I know, I'm not sure about it. I am confused. But I know I want it and knowing that much is rare enough. If he phones me again I won't say no. If I did it would be on principle, not because I don't want him."

Becky finished her coffee. "What's wrong with principles," she challenged.

Rachel was irritated. "There's nothing wrong with principles, but if you're not ready to give something up, you're not, and

that's all there is to it. To say no on principle is just suppressing
something I've discovered is part of me. Isn't that as dangerous
as letting it happen? Sex *is* potentially violent and it's certainly
got a lot to do with power. At least this is overt. We both know
what's happening. It's very self-conscious stuff. Anyway I've
spent years heaving men out of my life because they impose on
me, make demands, want intensity. You're always telling me I
don't see things through because I'm scared to get involved. So
I'm going to see this through because I'm not required to get
involved and the demon is certainly not going to get involved
with me. I get the best of both worlds."

"But it can't work long term."

"It doesn't have to work long term. Of course it can't. You just
won't accept that I'm not looking for a long-term relationship. I
accept that your marriage is what you want. Just because I don't
want it doesn't mean it doesn't have advantages. There's a price
to pay either way. You opt for whatever you can afford. I'm good
at being alone, it doesn't scare me; but that's just because I've
had practice, it's habit. You don't want to be alone because you
never have been. There's no big deal either way. Most people
are together to keep each other warm on a cold, scary planet,
and it makes sense if you can do it. I can't, but I don't keep
telling you that *really*, deep down you want to be alone, or
ought to be."

Becky was fully engaged in what had become a set-piece
conversation.

"Yes, but you've left out love. I'm in love, and have been for
five years of being married to William. It's been up and down
and the gloss has gone, and the sex sometimes goes off—inciden-
tally it's definitely on at the moment—but *you're* the romantic.
As soon as the big thrill goes you close down the relationship.
You're the one who lives in fairytale land—and at the moment it
seems to be 'Beauty and the Beast.' "

Rachel smiled. Becky viewed the world from some point
quite alien to her but managed sometimes to hit a bullseye on a
target that Rachel didn't even know existed.

"There is truth in what you say, O Wise One, but I don't like
it. Look, we're stuck with what we are. That, at least to some
extent, is someone else's fault, so we have to live with it. There's

always a price to pay. You pay with periodic boredom, I pay with a degree of isolation. What the hell? I'm not really as sanguine about this as I seem, but what else can I do? What else, Becky, can you do?"

Rachel looked at her watch, as Becky replied, "All right, but keep me posted. There may be an article in this for me. And anyway I want the sordid details. But don't get out of your depth. You can't live *The Story of O* and be Rachel Kee all at the same time, you'll get confused."

"Don't worry, Auntie, it's simply a question of knowing the difference between fantasy and reality."

Becky pointed an emphatic finger at Rachel. "The mental hospitals are full of people who thought they could do that and were wrong."

Rachel gathered her things together and put some money on the table. "But I'm famous for looking reality hard in the eye, I couldn't avoid it even if I wanted to. It's a failure of imagination, I think. Got to run. Reality right now is a sixteen-year-old who's spent his life in care and wants to get some pointless CSEs so he can be half-educated as well as unemployed. I'll ring you. Glad to hear your sex life's going well, by the way. Bye."

Rachel left the café and drove down the hill to Wentworth House where she found Pete waiting in the kitchen with Dick, the residential worker she had met on her first visit.

"He's all yours," Dick smiled, putting his arm around Pete and pushing him forward, "and you're welcome! Make sure he works hard, he's got too good a brain to waste, even though you'd hardly tell from his grunts."

"Yeah, yeah, yeah," muttered Pete, grinning at Dick.

"You might teach him respect for his elders too, while you're at it."

"Well, I'll try. Don't promise anything though," said Rachel. All three laughed uneasily. "What is for dinner?"

"Shepherd's pie, or it was until Pete started waging culinary war on it," Dick answered.

"Culi . . . what?" Pete demanded.

"He means cooking," Rachel offered. "Do you like to cook then?"

"Yeah, a bit. I'd like to be a chef." Pete mumbled to the floor.

"He's really good," Dick put in. "He helps out a lot with the meals."

"Right," said Rachel, "we'll put it on the curriculum. I can use some help with the cooking at my place too."

"I thought I was supposed to be getting an education, not becoming a servant."

"They call it Work Experience these days. There's no reason why you can't get an education and enjoy some of it too. Come on, let's go." Rachel led him out to the car.

Pete crammed himself into the 2CV which was not designed for long-legged six-footers, and they set off. Rachel noticed as they were going along a stale smell in the car, a smell she half-knew but couldn't quite put her finger on. She wondered how the clothes got laundered at the home, then remembered that she had seen a large washing machine in the kitchen. She wanted to open the window to get some air into the car but thought it would be too pointed. She made a note to remember to open the window as soon as they got in the car for the return journey.

Shamus, the cat, greeted them on the stairs. Peter bent to stroke him, then made to kick him, his toecap falling carefully short of where the cat stood.

"Don't you dare," Rachel warned, half-joking.

"Bloody cats," Pete said, as he stroked Shamus again.

Pete sat himself at the living room table, and Rachel went into the kitchen. "Want some tea?" she asked over the half-wall.

"Yeah, three sugars."

"Remind me to double the sugar on my shopping list," Rachel said, as she put the kettle on.

Pete looked around the room, checked out the records which he pronounced old-fashioned and boring, looked over her bookshelves.

"Have you read all these?" he asked.

"Most of them. It's taken a long time though. Do you read at all?"

"No, not much. I read cookery books, and I like detective books. Ed McBain and that."

"Well, maybe we should read some Chandler. If you like crime stories he's the best," Rachel suggested.

Rachel produced the tea and put a plateful of biscuits on the table. When he polished off the plateful she made a mental note to double the biscuits too. She wondered if he was still growing; he was probably in a state of perpetual hunger however much he ate. They sat across the table from each other and Rachel talked about CSEs, what he could and should take if he had any plans about further education.

"If you're really interested in becoming a chef, you might think of doing a catering course at college next year. My guess is you'd need at least English, Maths and probably Home Economics. I'll write off and find out for you."

"Did you mean it when you said we could do some cooking? I was only joking when I said about being like a servant," Pete asked.

"I know. Yes. I think it's a good idea. Perhaps you should make a list of dishes you'd like to make. Then we can work out what ingredients we need, and shop for them and so on. You can take what we make back home and share it."

"Share with that lot? Not bloody likely. Well, maybe I'll let Dick have a taste. What about the money?"

"Don't worry about that. I'll speak to Dick; there's probably some money available from them, and the Home Tuition centre might cough up."

"That sounds all right. Can we start tomorrow."

"OK," Rachel agreed, "but you also have to do the other work. I think you ought to try for college. It'll mean some boring slog, a lot of effort. But it's just something that has to be done if you want to get anywhere. You have to decide you're going to really work because it's for you, and then just get on with it. But you might actually enjoy some of it. There'll be projects you can work on, that sort of thing."

"Yeah, all right."

The energy of starting something new, Rachel thought, wondering if it would last, if he would have the confidence and stamina to stand the low-key dullness of working every day for CSEs. They could only try.

"I like your place," said Pete, "but it's a bit small."

It dawned on Rachel that it must seem minute to Pete. It wasn't large: the living room was about thirteen feet square, big enough; but to someone of Pete's size things probably looked smaller than they did to her at five foot three; and having spent his life in residential homes, which however homelike they are made to seem, are always to some degree institutional and must by definition cater for unfamilylike numbers, her flat, carved out of a small terraced house, must seem a dollshouse. She wondered if he was claustrophobic, or if the domesticity of it brought on a psychological claustrophobia. Very likely. How often had he been in someone's home, in a normal domestic scene? Maybe very little indeed; if he hadn't been at school for years all his friends would be in care also. It was possible he hadn't been a visitor to an ordinary house for years.

He asked her about her family and she told him about Carrie, and that she didn't live with Carrie's father. She felt slightly relieved at not having to give him a picture of domestic bliss. But at the same time she found herself explaining that she and Michael were friends, and that he would probably meet Michael one of these days. She wanted to welcome him into a home, make him a welcome visitor to a place where, if things were not exactly the national average, they were amiable, and settled enough to make him feel secure.

For God's sake, she thought, I'm not adopting him. Careful. She led back to the topic of work.

"I'll go and see Mr Soames this afternoon and get some old CSE papers and textbooks, and we can start work tomorrow. You can make a list of things you'd like to cook and we'll work out a shopping list tomorrow as well. OK?"

"OK. How come your cat doesn't eat the fish?" he asked.

"Because he's not bright enough to figure out how to get it," she answered.

"Bleeding stupid animal."

They had already got an easy joking relationship going. Teasing her with her affection for Shamus was obviously going to become a motif. She was pleased because he could allow his liking for animals to show itself clearly through the surface banter. There was a warmth and gentleness about him cased in a very thin layer of tough. It was remarkable. She wasn't sure about the work side of it, but she knew they were going to get on well.

THREE

The shopping spree was not a success. Rachel wandered up and down, gazing into familiar shops, hoping that something unmissable would catch her eye. The clothes all seemed too ordinary. She couldn't imagine why anyone would pick out this or that particular garment feeling that it was exactly what she wanted, would provide precisely the desired image. Everything was grey—literally; shockingly so after the greenness of Cornwall. The now cloudy afternoon was complemented by uniformly dull shop windows selling dresses, sweat shirts, skirts and shoes in every conceivable shade and combination of grey. She thought, maybe it's my imagination. But she had the colour right. She wondered how it would be perceived by someone whose frame of mind was different from her own. Would the contrast between light and dark grey look vivid and interesting if you were idling down the street with plenty of money in your pocket, feeling at one with the world?

It was remarkable for Rachel not to be interested in clothes. She had a wardrobe bursting with ill-gotten gains from unnecessary shopping expeditions. The sudden urge to buy clothes would come over her and when it did it was only a matter of time before she set out. She felt deprived unless she had something she felt to be exciting to put on in the morning. It didn't have to be new, but when new and interesting combinations of old clothes failed to work, it was time to get something else.

She dressed, she was convinced, for herself. How she looked to others was secondary. Lately, in line with fashion and her own inclination, she wore layers of loose all-encompassing clothes. Huge baggy boiler suits, sizes too large, enclosed her airily, while she flung strange shaped scarves and wrist warmers about. She disappeared into her clothes like an orphan seeking refuge. Her frizzy hair, which she brushed with her head upside down to make it all the frizzier, hid most of her face so that she often had to peer through the fringe to see who she was talking to. She bought American dungarees cut for men with enormous bellies, rolled the bottoms, pulled on her stomping boots and strode about London like a shrunken Huckleberry Finn, lacking only a straw to suck. Becky said to her, "You're crazy. If I had a body like yours I'd be wearing pencil skirts and tight jumpers. I'd show it off."

"Too obvious," Rachel retorted. "Only someone with a body like mine would dare walk around in clothes three sizes too big. It's Implicit Dressing."

Which was only partly true. If she was dressing to be attractive it was to attract someone who would see beneath the layers. This was a challenge to which few men would rise, so in addition it made her safe. She was fed up with taking her clothes off only to find that the trouble of stripping them away was never really worth it; not for long. So she piled on the layers; the more trouble it was to undress the less inclined she was to do so. It saved disappointment in the long run.

Today, however, was a washout. There was nothing she wanted. Nothing, even, she could imagine she wanted and be sorry about afterwards. Things had to be pretty bad for her to find nothing at all.

Things were pretty bad. She had to face that she was quite as depressed as she had been before she went to Cornwall. The holiday had been hiatus, not change. The only man in her life was a sadist who might also be a rapist. She had a bloody great hole outside her front.

She also had a voice in her head that whispered into her right ear, "Why don't you kill yourself?"

Not that that was new. The voice had uttered the toneless question for years, for as long as she could remember. It was like a tape loop which repeated itself over and over. Normally she ignored it, brushed it away automatically like a cow swishing its tail at the flies that perpetually buzzed around. When she was at her most depressed, when she was immobilized with it as she had been before Cornwall, the voice disappeared because, she had come to understand, it became her: the quietly malevolent *thing* that wanted her dead moved in from the periphery and took over her being. She suspected, was sure, that that was what depression was.

But the voice was back, so she was at least walking wounded. She supposed that things could be worse. There was a fear, though, that it would move in on her again. Having been so recently incapacitated she didn't think there were any resources left to fight it.

Depression had been part of her life from way back. She remembered as a small child sitting stuck inside herself, unable to answer the "What's the matter?" from her mother or father, there being no answer that she could think of. Then she had been called "moody." "She's in one of her moods."

She recognized now that she had been depressed, as real and palpable a condition then as now, but unacceptable in a child. Moody made it her fault somehow, part of her character; she just was like that. Well, perhaps that was true too.

She had had every reason to be depressed. Life wasn't good. For the first ten years of her life her parents had conducted a war in which there were no innocent bystanders. The devastation was total, civilian casualties to be expected. She had been conceived as a kind of UN peace-keeping force and had failed as completely as the one out there in the real world. As the battles raged she ran back and forth in the tiny flat delivering messages, ultimata. Mummy says . . . Daddy says . . . In the very early days she made some attempt to make peace.

"Please don't fight. Let's make up. Let's be happy."

But that was always the cue for a stream of abuse and recrimination.

"*I* don't want to fight. It's him/her. Go and talk to him/her about it if you want it to stop. How dare you blame me for his/her behaviour. That bastard/bitch wants it to go on, wants to drive me mad, wants me dead . . ."

And on . . . and on . . .

It didn't work, it simply drew her in. So she stopped. And her mother, at least, never forgave her.

"You hard, unfeeling little cow. You don't care. You don't love me. I could walk out of this flat and you wouldn't lift a finger to stop me. You're just like he is—no good. If I'd known what you were going to turn out like I'd have strangled you at birth."

This catechism was screamed at Rachel many times, sometimes daily. As a child Rachel had had an image of maternity wards as long rows of beds in which sat women whose hands encircled their babies' necks, throttling them. She half-imagined that it was an option open to all new mothers.

Once or twice her mother did walk out, never for long, but long enough to prove that Rachel had not lifted a finger to stop her. She sat huddled up against her father on the sofa as the door slammed and the footsteps echoed down the corridor. She never did say, "Please don't go," as her mother threatened over and over to leave, until finally, her back to the wall, faced with her daughter's refusal to beg her to stay, even to cry, there was nothing else for it but to slam her way out of the flat.

She always came back, she had nowhere to go.

By the time Rachel was five her mother had alienated all family and friends, picking quarrels, accusing them of bad thoughts or evil deeds towards her, sending them packing: "And don't ever come back here again with your pretended friendship, do you hear?"

They never did. When the last, bravest cousin went, so did any kind of normal social life. There were no visitors. Sundays, Christmas, birthdays, Passover were all grim three-person affairs weighted with the tensions of not saying the wrong thing, although when someone—usually Rachel—finally did, it was almost a relief to get it over with and to end the pretence of festivity.

Rachel had friends in the block of flats with whom she played in the stairways and corridors, sometimes in their flats, but she rarely had them in her home because they would inevitably be quizzed on how they treated *their* mothers and then treated to a list of Rachel's shortcomings. She played alone a lot, using every inch of the corridors and fire escapes as labyrinths and mountains. Great heroic adventures were played out and she recalled these times as happy, even thrilling. The landscape of the building was rich and mysterious—front stairs, back stairs, fire escapes, lifts, endless floors of corridors—and people got used to seeing her engrossed in her current fantasy. Sometimes some of them joined in and her landscape became peopled with travellers, witches and wizards who directed her to caverns of gold or princesses trapped in fairy castles (she was generally both rescuing prince and maiden in distress). Some of them invited her to visit them, and she would secretly go to their flats and eat biscuits and learn new ways of playing patience, or just sit and chat about their lives and what she planned for hers. She always pretended that she had a happy family, although some of the grown-ups she visited who lived on the same floor looked at her quizzically, having heard the shouting and screaming coming from her flat. Rachel always pretended she didn't notice.

She was never an innocent victim. If such a thing exists. She loved one desperately, not the other. She chose sides, and was chosen. *He* loved her, made her laugh, took her out, hugged her as the footsteps receded down the corridor, or the door to the bedroom slammed shut, leaving them alone together in the poisoning air that hung about the flat and seeped through the crack under the bedroom door—Rachel's bedroom, because that was invariably where her mother shut herself away, so that Rachel often slept with her father in the double bed. Even when she started out in her own bed she was many times woken in the night by her mother telling her to get into their bed, *she* wasn't going to spend another minute next to *him*. Rachel would push back the bedclothes and stumble sleepily into the other room where her father lay on his back smoking in the dark. She would climb into the big warm bed and cuddle up tight against him, watching the glow of the cigarette and listening to the sound of him inhaling and the long sigh as he let the smoke out of his lungs; and he held her, stroked her and rocked her back to sleep.

Once she had said to her mother sleepily before she could stop herself, "This isn't like real life. It's like a story in a book."

This, for some reason, had been a hammer blow to her mother who never forgot it. It figured in the catechism regularly after that: "A bloody storybook! You think this rotten life is like a bloody story? Well, it's real, too bloody real. If you only knew how you and he have ruined my life. One day you'll be sorry, when I'm dead. If I'd known how you were going to turn out I'd have . . ."

Rachel was usually very careful about what she said, but sometimes the most innocent-seeming things began the recital. You could never tell, you had to tread so softly as if walking on eggshells. Things from outside were dangerous too. If on the television someone expressed love for their mother in words or music, it would begin:

"You see, you see that? She loves her mother . . . Not like you."

You couldn't control the outside dangers, she learned, but you could think very carefully before you spoke. And there was always the lurking suspicion that her mother was, after all, right. Rachel didn't know then about self-fulfilling prophesies, but she did know, guiltily, that she didn't love her mother. She wasn't actually sure what loving her mother meant, or was supposed to feel like, but her constant failure—refusal—to be what was wanted seemed proof enough to both of them that she didn't. She was pretty sure she loved her father, but that in itself was evidence of her failure towards her mother. They were, Rachel and her father, "two of a kind," "no good," both of them, so loving him was an act of treachery. It was, too, because he *was* a bastard.

"He's a rat," her mother used to say. "If I saw him lying dead in the gutter I'd step over him. I'm no hypocrite, you know that."

Rachel's father was debonair, smooth and very attractive to women. He was a creature of his time, a crib on the suave Englishman of the forties and fifties, a mixture of George Sanders and Errol Flynn, whom he resembled. In the argot of the time he was a cad; now, hustler seemed more appropriate. He stayed out late, told lies, had many affairs, had twice left home for several weeks and once, Rachel remembered, a woman had arrived at their flat from Plymouth and told her mother how he had run off with several thousand pounds of *her* mother's money, having in the terminology of the time seduced her. The woman was about Rachel's mother's age, so *her* mother must have been well into her sixties. He had been a clever East End boy, her father, lots of promise and scholarships, but had turned his hand in the end, thanks to his looks and charm, to being something of a crook.

While he conducted his affairs Rachel's mother had, as she had many times pointed out, taken care of Rachel, sat with her when she was ill, explained away—at least at first—his absences, cooked, cleaned, "skivvied for him" as she put it. She *had* been the martyr she portrayed herself to be. There was justice in her accusations, he was not a good man, he had truly made her life a misery. His single virtue was that he loved Rachel. So he said and so Rachel thought. Even her mother acknowledged that—insisted on that. And Rachel loved him, who so patently mistreated and did not love her mother. She understood the injustice of this, the pain it must have given her mother. They had an alliance, Rachel and her father, but it turned out finally that she had no power over him. No power to make him stay, no power to make him go on loving her.

When she was ten he left suddenly and for good. Rachel was left alone with her mother who railed and raged against him and her and life itself. He, Rachel, their relations, their ex-friends, the Jews, the world had ruined her life—nobody cared about her at all. They heard nothing from him and received no money. Rachel's mother had never had a job, was completely uneducated, having left school at twelve to bring up her sisters and brothers. She had lived entirely as a household servant, first to her own motherless family and then to Rachel and her father. She couldn't and wouldn't consider working; nor would she ask for social security, she would not, she said, "stoop to that." So they had nothing, no savings, just a few pennies. They lived on potatoes and bills went unpaid. The rent was in arrears and finally the bailiffs were sent to repossess their furniture. After that they walked around the flat barefoot because Rachel's mother feared the people downstairs would hear that they hadn't any carpet. Rachel was not to tell anyone at school what had happened: her father, she was to say if anyone asked, was dead. The keynote of the time was shame and rage. Finally they were to be evicted.

One morning, two weeks before the eviction was due to take

place, Rachel walked into her mother's bedroom and found her
naked in bed, rolling wildly from side to side. Saliva spilled from
the corners of her mouth as she wailed and moaned incompre-
hensibly to someone whom Rachel looked for but could not see.
At first she was terrified, faced with this crazed creature, and
moved towards the bed to touch her mother, more to take
comfort than give it. She put a hand on her shoulder and asked,
"Mummy, what's the matter?"

Her mother stopped rolling for a second and stared at her
without recognition. "Who are you?" she demanded. "Go away.
I don't know you." Then she jerked her shoulder away and
continued with the obsessive rolling as she wailed and screamed
her stream of complaint and misery.

Rachel took a step back and looked at her for a long moment
until something strange happened to her vision, and the bed
with her mother writhing on it seemed immensely distant. Just
a moving speck, very, very far away. Then she straightened up,
like a soldier, shoulders back, head balanced perfectly over her
spine, and turned briskly on her heel to walk quietly from the
room, her face impassive. She knocked calmly on a neighbour's
door and explained politely that something was wrong with her
mother, she was sorry to bother them but could they please
come and see. Feeling nothing, doing what was obviously necessary, quite cold. The neighbours remarked to each other in
whispers, as they watched her mother being carried off on a
stretcher, how strange the child was; quite hard, not a tear or a
question.

They took her mother away to a hospital and Rachel was sent
—God knows where. They said it was an aunt, but it wasn't any
aunt she had met before and the area was completely unknown
to her. Later, as an adult, she realized it must have been a foster
home, but at the time it was simply strange and unknown. She
lived there for months, unhappily, feeling she was in the wrong
place, quite alien and alone. There were other children there,
children of the woman who looked after her, but she didn't
know them either, though she joined in their games sometimes.
She had nothing of her own there, just some clothes, and there
was no one she felt attached to or able to talk to. She was cool
and polite and went daily to the local school. It must have been

autumn because she remembered sitting on the floor in assembly singing "We plough the fields and scatter the good seed on the land." She wasn't interested in the words, but the tune had a strange quality which made her think of space, infinite emptiness, and gave her a wrenching feeling somewhere in her diaphragm. No one seemed to notice that she walked around frozen inside, a small, angular block of ice.

Then, after what seemed forever but was in fact a few months, her father suddenly turned up—had presumably been found by Social Services. When he walked into the room, unexpected, unannounced, it was, for Rachel, like living all the happy endings in all the fairy stories she had read. All of a sudden everything was all right. The thaw was immediate. They fell on each other, and held on and kissed. She cried, "Daddy, daddy, daddy," as she hung tightly to his neck and felt for the first time in so long his rough cheek against hers. The "aunt" looked on astonished at such a display of affection from the tight little girl who had been in her care. Then, dreadfully, her father was on his knees in front of her, tears streaming down his face. "Forgive me, darling, please forgive me. How could I have done this to you. I swear I'll never go away again."

The tears terrified her and the apologies were worse. She begged him to stop and there was something secret and dreadful inside her that hated him for doing it, but he got up finally and they held and hugged and touched each other while the "aunt" gave them tea, and the anger she had suddenly felt when he was on his knees was forgotten. It was all right now, her daddy was back, the one person she loved and who loved her.

But it turned out he wasn't going to take her with him; he would visit her weekly, he told her, and they would go together and see her mother. She was disappointed, but the prospect of seeing him regularly and eventually living with him again satisfied her. There was a future to look to.

Once a week he came and took her to see her mother in the hospital who received them always in drugged, remote silence. She recalled walking up the long driveway clutching her father's hand until they came to a courtyard, tarmac and formal, brightly coloured flowerbeds. Her mother waited on a wooden bench with a nurse and gave no indication that she noticed them as they came into view. Rachel would put the flowers her father bought outside the hospital gates on her mother's lap, between her limp hands where they lay unnoticed until the nurse took them away saying how lovely and cheerful they were and that she would put them in water. Very gradually, over a period of months, her mother began to show signs of recognizing them and started to respond very wearily to their conversation, and occasionally asked questions, though with little enthusiasm. In spite of the visits meaning that she saw her father, Rachel dreaded them. She hated the discomfort of sitting with her silent, absent mother trying to make the bright conversation her father coached her in as they rode to the hospital, trying to pretend she was a proper daughter. What Rachel dreaded was seeing her mother at all, ill or well; she didn't feel any happier when her mother's face eventually creased into a semblance of a smile—she had merely regained the memory of smiling, the muscles recollected how to go about it, there was no meaning behind it. Rachel didn't care about her, didn't want to see her, didn't even want her to recognize her. Visiting her mother was the price she had to pay to see her father. Rachel had switched off long before on the morning she had walked into the bedroom and found a bizarre stranger.

Then, as suddenly as he had returned, her father disappeared again. There was no explanation; he just didn't come one weekend and that was that. The "aunt" simply said she didn't know and Rachel didn't enquire any further. Deserted again, she became a tight, unloving, unlovable little island. She didn't want her mother and refused to think about her father—there were no questions she could ask that had satisfactory answers, so she simply would not allow herself to think about it. All the while she remained polite and did what it seemed she had to do.

Eventually she left the "aunt," who apparently hadn't taken to her, and was put into a children's home while her still-fragile mother was set up in a bedsit. From time to time there were visits which neither of them relished. The home itself wasn't a terrible place, the people were kind enough, it was only that she was alone and had nowhere to go. It was a huge Victorian structure designed with large numbers in mind which pro-

vided, in Rachel's time, for the care of forty or fifty children who
were permanently or temporarily unable to live in their own
homes. There was no attempt to pretend it was other than what
it was—it didn't have the compromised domesticity of Wentworth House.

She was by now eleven and a half and attended a grammar
school near the home. She survived by being tough, isolated and
clever, and while she remained quite separate from her classmates she engaged the interest of her teachers with her preco-
ciously cynical comments on life. She questioned everything
from the contents of their lessons to their assumed right of
authority and used words as if they were explosive devices to
attack and destroy everything in sight—but carefully, accu-
rately, so that her logic was always infuriatingly unassailable.
She was interesting but not likeable: a sharp, skinny creature
with a strained much-too-old face and a verbal style like razor
blades. Her teachers recognized a quality in her that they de-
fined as "remarkable," but also sensed a dreadful, consuming
need, of which Rachel knew nothing, that kept them at arm's
length. She saw the distance they kept but had no idea why, and
sometimes she ached to have one of them put their arm round
her, but of course had no notion of the pain she would have
extracted from them if they had.

What Rachel experienced from inside herself was a cosmic
sense of not belonging. She was everywhere in the wrong place
with the wrong people, though this was merely an extension of
how she had always felt. When things were bad at home in the
old days with her parents she had raged inside at the unfairness
of having been "placed" with these people, having to suffer the
misery they created, because she had nothing to do with them.
They were not the right people, a mistake had been made
somewhere, she didn't belong with them and *it wasn't fair*. At
the children's home she experienced homesickness and
couldn't for the life of her understand why. Homesick for what?
For whom? She wanted to get back to . . . but she had no idea
what. Not her mother, not the old days of the three of them
living unhappily together. She wanted just to get back to something familiar. She ached for her mother but not the flesh-and-

blood mother she had known and failed to love. She just ached
and could think of nothing real that she ached for.

So what's changed, Rachel thought, as she sat in the café, having
given up her quest for clothes. I'm still aching, I still don't know
what I ache for.

Joshua. I ache for Joshua. Who couldn't give a shit about me.
Whose picture I see in a newspaper and know immediately he
could have done that, raped and assaulted and frightened a
sixteen-year-old kid. Whose deliberately infrequent calls I wait
for desperately. That's what I ache for, she told herself, that's
how far I've come in the last twenty-five years. It's not exactly
travelling at the speed of light, kid!

When she got home she took the cutting from her diary and
dialled the number the police gave for anyone with information. The electronics pinged and echoed as they connected her
to the police station at Inverness, and her heart thumped as she
wondered what it was she was intending to do. Find out. Get
information. She wanted information.

"Hello, Drumnadrochit Police. Can I help you?" said the
broad Scots voice.

"Yes. I don't know. It's about the man you want for assault . . ."

"Yes, madam. Do you have some information?"

No. She wanted information. She didn't have any.

"I don't know. I mean I can't . . . The man, was he a Scot?"

She suddenly wondered if they could trace the call, her mind
filled with images from television cop programmes, sifting the
nonsense to see if she had any knowledge about it. She didn't
now feel safely anonymous. How long did they need? Did local
police stations have that kind of equipment?

"I can't say very much about the man. What is it you have to
tell us, madam?"

"I can't tell you anything unless I know whether the man was
local or not," she said. She wanted to explain that she couldn't
give information about someone who was not the man they
wanted if they were looking for a Scot. She wanted the policeman on the other end of the line to understand that. This is
insane, she thought.

The policeman said carefully, "We don't think the man was local. What—"

"Right. Thank you. Sorry."

She put the phone down fast. They couldn't have traced the call in that time. But what had she found out? Nothing. What did local mean? Local to Drumnadrochit? To Inverness? To Scotland? She meant did he have a Scots accent or a plummy Oxbridge one? But so what? Joshua's BBC English was an invention anyway, he could have used a Scot's accent well enough to fool a frightened little girl. It was a pointless enquiry. What did she think she was doing? Supposing the policeman had said, "Well, madam, he had an Oxbridge accent." What would she have done then? Put the phone down. Supposing she knew for sure that it was Joshua, what would she do? Phone Inverness and say, "Excuse me, officer, there's this man I've known for three years and I think he's the man you're looking for. His name is Joshua Abelman and his address . . ."

It was unthinkable. But why was it? She didn't think it was all right for men who were a danger to women to be roaming free. She could speak to Joshua, let him know she knew (clever girl, powerful girl!) and make him promise to go and see a shrink. A laugh burst out of her at that. Try again. Think reality, Rachel. But how do you think reality about something like this. It wasn't real. It couldn't be real. And if she made it real by making her fears public what was she doing? Paying the bastard back. Did she really care about an assaulted sixteen-year-old more than theoretically? And if it was reality that was being thought then what about the sixteen-year-old herself? How did she get into the car with the two of them in the first place? Voluntarily, eased in by Joshua's charm. Attracted in. Was she an innocent victim? No one's quite that. She could imagine her excited and cooperative—up to what point? When exactly did she start to get scared? Rachel remembered reading about another rape recently where the girl had described what the newspaper called "her appalling experience." "He explained that he was going to tie me up," the girl was quoted as saying, "which he did, quite carefully. Then he raped me. He told me if I did as I was told he wouldn't hurt me. His voice was very calm and firm.

He didn't hurt me when he raped me. He was almost considerate. Then when he'd finished he said goodbye and left."

If Rachel had read that before she knew Joshua it would have been another description of another bloody rape. Made her angry, as any rape would. But now she thought she detected something almost wistful in the girl's account. Sex will never be the same for her again, Rachel had thought, not because she's been raped, but because she heard that tone in his voice. She'll spend her life hankering guiltily, if not consciously, after it. The real violation is that she's been shown *that* side of herself. The really appalling experience is that she's been turned on.

Obviously Rachel was projecting. The poor girl had probably hated every moment. Rape is rape. It is completely unacceptable. But that being true there remained in Rachel's mind at least a question about herself. If that man had done that to her, her emotions would not have been unmixed. Had she been speaking those words there *would* have been a quality of wistfulness, a sense that nothing would be the same again. That, after all, exactly described what had happened to her with Joshua. Was she unique? Obviously not. Joshua had recognized it in her, she had given implicit permission. She was *not* an innocent victim.

But Joshua did not do what he did to her against her will. She had always felt that if she said "no" at any point (in a way that really meant it) he would stop. At some point the girl in the car had said "no" and the man had not stopped. It didn't matter at what point she said it. No is no. The girl was raped, forced to do what she didn't want. That was that. Whoever did that was dangerous and violent and might do it again. Or worse.

There was something else, something that she identified as "betrayal" in the confusion of her thoughts. Apart from a natural disinclination to tell the police anything about anyone, she felt vaguely that it would be an act of treachery, that she couldn't do that to him. But who was this man she felt so protective towards? Someone who hurts people wilfully? There was, at the back of it, some childlike notion of not telling tales. It was the same prohibition that functioned in the idea of "professional ethics," that kept incompetents in their jobs in spite of their colleagues' knowledge that they performed badly, sometimes even dangerously.

So now there was Joshua. Well, she could justify her silence because she didn't know the truth, she could not wreak that kind of havoc in someone's life if they were innocent. She wasn't sure she could do it if she knew him to be guilty. What a *nice* person you are, Rachel, she heard her scathing voice tell her. And if you didn't, and he did it again and really damaged someone, what then my tender-hearted friend?

She decided that she wouldn't do anything until she heard from Joshua; he was due back any day and she supposed he would get in touch. She would wait, as she'd done for three years, for Joshua to ring. Uncertainty, as ever, was the name of their particular game.

FOUR

Waiting was what characterized the three years of Rachel's involvement with Joshua.

At different periods of her life time was divided into segments which varied according to the circumstances. At school, and later as a teacher, term-time and holidays alternated, the one leading unstoppably into the other; a period of activity and routine followed by leisure, and both when their time came were welcome. The change was welcome.

Then there was the period in the children's home when time had seemed endless, and she waited for something which she knew wasn't going to happen; there was the feeling that, by its nature, the home was a temporary solution to an immediate problem, yet everyone knew that there was no resolution in sight. She had no idea what she was waiting for, only that something *had* to happen because no one can live without any kind of expectation, some notion of a future. And eventually that time too stopped when, at twelve, quite miraculously, Isobel, in search of a bright interesting child, had scooped her up and given her a home.

Time. Periods of waiting for the next episode. Perhaps change is a definition of time. And at the very best of times there is still waiting—call it dread—that that period too will pass and whatever it is that is good will become a memory bounded by a beginning and an end.

The three years of Rachel's life that were Joshua's time were spent in waiting; the segments bounded by his visits. Life took on another rhythm, a counterpoint to the to and fro of Carrie's school and holidays, her teaching, the daily need for shopping and cooking and cleaning the flat. Beneath all those activities, all the three years of everydayness, Joshua's rhythm was a continuous and powerful presence. Life was a series of more or less likelihoods. Once Joshua had been round there was a week or ten days when she knew there was no possibility of his phoning, although the certainty decreased as the days went by and gradually shaded into expectation. The best times, the quietest, were in the week after he had visited: she was released from the tension of listening for the phone, wondering when he would. As time went on, as it came up to the two-week mark, she began to wonder when, and then if, he would call. Perhaps this was it. Perhaps he'd never come back again, and the tension became anxiety if she hadn't heard from him for a fortnight. Where other women suffered premenstrual syndrome she had Joshua to provide the ebb and flow of her moods.

He came at about fortnightly intervals; never less than ten days, and usually between twelve and fifteen. Although sometimes the spaces were longer. Sometimes three weeks, once or twice four. (Then that appalling gap of six months, when she knew that reason demanded she recognize that he wasn't coming again but nevertheless was somehow certain that he would. Wishful thinking, she told herself over and over, but eventually he called.)

"Whim," he explained, "nothing more complicated. I get a whim and I call you. If you're available and want to see me I come round."

So honest, so straightforward, their relationship. But what about Rachel's whims? Not part of the contract. She had phoned him one night when she was a little drunk.

"Joshua, I wanted to have a chat."

Liar, she had phoned because she wanted him to come round and fuck her.

"Perhaps another time. I'm extremely tired. 'Bye."

The voice so cold that she actually shivered as she put the receiver back. He hadn't called her for three weeks after that. Contracts don't have to be written, they can be etched into the brain by small icy experiences.

But although random whim was the acknowledged rule, the reality was not quite so simple. Joshua made reference from time to time to the haphazardness of his visits, and also, when it came up in conversation, to the fact that he saw her "once a month or so." She never queried this except for the brief amused look that passed between them each time; she knew, and she supposed that Joshua knew, that in fact he came with surprising regularity. The intervals were almost always fortnightly or thereabouts, neither random, really, nor monthly. The rules of the game required, however, that it was "as if" he visited her infrequently and with no detectable pattern. In that way the thing was kept light, she was given no excuse for thinking that anything other than occasional lust was operating. He didn't *need* her in any way. He had no needs, only whims. The nagging woman was kept at bay by this superstructure. She could never think of saying with any sense of justice, "Why didn't you come last week?" or "You are treating me badly, I have a right to some consideration," because she had no rights to anything, never having been promised anything. So if the reality was different from the apparent structure it was never tangible enough to be evidence of commitment or affection. There were several occasions when he did respond to her requests, but the requests were oblique and his response was never officially recognized as such. Sometimes she sent him cards when she found one funny and appropriate enough: a fifties photo, presumably an advertisement, of a woman in shirt and jeans holding an electric drill on which the contemporary cardmaker had written, "Women need this kind of relaxation too." On the reverse she had scrawled: "A woman's right to do it herself. Love R." He called the following day though no reference was made to the card. Once or twice she phoned him and replaced the receiver before the tone on the machine. Click. On both occasions he called in the evening and came round. She was sure he knew it had been her but nothing was said beyond a grin. And, of course, there was what she felt to be the inordinate power of her fantasies. This was probably delusion, she knew that, but there were enough times when she had concocted one of her scenarios, so strong that she sleepwalked through the rest of the day, and then Joshua had turned up and uncannily proceeded to act them out, sometimes using the very words she had imagined to go with the action. In some way, she supposed, she must have influenced what happened, how it happened, pushed it somehow in the right direction, and in any case there are only so many things two people can do with each other's bodies and only so many clichés appropriate to an activity. Coincidence.

It continued like this for two whole years, during which time Carrie learned to read and tie her shoelaces and draw people with features on their faces. While she changed from a five-year-old, half in, half out of babyhood, to a self-possessed, competent seven-year-old, Rachel learned how to wait. He called, she said yes. There were no other men in her life—she met few people, no one who interested her enough even for a single night—so she was always available, a fact which discomfited her a little. At first she was jubilant and maintained the story of a free and sexy affair with no strings.

"How's the Demon?" Becky would ask over the phone.

"Wonderful. He turns up late, we have great sex and then he goes before breakfast, just like any respectable Demon Lover should. Who could ask for anything more?" Rachel answered gaily.

"Does he just arrive?"

"Lord no! He always calls first to see if I'm free. He's nothing if not civilized."

"How exciting," Becky would say, "but it can't last."

"Idiot," Rachel laughed.

Rachel, in fact, was divided. What she told Becky was true as far as it went. She didn't want *more* of him, not inasmuch as more meant going to the movies, to restaurants or for long walks in the park together. They had created a time-out, a hole in space where they met to do only what it was they wanted to do. The social niceties were not necessary. It was a secure haven away from emotional entanglements. Sometimes Rachel imagined starting a new relationship—the traditional kind where two people meet and create a misty, emotional bubble, murmur sweetnesses to one another, walk in the rain tense with the anticipation of a hot bath and sex, linger over long meals in dim sympathetic restaurants aching with need for one another. Rachel remembered it well, she had done it a time or two. She remembered how time—and not much of it—had blown the mist away to reveal just two needy people with nothing in common, the moment when she woke in the morning to find herself wondering, as she glared at the man in her bed, "What am I doing with this person?" Then the embarrassment of extricating herself, of rescinding the whispered words of love and promises of future. God, how do I get out of this? Awkward, ugly business. The memory of it, the thought of it in the future, made her shiver with distaste. The misty, sexual excitement which was certainly fun at the time was now forever contaminated with the knowledge of how things turn out. Not something to yearn for, something to dread. There was, thank God, none of that with Joshua. "Games for children," was how he described conventional love.

So she didn't want that. A sexual affair, not a love affair, was what she had and wanted, but her total lack of control over the conduct of the affair began to bother her more and more. Of course her lack of control was the *sine qua non* of the sex they had. To be consistent his dominance, her submission, should be echoed in the way they arranged their meetings too. She didn't, however, feel consistent about it; she wanted, needed his control over her body but not over her life. She concluded that she was a part-time masochist, an amateur. The part of her that lived from day to day did not want to be at the beck and call of some man and began to rage against it. Quietly. She didn't want to lose Joshua, not yet. She knew the rules and for a while felt that she could put up with them. She squeezed a little self-esteem out of the notion that in acceding to his game plan she was actually using him as much as he used her. It was a bit theoretical, but it did for a while.

In the meantime he arrived pretty regularly and they sipped wine, joked, prodded each other's intelligence and performed their ceremonies. Nothing changed, there was no development, nothing residual. Each visit stood alone. Certainly they learned more about each other, but it had no obvious effect on the tone of their meetings. Nothing grew, they had a series of one-night stands, there was none of the familiarity that one expects from years of repeated meetings. She marvelled that

Joshua managed to keep the situation so cool and stable. Because it was certainly his doing. She was inclined towards private jokes and intimations, enjoyed comfortable familiarity—for as long as it lasted. It was quite clear that Joshua's way made for longevity. The scales weren't going to fall from her eyes because she didn't see enough of him to pick up the cues that made it happen. Clever Joshua, the man's a genius, she thought glumly. She might have spent the day angry, or longing to see him, aching for him; but each time she opened the door he stood there so bland, the casual acquaintance—and the fury and the longing dropped away. If she longed for anything seeing him standing in the doorway, she longed for anger, or lust, or rage. What she got from herself as well as him was urbanity.

What was true of the tone of the relationship was also true of the sex. She had, each time, to be eased into it anew. She was always the friendly, unflirtatious cynic with anything but sex on her mind—although perhaps it flickered around the corners of her mouth—who needed to be touched and commanded into sensuality. The switch had to turn first in Joshua's voice, then in her whole being. She had to be broken down, her self-possession dissolved and destroyed. What Joshua revelled in was the wreckage of a tough, clever and equal human being; a sex-change into a child-whore who was rendered inarticulate with wanting, overcome by her own sexuality, made to beg for pain and satisfaction. Joshua the magician, the wizard, with the magic wand and secret rituals that turned form into formlessness.

And it was precisely what Joshua revelled in that she wanted too. Sex, for Rachel, was a way, the only way, of slipping out of the controlled, armoured person she was. Sex was permission to let go, to be a wanting, hungry little girl who made demands and had them satisfied. It was safe to let go because Joshua was in control and it was the only way she could say or feel things that were impossible in everyday life. Rachel had never said, "I love you" to any man. Not since her father. The phrase, she would explain if necessary, was meaningless. Had no meaning. But that justification apart, the phrase "I love you" simply would not have come out of her mouth; she could not utter it in the cold light of day, as if a spell prevented that particular

combination of words from saying themselves. During orgasm
she could say them; not easily, but as if they finally burst out of
her. They came from the contractions in her womb and from
her tightened cunt, not from her head. Orgasm gave permission. Afterwards, after she had gasped, "I love you, I love you"
over and over and clung tightly to Joshua, she lay ashamed,
embarrassed at the echoing words.

"I assume that what's said during orgasm is under special
ordinance. I take it that it's expunged from the records," she
said lightly into the silence the first time it happened.

"Absolutely," smiled Joshua in the half-light.

She assumed he wanted that capitulation and resisted it for a
while, but not for long. She never resisted for very long.

The fatal flaw in sado-masochism, in dominance and submission plays, lies in the willingness of the victim. The last thing a
sadist needs is a masochist; the one person who cannot rape a
masochist is the chosen sadist. They can collude in the pretence
that one is wholly dominant, the other submissive, but the permission each gives the other denies the simplicity of their roles.
Rachel began to see that her willingness to be beaten and over-
whelmed gave her, paradoxically, a power over Joshua. If he
was to contain and act out his fantasies he needed someone like
her to permit, to understand and to react appropriately, while
at the same time her acceptance of him denied him what he
really wanted—to give real pain, to destroy. They were acting
out a pantomime and they both knew it, although it wasn't to be
said. As a pair of sophisticated post-Freudians they were giving
each other therapy. In the end, if they cared to think about it,
they were doing each other a kindness. Or so Rachel came to
understand. What Joshua chose to understand was uncertain.
She assumed he must know and made do with ritual. That was
what ritual was for: to conceal the underlying inconsistencies
with the theatre of black and white.

Then after almost two years of this seemingly endless, un-
changing relationship, Joshua suddenly stopped calling. There
was no obvious reason; the sex, the humour had been as usual,
she had made no demands. There was no reason to think as he
left on the last occasion that she wouldn't see him in another
couple of weeks.

The problem with the kind of relationship she had with Joshua is that there is no way of gauging when exactly it is over. He didn't call for a month, longer than usual; then two months, unprecedented, but still no reason to suppose that he might not call tonight, tomorrow night. At what point do you say, no, that's that, it's finished he won't call again—and believe it? Especially if you don't want to believe it. Sometimes she allowed the thought to creep around the corner of her mind, tried to make it real: *you will never see Joshua again.* She couldn't bear it, she was just not ready never to see him again; if she didn't have Joshua she had nothing. The idea of no more Joshua from now on gripped her with terror; the rest of her life became a void, an emptiness that was unsurvivable. Common sense offered the comfort that other things inevitably would happen, other men, or just the passage of time weaken Joshua's hold on her. While at some level she knew this to be true, it did nothing to allay the desperation she felt. Other men would not be Joshua; she imagined that from now on when she fucked other men some part of her would want *him*; whatever anyone else was or did, they would always be measured against Joshua, what he did for her. The future became a life sentence and she dared not think about his permanent absence for very long. The thought was stuffed back underneath the feeling that he would turn up again, if not tonight, then next week, or month.

This was not like Rachel, it surprised her as much as finding herself bending over to be smacked. A central tenet of her life was that you looked at the hard reality whether you liked what you saw or not. You examined first the thoughts that didn't want to be thought, because it was likely to be there that the truth, if such a thing existed, was found. Seeing how things *really* are may have been Rachel's chosen way of tormenting herself, but nevertheless she knew it was of the utmost importance. Human beings told themselves stories, reshaped reality into an acceptable form in order to survive, they beavered away creating hope, expectation and future from everything but the evidence of their eyes and experience.

Rachel's rejection of institutionalized hope was an essential part of who she was, but perhaps stemmed as much from fear as did compulsive optimism. Becky pointed this out to her once as she sat with her during one of Rachel's more massive depressions. Rachel, locked in and unavailable, had muttered over and over, "You have to tell yourself the truth. You have to face the cold hard ugly facts. Or you get lost in a web of sentimental lies."

Becky had interrupted gently, "But you assume the truth can only be ugly and painful. Perhaps that's the way you lie to yourself. You don't allow in any truth that may be positive. There may be pleasant truths too."

Rachel acknowledged the logic of that with a pause, but it had no inner reality for her then or later. She couldn't move beyond the fear that a belief in generosity, love—goodness—whatever Becky was talking about, was terminally self-deceptive, a way of comforting oneself for the unhappiness of being alive. It was a form of voluntary blindness that Rachel feared above all else. Still, from time to time it occurred to her that her stubborn commitment to bleakness might also be a truth she had to face.

However, committed to bleak reality as she was, she could not, try as she might, hold the permanent disappearance of Joshua in front of her eyes for more than a few panic-stricken moments. And it frightened her. It was a measure of her obsession, and made it finally necessary to see that she was in a condition she had never been in before. She felt devoid of experience or guidance. She was lost in a place she had always imagined she would never go. This does not happen to me, she thought over and over again; this isn't *me*. And I don't know what to do about it. Well, it didn't matter what you called it, impervious Rachel's walls had been breached, and if they didn't exactly come tumbling down she was having the hardest time of her life cementing the cracks.

Isobel wasn't much help; she was as committed to independence as Becky was to love. Rachel had told Isobel about Joshua in the early days of the relationship although in pretty general terms.

"Got this new man in my life. Well, 'in my life' is putting it a bit strong. There's this man around. He comes and goes."

"Well," said Isobel briskly, "I hope he treats you properly."

Whops. Not exactly.

"It's a sexual thing, not the Big L. We have a good time with each other and it's, um, interesting."

Isobel, drinking tea on Rachel's sofa, caught the look that Rachel's eyes were only half-attempting to conceal.

"Interesting?" she asked, sipping tea carefully

"A bit kinky. Nothing I can't handle," Rachel reassured quickly, "really quite safe. Just a little ritual violence. Well, one has to look at these things in oneself if they come up, doesn't one?" she invited, "and it's come up." She appealed to Isobel's equal commitment to telling oneself the truth. It didn't work. The Isobel who had been her mother for much longer than her real mother had, was engaged.

"What, exactly, do you mean, 'kinky'?"—her face tight with the effort at composure, the tone over-careful. She didn't want to hear the answer.

"Well, he's something of a sadist. Look, it's all right. It really is."

Isobel looked hard at Rachel, her lips pressed firmly together to prevent an unconsidered response. She was a woman in her early sixties, dressed in the careful elegance of a successful academic, the clothes expensively designed not to draw attention away from the presence of the substantial woman who wore them, her grey hair subtly cut to a sensible but attractive crop.

"I'm very surprised that you, of all people, should get involved with that. It's not like you. Rachel, it's dangerous!"

"No, it's not. Believe me, it's not. It's a kind of ceremony. And he's completely under control. I can't really explain this, but I do know. It's not just the sex, I get on with him; I mean when we're not fucking and so on, we talk—as if sex hadn't happened, and he's witty and funny and so am I." Rachel felt idiotic. She'd let the side down. Isobel was anxious but also disappointed in her.

"So you're letting this man do God knows what—tie you up and whip you for all I know—so you can have a witty conversation. You're crazy."

"Possibly," Rachel said, tightening up. "Anyway, it won't last. If someone else were doing it we'd be sitting here gossiping and laughing about it. And you'd be shaking your head saying, 'Well, people just have to do whatever it is they have to do.' We'd be amused and philosophical and wait for them to be finished with it. Why is it different for me?"

Silly question. But then Rachel was never quite sure which Isobel she wanted to address herself to and that was complicated by her uncertainty about which one Isobel was at any given moment: a confusion she imagined Isobel also experienced. Rachel never really knew how to describe her to other people—my friend Isobel, my adoptive mother. The difference in their ages and the length and depth of their relationship made "friend" a weak, unsatisfactory description; but then for a woman of thirty-one to speak of her "adoptive mother" was ridiculous and pedantic.

Isobel, sitting across the room in Rachel's flat, was clearly "mother," and had to say more than, "Because it is," to Rachel's question.

The topic of conversation changed at that point and Joshua was not mentioned again. Occasionally, during those first two years, Isobel would ask in a voice that made it clear she wanted no more than an exact answer to her question, "Is that—man— still around?"

Rachel would offer a clipped, "Yes, he's around," and the subject would change. Isobel never discovered Joshua's name.

But now he wasn't around and Rachel had to decide at what point the answer to Isobel's question was, "No, I'm not seeing him any more." She was loath to see the relief which would spread over Isobel's face at that and loath to admit to herself, as confessing it publicly essentially did, that it was finished. At three months she did make a declaration, "No, he's not coming round any more," and Isobel, who was not given to wrapping life in rose petals, said, "Good" firmly and finally.

"As a matter of fact it's not good," Rachel responded with a long, straight gaze at Isobel. "He's stopped seeing me. I didn't stop seeing him, because I want to see him. I can't just say 'no,' I don't mean it."

"Well, I'm sure he'll be back. I know the type," Isobel answered. This wasn't consolation, more a grim reminder to herself how impossible human beings are, particularly when it

comes to sex. She regarded Rachel as too informed, too knowl-
edgeable about life to waste time getting emotionally involved.

"You're in the grip of a sexual obsession. There's nothing to be
done about women in that condition," she said.

Oh dear, demoted to one of the "women." Where was strong,
free Rachel who had survived against improbable odds, to become more than the subject of mere physical hunger? Shame
on you Rachel, who of all people should know better!

"Well, I hope you're right, Isobel, because I want him back,
and I'm not suggesting that my obsession is anything more than
low-life sexual. I'm not under the impression that I've found my
mystical other half. If you know of a way of getting rid of sexual
obsession I'd be pleased to hear it, because it's bloody uncomfortable."

Rachel, fighting for her right to be an average klutz, just like
everyone else, sounded equivocal even to her ears. She wanted
out, but she wasn't out, that was that. She was as sick at herself as
Isobel was. I don't want to be this, she would mutter to herself
after an afternoon of masturbation and fantasy, how do I make
it stop? Strength of character, of course, but for the first time in
her life strength of character didn't apply. She either didn't
have any or it simply wasn't applicable in this circumstance.
How then had she managed to live through everything else?
Was it, after all, just luck, nothing to do with who she was? She
remembered a psychiatrist saying to her once after she did a
quick gallop through her childhood and adolescence, "You are
remarkably fortunate not to be psychotic. I think only your
powerful sense of reality prevented it."

Luck or character? Where was her powerful sense of reality
now, when she needed it most?

Not a day of those six months passed when she didn't think of
Joshua. She woke in the morning with him etched on her mind,
some memory or desire already half-thought. She got through
the days, worked with Pete, was involved in things; but there
was a small compartment always that contained Joshua like a
computer, humming quietly away sorting, sifting memories,
dreams and hopes. She didn't spend much time wondering *why*
Joshua stopped coming round, she assumed boredom and found
that reasonable—everything gets boring. She didn't actually

concern herself much with Joshua's life at all; her fascination was with what he was, not what he did. She knew he had other women, imagined it possible (though unlikely) that he had fallen in love with someone, was ill, had died. But jealousy and concern loomed small in her mind. She really didn't care who else he fucked, or how, or if he went to the movies, or had a temperature; she simply wanted him, there, fucking her, joking with her in their isolated little compartment. Once or twice she screamed aloud in her empty flat, "I want Joshua" and felt only slightly foolish afterwards.

Time didn't heal a thing. She waited for six months for the phone to ring with the same intensity throughout. She found a couple of men to fuck but it was never satisfactory. She came all right, but it wasn't enough. The time when just having one orgasm was sufficient was over. She was left in a more wretched condition when they left and lay alone in bed feeling as frustrated and needy as if they'd never been. More so because she knew she could not have what she really needed. Sleeping with other men was a travesty of what ought to be happening, a reminder of what she didn't have—any more. Her orgasms became mixed with rage, they became anger, bursts of fury. She decided she was better off without them and dealt with her sexual needs herself: it was hardly less satisfactory.

"He obviously isn't coming round because he was getting too involved with you and he's scared of that. You got to him," Becky consoled.

Rachel took a deep breath. "That won't do. He obviously isn't coming round because he doesn't want to, and that's that. The Mills and Boon version of Joshua Abelman is very attractive but it just doesn't fit. This is not some dark romantic hero who's struggling with a great inner need for me. And, what's next? Oh yes, he's been terribly hurt by a woman and dare not trust himself to anyone again. Probably in some deep structural way that's true, but it's not relevant, nor is it helpful. He came round for the last two years to fuck me, because I'm a good fuck and he likes my body. And he got bored. End of story. No big finish."

"I don't believe that," Becky insisted as she spooned the froth from her cappuccino. "He did come round for all that time, and you did get on. He doesn't want to admit it, that's all."

"And that's enough," Rachel responded grimly. "He's a finished product. If he's been damaged, which he has, then it's done. He doesn't get involved. It doesn't matter why. He isn't involved. It's just not useful to me to evoke feelings in Joshua. There's nothing to be hopeful about and I'm not going to start weaving dreams of 'deep down he loves me' into the unpleasant truth. It'll sink me."

Becky looked disappointed. Rachel's minimalist view of life chilled her. "Well, what are you going to do?" she asked.

"Nothing. There's nothing to do except shut up about it. There's nothing more to say. I don't want him secretly loving me, I just want to see him. Since I can't I'll settle for not being obsessed. Why can't I leave it alone?"

Becky didn't dare mention love, which seemed to her to sum up Rachel's condition. Becky had always rather enjoyed being in love. Rachel, she knew, regarded it as a kind of influenza, a sickness from which one recovered more or less quickly. Becky could say, "I am in love" and it was an act of pleasure, not something that had to be wrenched from her when she could no longer hold out any more. Becky wasn't at war with love, she just enjoyed it. She had only ever been involved, in love, with three men in her life; one she had lost to someone else, another she had left for her current love, William, with whom she had been living for the past five years. The rejection by the first and rejection of the second had given her pain in different ways, and the excitement with William was no longer bright and glossy new. She knew that things could go sour, that feeling changes, but she didn't accept that this was a necessary condition of love. She had no sense of the inevitable end as Rachel did. Because things had gone wrong twice didn't mean that her love with William was doomed. Even the loss of intensity wasn't fatal, she saw it as a reversible process; unlike Rachel who knew in her bones that once the glow had gone that was that, it was finished and time to get out. Becky was convinced that her relationship with William would continue, if differently. She never thought about endings, only continuations, and if things finally went wrong they were to be adjusted to as and when necessary, not something to plan for.

The dialogue between Rachel and Becky had been ongoing

since their early twenties, their positions fixed even then. Becky
often wondered if there had ever been a starry-eyed little Rachel who believed in fairies and the inevitable visits of Santa
Claus. Rachel wondered how it could have been that Santa
visited Becky so unconditionally that she should still believe in
him. But she counted herself lucky in the end that she had
learned that you couldn't rely on the magic out there, and so
avoided the awful pain when that Christmas morning came and
Santa hadn't made a delivery. Each woman could see the attrac-
tion or sense of the other's position; with a small part of themselves one wished herself a little more armoured, the other a
little less wary, but fundamentally each knew that *they* were
right.

Becky changed direction. "I'm going to the launch of Donna
Saunders' new book next week. Want to come? It's women only,
but I can bring a friend! Cissy phoned me and said she was
inviting lots of people but no men. It's a third sex party."

"What a treat! Yes, love to. Are we going as closet heteros?"
Rachel grinned.

"Right. They'll be very tolerant as long as we don't flaunt it.
It's on Tuesday. Let's meet for a drink before. How's the kid
you're tutoring, by the way?"

Rachel pulled a face.

"Maybe we should take him along to the party. That would be
very educational. Well, he's turning up more or less regularly.
He's a really nice kid, quite special, but I don't think he's going
to make it. He's permanently teetering on the edge of himself,
and the set-up at the home is getting worse. It's not looking very
good."

"Not make the exams you mean?" Becky asked.

"No, they're long since out of the window. Make life, I think I
mean. He's such a mess and he really hasn't got anyone."

"He's got you."

Rachel answered slowly. "Yes, but not in the way he wants or
needs. I'm a friend, I think, but what I've got to offer is terribly
limited. He needs a home, to be taken on full time and cared
for. I can't do that, it wouldn't be fair to Carrie, and anyway he'd
act out like mad. Somebody would have to engage him in battle
and I couldn't cope on a twenty-four hour basis."

"But he's not your responsibility for more than two hours a day. You're not employed to save him, just to try and teach him something. I don't think you're in any kind of shape to take on someone else's wreckage," Becky warned.

"Oh, ta. No, I know. But he bothers me terribly. You're right, I can't adopt him, it's just not on and anything less wouldn't be enough." They were silent for a moment, then Rachel smiled, "Do you remember the day we met, our first day in the staff room?"

Becky groaned. "God yes, hours of staff meeting and that dreadful woman instructing the new members of staff about the 'chain of command' and discipline and order."

"Come to think of it," Rachel said, smiling wickedly, "I don't know why I objected to it so much; it sounds right up my street when you put it like that. But then the kids arrived, remember? And all that either of us could do was survive the chaos. Hundreds of illiterate hopeless kids and all we had to do was contain them."

Becky closed her eyes at the memory.

"I was in shock for the first half term. I was so innocent. I'd only ever taught in that private school. I'd never met kids who thought there was no point in learning anything."

"We sat in your car at the end of the day, do you remember, and just laughed. We sat there for ages howling with laughter. I don't think I would have survived that place without you."

"And Amanda," Becky recalled. "When Amanda stormed into the staff room after a lesson with her remedial class and yelled, 'These kids are no good to Socialism!'"

"The good old days." Rachel smiled wanly. "Must go, I've got a lesson with Pete in half an hour."

"Take care," Becky smiled back. "See you Tuesday if not before."

Rachel waved a hand in farewell, paid the bill and left the café. Leaving the warm, fuggy air of pseudo Paris, the cold, clammy air of leaden London hit her like a ton of bricks.

Pete's crisis came to a head during the period of Joshua's absence. He had been coming to her for two years now and in the initial stages they had attempted to work towards CSE exams.

He was intrigued in particular by the Social Studies work, especially when they started to discuss group identity. He objected at first to the idea of his appearance being a badge of conformity to a subculture.

"I really like what I wear."

"Yes, but what if you'd been sixteen in 1969. Do you think you'd be wearing that stuff?" Rachel asked.

"Well, I wouldn't be dressed like a bleeding hippy which I bet you were," he grinned.

"Absolutely right, I was. There were other styles to choose from though. But there wasn't skinhead. And what people wore then looked right at the time, just as you do now. So in '69 we had a choice: we could be hippies, or mods, or straight. But each style was a uniform that told people who we'd decided to be."

"Yeah, all right," he conceded, "but just because I wear these clothes don't give people the right to think I'm just like everyone else who wears them. I don't go around beating people up, or Paki-bashing or anything. I got nothing against blacks, but when they see me walking down the street and there's more of them they start something."

"Well, what do you want people to think of you? Why wear those clothes and shave your head? And what about that swastika on your hand?"

Pete looked impatient with her. "They don't mean nothing. They're just what I wear."

"You can't get away with that, Pete. Look, I'm a Jew—"

"You're not!" Pete interrupted. "Are you really?"

"I'm a Jew," Rachel repeated. "What do you expect me to think when I see someone with a Nazi sign on their hand? Forty years ago people who wore those signs were killing people like me. The sign has a meaning. If *you* don't mean it why wear it?"

" 'Cos everyone does. And you're not scared of me, are you?" he asked.

"No I'm not, but I've got to know you. When you come here I talk to you, not your clothes. And now that I do know you it helps to stop me making assumptions about other people I see in the street dressed like you. But that still doesn't explain why you dress in one way and then act aggrieved when people take you at face value."

"All right, yeah, I want to look like my mates, but I still think people ought to take the trouble to find out about you."

"I agree, but you don't make it easy for them. Anyway, why do you want to look like your mates? That's what the textbook is talking about. We all do. We all have uniforms of some sort."

They began to make a list of all the things Pete saw in Rachel's flat, and clothes that typecast her, then looked at other people—pop groups, politicians and so on. Then they got back to Pete and his friends.

"Well, I suppose," said Pete finally, "you've got to have a group of friends you feel you belong to. You got to feel you're part of something."

"I think so," Rachel replied. "I think it was perhaps the way the human race got started. People make signals to each other that say, 'Hey, I'm one of us.'"

"Well, what's wrong with it?" Pete asked.

"Nothing, except when people don't know why they're doing it and start to really believe in the signals and acting on them. Then you get Nazism and Paki-bashing and religious wars."

"And all they really wanted was to be part of a group?" Pete offered.

"Maybe," Rachel shrugged.

"I'll wash the swastika off if you don't like it."

"I don't. I'd appreciate it." Rachel smiled. "Want some tea?"

They cooked a lot too. Rachel and Pete pored over recipes and made the ones that were most interesting and exotic, which Pete took proudly back to Wentworth House for Dick and the others. Pete wouldn't eat most of what he cooked.

"I hate foreign food," he explained, his hands covered in a mysterious and pungent concoction of spices he'd mixed to make an authentic curry.

They had their conversations, read through some textbooks, Pete even began a project on the history of cooking; it was positive up to a point. But he found it hard to write down his thoughts and ideas and was easily bored with anything that didn't grab his attention. Rachel decided not to push; she explained several times that passing the exams required he do the boring stuff and a lot of written work but that she wasn't going to force him—couldn't anyway. It became clear that he couldn't

cope with the work and wouldn't manage college; he was quite
bright enough but simply unable to concentrate on the dull bits.
Underlying that, it was increasingly obvious that there were
very much more important problems in his life that made the
idea of hard work and college out of the question. So they
continued with the cooking and quietly dropped the textbooks.
The daily sessions went on, Rachel made tea and provided biscuits, and they sat at the table and played chess or Scrabble and
talked about anything and everything, but most often about
Wentworth House and what went on there. Pete brought his
anger and resentment to Rachel but was careful not to release
it. Sometimes during their chess games Pete engineered an
early exchange of queens which never failed to irritate Rachel.
A small battle would ensue.

"Look, you can't play chess like that. You can't have a decent
game if you just swap pieces."

"That's what I want to do. I can play how I like," Pete would
mutter back at her.

"Well, you can play how you like, I can't stop you. But it won't
be chess," Rachel would answer, feeling a bubbling rage.

"I don't care."

Rachel would take a deep breath, remember which of them
was which and say, "OK, but next time why not think about
another way of getting out of the situation that doesn't mean we
both lose our queens? There are other ways to win."

She avoided confrontation not because she was scared of him,
but because she didn't want him to get into a situation where he
stormed out and felt he couldn't return. It was clear also that he
didn't want that to happen. To the degree that each was capable
they controlled their anger and maintained contact.

Pete's anger centred initially around his social worker, Mary,
who visited him weekly at the house.

"She doesn't bleeding care about me. It's just a job," he'd
complain.

"Well, of course it's a job. Teaching you is my job, it doesn't
mean I don't care about you," Rachel tried.

"Then how come she ain't found me a foster home all this
time? She talks a lot and does fucking nothing."

"But Mary's only been your social worker for a year. You can't blame her for what didn't happen before."

"All right, so it's not just Mary-bloody-Jackson. It's bloody Social Services. It's all of them. Why don't they find me a home in all that time?"

And why don't I give you a home, Rachel heard beneath his complaint. Why does everyone give just so much but not enough, not what you really want? What is stopping you, Rachel, who's got such a comfortable home and who says how much you like me, from taking me on? Why don't you love me?

"I don't understand why they never found you a foster home, Pete. I don't know the details. Organizations like Social Services are very slow and clumsy and make mistakes. Would you like me to meet Mary and talk about it with her? Perhaps we can get a clearer idea of what's going on. I won't unless you say it's OK."

"If you like," Pete responded.

The next day he arrived with a piece of paper with Mary's work phone number written on it. Rachel called while he was there and made an appointment to meet her.

She was sent up to Mary's office where she was met by a pleasant woman in her early thirties. Mary Jackson wore dungarees and running shoes, comfortable, ill-considered clothes covering a plump homely body. Her hair was pulled back into an untidy bun and she wore National Health wire-rimmed spectacles over her watery blue eyes. She was friendly and harassed; her desk covered with files which spilled over onto the metal wastepaper basket beside it.

She brought in coffee in plastic cups and handed one to Rachel as she sat down on the green plastic chair in front of her desk.

"What do you make of poor Pete?" Mary asked, crossing her large thighs.

"He's extraordinarily likeable. Amazing really, when you think how little he's had in his life. I don't think he's going to do CSEs though." Rachel sipped her coffee and waited.

"I never thought he would. It's asking a bit much. But we're terribly worried about what's going to become of him when he leaves care. You know about his problem, of course?" Mary asked.

"Well, I know he's been in care all his life and he's pretty resentful that he was never found foster parents."

"No, I mean his physical problem," Mary said, "the encopresis."

"The what?" Rachel asked, mystified.

"He hasn't been too bad lately and the workers have been making a special effort at getting him to keep his clothes clean, but surely you've noticed the smell?"

"I've noticed a smell now and then. I assumed he wasn't washing much. What is encopresis?"

"An inability to control bowel movements. He's been like that all his life."

Rachel blinked. She remembered eneuresis was the term doctors used for bedwetting. She had noticed that Pete smelled sometimes, often opened the window after he left to air the room, but it had never been really obviously a smell of shit.

"You mean he shits in his pants? Is it a muscular thing or what?"

"No one really knows. He's been to endless doctors and even spent six months having behaviourist therapy at the Maudsley children's unit. That was a disaster, he came out much worse than he went in. It seems generally agreed that there's no physical reason for it. As I said, it's not happening much lately, but his clothes do have that stale smell. When it's bad there's no mistaking it."

"Poor kid. What happens when he's with other kids?" Rachel asked, beginning to imagine the impact that would have on someone's life.

"That's why he's not in school. The other kids gave him such a bad time we decided it was best if he left. They called him names and wouldn't sit near him, that sort of thing. At the home the workers make sure his underpants are washed, because he doesn't really make the effort, but the kids laugh at him when he's going through a bad patch. He's the oldest one there, and the biggest too. The younger kids tease him and then he beats them up."

"Does he hurt them?" Rachel asked.

"No." Mary hesitated. "It's more that he's making them see

who's boss. All his friends are much younger than him, as if he
can't stand equal competition."

"I'm not surprised. God, what a burden. Can't anything be
done?"

"Well, we've tried everything we can think of. If only he'd
keep himself clean it would help. It's only a matter of rinsing
the clothes out and then bunging them in the washing machine,
but he just won't do it. Dick and Maggie have to make raids on
his room and find piles of filthy pants and jeans lying on the
floor."

"It's hard enough for adolescents to keep things clean at the
best of times, but if you have to face the fact you can't control
your own bowels it must be . . ." Rachel was lost in the effort of
imagining what Pete must feel like. She wondered whether he
thought she knew about it and had been saying nothing out of
tact. She felt terribly unobservant.

"Yes, it's horrible for him." Mary agreed. "The kids yell 'time
for a nappy change' when it happens. They won't sit next to him
at mealtimes if it's happened in the previous couple of days, but
as I say he doesn't do the practical things he could do to improve
his situation."

Rachel wondered if being practical in that situation wouldn't
have been beyond her capabilities too. It must be so humiliating, and then to have to wash out the clothes—unpleasant and
difficult and constantly face to face with what you'd rather
forget. Suddenly Pete's future looked bleaker than ever.

"And you see why," Mary went on, "it's been so difficult to
find him a foster home. It's hard, in any case, to place adolescents, but with his physical problem it's practically impossible
to find the right family. It would be out of the question to place
him with a family where there are other kids—he couldn't cope
with that—but couples without other children probably
wouldn't have enough experience to deal with Pete."

"Yes, I see that, but perhaps the shitting would come under
control if he was living in a secure set-up?"

"Possibly," said Mary doubtfully. She was very much the professional now explaining reality to a sentimental onlooker. "But
first we have to find the family. The truth is that Social Services
really screwed up about Pete. He should have been placed with

a family when he was very young, it would have been possible then, but there was some kind of administrative cock-up. He was shuttled around from one residential home to another and no one ever seemed to get round to looking into the fostering or adoption options. Sometimes that happens in large organizations. His social workers kept changing, there wasn't enough continuity."

Who was to blame that Pete never got a home? *Them*, not us. Those in the past were responsible, the ones who had left. Social Services was a bureaucracy, the structure remained but the personnel changed over time. The structure—the current personnel—could freely admit to mistakes made in the past, they weren't their mistakes. There was no one to hold responsible, only the results of past errors to deal with. They, the current workers, had to clean up situations not of their own making, and sometimes it was not possible. Too much damage had been done, too much time had been lost. They were regretful about their predecessors but they were practical people, working with what they had in the here and now. Rachel felt vaguely helpless, like Pete. Being reasonable she could see there was no one to blame, but felt outrage that there was no way of pinpointing responsibility, of making someone correct the fault that had wrecked a person's life. She understood Pete's fury with a new clarity, and his resentment of Mary as the representative of those who had done so badly by him and the unreasonableness of that resentment. Almost worse was Mary's understanding of Pete's anger with her.

"Of course Pete is angry with me. It's inevitable that he should see me as useless and the reason why he has no home. Part of my job is to take that flack and not get emotionally distressed. But Pete is a bit different, he does have that seductive quality that makes you feel guilty even when you know you are doing your best. Sometimes I'm close to tears after a visit because I have to take his anger and know he won't understand it isn't really my fault. But, as I say, that's my job."

I don't want to know what a hard life it is being a social worker, Rachel thought irritably, I'm on Pete's side. She saw that she had to be careful, Mary was including her in on the "professional" side, inviting her to be one of them. In fact, she realized, she was the only person in Pete's life who wasn't "one of them." There was possibly Dick who he seemed to trust, but she was the only one fully outside the ambiance of Social Services. If she was to be a go-between it would have to be made clear that she was Pete's friend first and foremost, and was not to be used to "explain" Mary's problems to Pete and Mary's benefit. If she did explain, and she realized that there were explanations to be made, it would be because Pete needed to know what was happening, why and how things worked. It was not her role to excuse Social Services to Pete. She wasn't going to do it.

"What's going on at Wentworth House?" she asked. "I'm getting the impression that all isn't well there. There's some trouble between the staff and the new man in charge."

Mary looked at her sharply, assessing how much to tell.

"I don't think that Richard Pierce is handling things as well as he might. It's probably just initial settling in, he does seem to be getting on people's nerves a bit."

"I gather someone Pete rather liked has left because she didn't like Richard. Pete feels that maybe Dick is about to take off."

"Actually Dick has handed in his notice. He says he wants to travel a bit, but unofficially he told me he can't work with Richard. That's confidential, by the way."

Oh is it, thought Rachel. Here we go—I'll tell you what's really going on but you mustn't tell Pete, who really needs to know. Professional ethics.

"Mmm. Richard seems to be a bit rigid about regulations. Wants to keep the rules and invent a few more of his own, is that right?"

"That's about it. He's newly promoted and isn't all that easy about being in authority."

"Sounds to me that he's scared of things getting out of hand, but if you're running a home for disturbed children things will get out of hand. You can't regulate problems away. He's managed to scare off the only two people Pete trusts; there's going to be trouble, surely? Pete's sounding very angry."

"Yes, I know. We're keeping an eye on things at Wentworth

House. But for whatever reason, Richard was given the job and we have to allow him to *be* the head of home."

"Why was he given the job? It doesn't sound to me as if he's suitable," Rachel queried.

Mary didn't answer. She had gone as far as she was prepared to go with an outsider. Why Richard Pierce got promotion was restricted information—presumably because someone had made a mistake which couldn't now be rectified. Was Richard's job a way of getting rid of him somewhere else—the bureaucratic solution. It seemed that the errors were not just in the past, although the error-makers were equally obscured from view.

As she left Mary's office, Rachel had the uneasy feeling that she was thoroughly involved in something that was going to become increasingly dramatic. She had an urgent desire to get out of the whole thing, find a way of sliding out of any commitment she had to Pete. She could tell Donald Soames that the CSE business wasn't working, that Pete was too disturbed to deal with education. That *was* her job after all. She didn't want to be part of whatever was going to happen, she didn't want entanglements. She could phone Donald when she got home. But she didn't.

The next day Pete was an hour late for his lesson, and as she opened the door and saw him standing there she realized the drama had started. He looked terrible, she had never seen him like this before. His clothes, though the same ones he usually wore, were filthy and somehow limp, and his face was several shades darker than his normal fair colouring. It wasn't just dirt although there was that, it was as if the actual skin had changed tone, as if the greyness of his face came from the inside. His features were pinched, closed off; he glared at her through narrowed eyes as he stood in the doorway, and the anger seemed to come from them like a shaft of light through a crack in a door, from deep inside himself. She immediately cut off the complaint she had planned to make about him being late and wasting her time and opened the door wide.

"Come in, Pete."

He strode past her and up the stairs, ignoring Shamus who arrived, as usual, to greet him. As he passed she caught the smell

—unmistakable now. He must have soiled himself on the way. He sat down heavily on the chair on his side of the table and began to pick at a loose bit of paint on the window-frame. After five minutes of silence as Rachel busied herself making tea the stripped area had grown to the size of a matchbox.

"Don't do that," she said.

Pete pulled his hand away and looked up at her angrily. "If you're so fucking worried about your paintwork I can go."

"Why don't you tell me what's wrong," she suggested, as Pete picked up her lighter from the table and began to flick on the flame over and over. After a moment he held the flame to a hole in his jeans and started to burn away the threads. A smell of burnt fabric and shit filled Rachel's room. She took a deep breath.

"What's happened, Pete? Stop fucking about with the lighter and tell me what's happened." She sat down at the table opposite him. He simmered with aggression, but he was holding on to it as well as he could.

"Dunno." He could hardly get the word out of his rigid lips. "It's them. It's those fucking bastards."

"What? Tell me what's happened," Rachel insisted.

"I had a fight. It was her fault, she fucking goaded me. That cow, Maggie. She wants to get me in trouble. She hates me. And I fucking hate her too. I wish the bloody vacuum cleaner *had* hit her. I wish I'd fucking killed her. Fucking cow."

"What vacuum cleaner."

"She woke me up. She went on and on and I warned her to stop, but she just went on hoovering. I was out late last night with my mates and this morning she knocked on my door and went on about how I had to get up and come to you. I was dead tired, I didn't want to get up. And then she got the hoover and started with it outside my door. She went on hoovering for twenty minutes and banging the bloody thing against my door, and I warned her to stop. She's not even supposed to do the hoovering, there's a fucking cleaner to do that. She was just getting at me."

He stopped and began flicking the lighter again.

"What did you do?" Rachel asked.

"I fucking leapt out of bed and pulled the door open and got the hoover out of her hands. I was just getting it away from her and I sort of chucked it out of the way. Then she rushed downstairs and said I'd thrown it at her and that I'd hit her with it." He looked at Rachel levelly.

"Did you throw it at her?" Rachel asked.

"No I fucking didn't. And it didn't hit her, I just threw it out of the way, it didn't go anywhere near her. She's a fucking liar. She started it. She should have left me alone."

"Maybe," Rachel said, "but that's not a good enough reason for throwing a vacuum cleaner at her."

"I *didn't* throw it at her. Don't you start on me." He was on the edge of the seat ready to storm out.

"What happened then?"

"Nothing. I ran out of the house while she was still crying in the kitchen with Dick and Richard. Dick called me and told me to wait but I just walked out. They wanted me to come here, so I came. Dick's leaving. He told me last night," he added, as if he was starting another conversation.

"Yes, Mary told me yesterday. You must be very sad about that."

"I couldn't give a toss. They're all the same. I couldn't care less what any of them do as long as they leave me alone."

"That's not true, you're very fond of Dick, and you know he cares about you."

"Yah? Well why's he leaving then if he cares so much?" Pete demanded.

"Because he can't get on with Richard. They don't see eye to eye about how to run the place. It's got nothing to do with you."

"That's what he said last night. Richard's a prick, all he's interested in is rules and rotas. But I don't see why I should suffer."

"No, it's not fair," Rachel agreed, "but what happens between the staff will obviously have some effect on you. It's like in any home; if the grown-ups don't get on the kids suffer too. It's not their fault but they're part of the place."

"But if bleeding grown-ups can't get on why should they expect us lot to be any different. They're always telling me I've got to learn to control myself, but what about them? If they really want me to control myself why do what Maggie did? She should have just asked me to get up."

"It sounds like she did at first. Would you have?" Rachel asked.

"No." Pete grinned for the first time and Rachel smiled back, pushing the biscuits towards him.

"Why didn't she know that all that hoovering and crashing against my door was going to drive me wild?"

"Come on, Pete, you're not stupid. You know perfectly well that you can wind them up. That adults lose their cool and do stupid things. If things are very tense at Wentworth House then that's going to affect their behaviour generally. The world's not peopled by saints who never make mistakes or who only think about others, not themselves. You're living with real people who are going to fly off the handle sometimes, just like everyone else. That's the only kind of people there are. The best we can all do is learn how to make allowances for each other."

"Well, they should have made allowances for me. They don't give a fuck about me," Pete muttered. He wasn't hearing her. He was a needy, angry six-year-old who couldn't take the needs of others into account. He wasn't going to admit anything. He was the aggressed innocent. Full stop.

"Why don't I drive you back home and have a word with Dick and Maggie?" she suggested.

"There's no bleeding point. They don't care." But he hadn't said no. They finished their tea and left the flat. This time Rachel firmly opened the window as she got into the car. The stench was awful.

Back at Wentworth House Dick and Maggie were still sitting in the kitchen. Pete marched past and stamped upstairs to his bedroom, slamming the door. Rachel stood in the doorway to the kitchen, smiling ruefully.

"Hello . . . Trouble I hear? Can I come in and have a chat?"

Dick got up and smiled back at her.

"Yeah, things are a bit grim today. I shouldn't have told Pete I was leaving. Want some tea?"

Rachel smiled hello at Maggie as she sat down opposite her, and while Dick busied himself with the tea Maggie told her all about the morning's events. She described a huge, violent boy's deliberate attack on her and was clearly still shaken.

"I was so scared, he could have killed me," she finished.

Yes, but he didn't, Rachel thought.

"Has it happened before?" she asked.

"No, not like this. Not to me. We usually get on well, but lately Pete's been getting more and more disturbed. He locks himself away in his room and won't let anyone in and he winds up the younger kids. He's older than them and ought to know better. He's really challenging our authority, it's as if he's trying to establish his power over the others. He's violent and potentially dangerous."

Dick turned round.

"He's not a bad kid. This has all started since Richard came and there's been a lot of tension here. Sally left and now I'm going. He's obviously upset by it all. He just isn't emotionally old enough to cope with losing people."

Rachel, wondering who was, asked, "Did he really try and hit you with the vacuum cleaner, Maggie?"

"I don't know. I suppose if he'd wanted to he could have. He was trying to scare me, and he did. I'm scared of him, he's a very strong boy. Next time he may not miss."

Pete came downstairs and stood slouched against the open doorway. He glared at all of them in silence and then muttered something inaudible.

"What?" Rachel and Maggie asked together.

"I said," he spat out loudly, "I'm bleeding sorry. All right?" he contrived to look angry and anxious all at once.

"That won't do," Maggie said immediately. "You could have really damaged me."

"I said I was fucking sorry. What else do you want?" he grumbled.

"I want you to stop behaving like this and pull yourself together," Maggie answered. "The next time anything like this happens I'm going to charge you with assault and the police will deal with it."

Rachel tensed, and Dick moved forward.

"Maggie . . ." he began.

"Do what you fucking like!" Pete was animated now, shouting and close to tears. "I apologized and all I get is being threatened with the police. I'm not scared of you or them or anything. You think being in prison is so awful? It ain't any worse than being in this stinkhole. None of you lot care a fuck about any of us. It's just a job to you, you cunts!"

Dick tried to calm him. "Maggie didn't mean that. She's upset. But you've got to talk to us about how you feel, not just throw things around."

Pete deliberately marched over to the table. "What's the point of talking? You're not going to be here. You just want a quiet life." He picked up Maggie's empty teacup and threw it with all his force across the room. It hit the glass door to the garden and there was a deafening crash as the glass shattered into thousands of pieces.

"Pete! Stop it! Don't!" Rachel said, moving towards him.

"Leave me alone! All of you. You're all useless!" he wept, and ran from the kitchen. They heard the front door slam and then the glass in that break as his boots clattered down the path. Dick ran out after him and came back a few moments later.

"It's no good, I couldn't catch him."

"You see?" said Maggie. "You see what I mean? He's dangerous."

"Well, I see he's angry. He still hasn't hurt anyone, though, and as you say he's a big kid. I think maybe we could have handled it better," said Rachel carefully, marvelling at her capacity for understatement.

Maggie burst into tears. "Oh, Christ," she wept, "I can't cope. That bastard Richard has changed the rota and I've been on nights half this week. I've got a six-month-old baby and my husband is going crazy. He's been putting pressure on me to leave, and he's right, I can't cope with the work and the baby and everything . . ."

Rachel got a new cup and Dick poured tea for them all, stroking Maggie on the back as he did so.

"This place is falling apart. It's insane. We've got a house full of disturbed kids and we're all at each other's throats. They're only acting out what's happening to us."

"What's to be done about Pete?" Rachel asked.

"We'll have to call the police if he doesn't turn up tonight," Dick said.

"But then what, in the long term?" Rachel asked.

"I don't know. Richard was furious about the incident this morning. He's phoned Al Stevens and demanded a case conference. He says that Pete is too disruptive to stay at Wentworth House. Yes, I know, but what can I do? Why don't you come to the conference? Pete could use a friend at this point."

"OK, what do I come as—the voice of reason?" Rachel lifted her eyebrows quizzically.

"That would do as a start. You're outside the situation, you see Pete differently. Maybe you could be useful. I'll phone you when the meeting's set." It was decided. Deeper and deeper. Dick added, "Look, I really appreciate your getting involved. I don't know if it will make any difference, but I know Pete likes you and feels that you're on his side."

Rachel felt like the clergyman who walks with the condemned man to the gallows. When the chips were down, when the trapdoor dropped, it would be only Pete hanging there, whatever pious sentiments she intoned.

She left the fraught atmosphere of Wentworth House with relief. When she got home she opened all the windows in the flat and put the chair that Pete had sat on out into the garden to air. It still carried the smell. Then she ran a hot bath and stepped gratefully through the steam into the nearly scalding water, feeling her body gradually warm through. She squeezed out the flannel and put it over her face and then lay there for the best part of an hour without moving. A comfort bath, not a business bath. Rachel Equivocal Kee, they should have called me, she mused under her flannel. She who wants and does not want. Cares and does not care. Do I care about Pete? I'm angry and helpless, but do I really care? And so what if I do? That's just my private emotion, it's no actual good to Pete. My caring doesn't improve his life, maybe it's purely for my own benefit. It makes me feel good to think I care. Do I feel good? No, I want to run fast in the other direction. It's when you have to put your money where your emotions are that things get sticky for you, Kee!

In the meantime Pete was wandering, filthy and stinking,

around London feeling—what? Hopeless, she supposed. She knew how hopeless felt and put herself there for a few moments. No one to go to, nowhere to go, most of all no solutions. What could happen for Pete that would be right; that would make things right? Being part of a family, having someone take him on who loved and accepted him. He might think that the fairytale ending, but Rachel knew better. You don't just slip into love and family without any practice. Being taken on can be a hell of anxiety and terror: how much are you accepted, when does "no" mean "I love you, but no" and when "get out"? How do you assess that if you've not had it before? You never really know if they don't regret taking you on; you never really know how to love back and what the right line is between gratitude and just accepting that you belong. You never quite belong. No fairytale ending. Finally, anxiety makes you test beyond endurance; you push yourself out because you can't stand the uncertainty. No saints, she had told Pete. If he was to survive he would have to understand that there are limits to everyone, he would have to learn how to settle for less than the ideal parent no one has ever had. But he couldn't know that, never having had the ordinary flawed kind. She didn't feel hopeful for Pete. She knew how close he was to despair and how few resources he had. She didn't think she would survive in Pete's shoes.

The water had cooled to blood heat. She felt clammy and uncomfortable, too cold to stay in the bath and too cold to get out. And she'd left the bloody towel upstairs. She made a chilly dash for it, wrapped it around her and climbed damp and cold under the duvet. It was a couple of hours before she had to pick up Carrie from school.

There was no sign of Pete the next day, and when she phoned Wentworth House she was told that they had had no word of him, but that the case conference was set for the following day. She said she would be there.

She arrived to find Pete slumped desolately against the hall wall. She smiled at him and received in return a brief glance of recognition from his completely impassive face. He was, of course, filthy from sleeping rough, but what shocked her were his eyes, which seemed devoid of any light. It was as if there was nothing behind them. Inside Pete and outside Pete seemed to

have been severed. And his skin again had that strange dark
greyish tinge to it. He looked as if he were dying. Dick was
standing over him, looking worried.

"The meeting's about to start. Pete came back about a quarter of an hour ago. He's been telling Al that he wants to leave
Wentworth and get a bedsitter."

"Do you think you'd manage, Pete?" Rachel asked gently.

"Don't bleeding matter. I'm not staying here and that's that.
Anyway that cunt Richard says I can't stay here any more and I
ain't going to another bleeding home." The voice was flat, he
really didn't care about anything.

Rachel walked into the meeting and looked around. Everyone was there: Richard, Maggie, the two other workers at the
house, Mary and Al Stevens. Al was the Head of Social Services
for the area and chaired the meeting. He was a large man,
bearded and shaggy haired, not unlike Joshua in type, but
blond. He had the air of a reasonable man who was used to
running things and took charge easily. Rachel liked the look of
him. She took one of the spare seats in the circle as Dick arrived
and sat down also. Al began:

"I think we should begin by introducing ourselves. I'm Al
Stevens, I'm head of the area Social Services." He turned to his
left and waited. Each of them in turn gave their name, position
and their relation to Pete. This was obviously the way all such
meetings started; it seemed to make everyone more comfortable, although the only real outsider in the group was Rachel.

"I'm Rachel Kee. I was Pete's Home Tutor," she said directly
to Al, who was the only person in the room she hadn't met; even
so, she felt more as if she were about to participate in an encounter group than a serious meeting about someone who was
not in the room. She was faintly anxious that they were about to
hold hands in the circle and *feel* each other's energies. However, Al clearly meant to get down to business.

"I've had a word with Pete. He's demanding that we let him
leave and live in a bedsitter," he explained. "I've got a couple of
thoughts about that but I'd like to hear from everyone involved
first. Richard?"

They were going to go round the circle again.

Richard sat nearest to the door. He was a slightly built man:

his greying beard counteracting the weakness of his watery blue eyes. He wore a shapeless cord jacket, faded matching trousers and brown suede shoes, that placed him instantly as either teacher or social worker. His speech was peppered with moribund colloquialisms.

"I'm afraid we've come to the crunch with Pete." He spoke directly to Al. "I won't have him here any more and I told him that. He's aggressive and emotionally unstable and the bottom line is that I'm not prepared to put the whole house at risk for one disruptive individual."

His voice rose several octaves as he spoke about his confrontations with Pete who "wasn't prepared to listen to the voice of reason." The security of Wentworth House was breached by Pete's presence.

"He's very dangerous, a lad that size could do a lot of damage and we've got to take on board the fact that he's a force for destruction. He argued with the staff and walks around the place as if he owns it."

Al asked, "Has he behaved violently?"

"Well, look at his attack on Maggie. He could bloody kill someone, a kid that size. He isn't safe."

Then Rachel listened astonished as Maggie outlined Pete's "totally unprovoked" attack on her. She stared at Maggie who looked at the floor as she spoke. Dick met Rachel's eyes for a second before he looked away.

"I'm sorry," Rachel said quietly, "but I'd understood that you'd been trying to get him out of his room to come to my lesson."

"Pete is a liar," Richard broke in, directing himself to Al. "Of course we understand that he's very disturbed and he's had a bad time, but when it comes to the nitty-gritty he's not socialized and we can't contain him in a normal environment."

"But this isn't a normal environment," Rachel insisted. "I had the impression that Pete was reacting to various difficulties that were going on here."

"There's nothing wrong with this place," Richard snapped. "It's Pete who's causing all the trouble, breaking windows and rushing out when he ought to be apologizing for his unacceptable behaviour."

"He did apologize," Rachel said, looking at Maggie. "I was there; but when he did he was threatened with the police. Is it possible that things might have been handled differently? Given that he is disturbed and we're supposed to be professionals with some sort of expertise."

Richard was white with rage. "I want him out before he kills someone."

"But he hasn't hurt anyone, only himself. I know he's big and angry, but he hasn't actually hurt anyone. The vacuum cleaner did not hit Maggie. He smashed a window and ran away. I think he's desperate. Couldn't we try to help him somehow?"

"I believe he has a relatively good relationship with you," Al said to Rachel.

She spoke very carefully; she knew she had said too much.

"My job was to give Pete some kind of education for two hours a day. He *is* disturbed and can't concentrate on work as such, but we got on well enough." She paused, then continued, "I understand Pete on a twenty-four hour basis is a very different thing from two hours a day, but in the last two years there haven't been any confrontations that haven't been reasonably resolved, and no violence. I don't think for a moment that I could manage him long term any more than anyone else seems to be able to, but what I want to say is that my experience with him might suggest another way of dealing with him. He *is* able to make relationships on a limited basis—he's proved that with me. Perhaps there's some way of using that information to help him. I'm not a social worker and I don't know what resources are available, but there's at least something hopeful about his ability to put himself across, at least to me, as a valuable, likeable person. Getting rid of Pete may or may not sort out the problems in this house, but it's Pete that worries me. What's going to become of him?"

Al smiled at her with studied warmth.

"It's excellent, of course, that he's been able to make contact with you and maintain it up to a point, but the reality is that he has to go out into the real world sooner or later and be accepted in it. At the moment he has no social skills. *And* there's the bowel problem; it puts him completely outside normal society.

He may be very charming, he seems to have charmed you, but we have to look at the problems."

"Yes, I see that," Rachel replied, "but isn't an ability to be charming a pretty advanced social skill? Being able to make people like him is quite a lot, given his deprivation. Maybe other people will like Pete enough to overcome their distaste for shit, and maybe that will affect the problem itself. Isn't there some kind of day fostering scheme or something, so that caring for Pete could be shared and he could be part of a family in some way?"

Rachel realized that as an outsider she was moving too far inside their territory. Al smiled again, clearly indicating that she was a biased unprofessional, not to be taken seriously.

"We have to express our care for Pete in the most practical way, and given that Pete can't stay here for whatever reason," he glanced at her, making it clear that he was not prepared to discuss the real problems at the Home, "we have to decide what to do with him. That means either we give him his wish and let him stay in a hostel, or we go for some kind of treatment. It's very unlikely that he would survive out in the world even with the support of Mary. We have to show we care for Pete even if it doesn't feel like that to him."

Rachel knew it was true that Pete wouldn't survive out on his own. Dick said, "Treatment?"

"There's a very interesting hospital I've been hearing about that uses behaviour modification with severely disruptive adolescents. It's a system of reward and punishment directed at socializing kids out of unacceptable behaviour. Pete could learn how to deal effectively with the social world and they would also sort out his encopresis."

Mary now looked startled.

"But he's been through that at the Maudsley. He went badly downhill."

"This is a more rigorous regime. As far as I can see it's his only chance of survival. He must learn to deal with his violence and he cannot go on walking around stinking of shit."

At this point Al visibly shuddered, and Rachel realized how disturbed he was by Pete's encopresis; it was that more that anything else that had decided him on the hospital. The whole

meeting had gone off at a tangent. She had imagined that something would be faced about Wentworth House. That the problem would be pinpointed and changes made that would allow
someone like Pete to survive in a place that had been designed
for people like him. Children in homes were likely to be disturbed but weren't the staff supposed to be able to deal with
that? Wasn't that what they were there for? In fact, Pete had
become a scapegoat and his misdeeds used to avoid the more
basic issue. There was a blank refusal to try harder with him—
he was being rejected like poison vomited from an already
infected body. The notion of Pete as violent and dangerous was
not, to Rachel, real. What was real was that he had been badly
handled from the start and that faces were going to be saved at
all cost.

"I heard," Mary said tentatively, "that they use drugs as well
as behaviour modification at St Stephen's."

Al gave her a sharp look; she was talking out of school.

"Only in an emergency. They do use Largactil to quieten
down the most disturbed kids, but as I said only in the most
severe cases," he said briskly.

"Only Largactil?" queried Dick.

"Well, they've done electro-encephalographs and find that
many of the kids have brain disturbance so they're all given
anti-convulsants. It's done under medical supervision of
course."

"It sounds like they are really controlled by the drugs, not the
psychology. How long do they stay?"

"Two years. Look, as far as I'm concerned this is Pete's last
chance. It's my job to take the final decision and I've decided
that he must have the opportunity St Stephen's offers."

Dick stood up white-faced.

"Pete's being used to cover up the mess this place is in. It's a
disgusting way to deal with administrative incompetence, sending the victims out to be brainwashed."

"How dare you suggest . . ." Richard began.

"I don't think emotive language is very useful," Al said quietly. "We are all concerned with Pete's best interests. It's my
decision and I've taken it."

Dick slammed out of the room and Richard turned a smug I-

told-you-so smile on Al, who did not return the look but got up
and said, "I'll go and tell Pete what's been decided. He must be
anxious to know what's going to happen."

The rest of the group sat in silence. Richard was clearly triumphant. After a few moments they heard Pete's voice shouting,
"No, I'm fucking not!" and then the sound of the front door
slamming.

Al returned looking a little shaken.

"He's upset of course. He'll be back and when he's calmed
down we can talk about it more seriously."

"Sounds to me as though he took it seriously enough," Rachel
suggested, glaring coldly at Al.

"Right," said Richard, standing up, "let's get back on with the
task in hand—running this place." He left the room and called
Maggie out after him. When they'd gone Rachel said, "Why
have you let Richard get away with this? You know perfectly
well what's going on here."

"Pete is simply not emotionally equipped to deal with the
stresses here. I agree that things aren't as good as they might be,
but that's a separate problem. I do appreciate your concern,
Rachel, but are you prepared to take him on yourself?"

Rachel was furious. And guilty, as was intended.

"I'm not equipped to do so. That doesn't mean I can't have an
opinion about how you're handling this."

"If you're prepared to give me a guarantee that you'll remain
involved with Pete indefinitely I might consider rethinking my
decision."

Rachel went rigid with rage. She understood clearly why
Pete hit out at these reasonable blackmailers.

"I'm not prepared to guarantee anything. I can't make commitments into an unforseeable future and my relationship with
Pete is not professional. If he wants to see me or talk with me
I'm around. I don't sign bits of paper to prove friendship and I
won't be bullied by you."

Al shrugged. Point proved.

"Well, in that case the decision stands. I hope you can visit
him at St Stephen's." Dismissing her.

Rachel fought back tears. Point proved. She wasn't prepared
to care for Pete any more than anyone else, so his future was to

be decided by the professionals. Had she allowed herself to be
pushed into taking Pete on on the most dubiously emotional
grounds they would have let her—as it was they sadly had to
take their painful decisions because it was proved no one else
would.

But Rachel, personally, was back on old territory. How much
was her refusal based on her knowledge that she wasn't able to
deal with Pete's needs; and how much was it Rachel once again
backing away from commitment? It was true the flat was too
small, Pete wouldn't have his own room; her income was minimal; she knew Pete needed a more sociable situation than she
could provide. It *was* quite inappropriate, but still, the note of
defensiveness in her voice as she replied to Al's invitation told
her that he had hit her where it hurt. She only offered Pete
partial concern. So did they, but they were justified by the
"objectivity" of their professional status. Little busybody Rachel
Kee had been revealed as nothing more than a troublemaker,
someone with plenty of washy emotions and minimal practical
use.

She called Mary and Dick every day for a week to see if Pete
had returned, but there was no sign of him. The police were
looking for him officially, but Dick thought that they were probably just waiting for him to get into trouble and could then pick
him up with ease. A couple of days later they did. He was
arrested in Woolworths in south London with 65p-worth of
stolen chocolate. He told the police he had been hungry and
apparently had seemed quite pleased to see them. The magistrates had ordered him to be sent to a youth detention centre
while they investigated his case with Social Services. Dick
phoned Rachel that night, and gave her the address of the place
in west London.

"I'll phone them in the morning and tell them you are a bona
fide visitor. He's allowed visits in the afternoons if you call first
and are OK."

"You mean not a friend of his," Rachel suggested.

"That's about it. But I'll point out he hasn't got any family and
that you're sort of official. I've spoken to Mary and she says that
Al is adamant about the hospital. Pete has really played right
into his hands, maybe that's what he wants. The magistrates will

probably make a court order that he has treatment at St Stephen's. Then he has no choice. My guess is he doesn't want a
choice."

"Well, thanks for letting me know, Dick. I'll go and see him
tomorrow."

"Right. I'm off next week to France. I don't know how long I'll
be gone but I'll call when I get back. 'Bye Rachel and thanks.'"

Rachel put back the receiver. Professionally her relationship
with Pete was over; she would have to call Donald tomorrow
and tell him that Pete was off the books. She spent the rest of the
evening switching channels on the television, finding nothing
she could be bothered to watch but determined not to do anything else. At eleven o'clock the phone rang. She reached for it
without thinking and said hello.

"Busy?" said Joshua's voice.

"No," she replied, voice calm, heart leaping.

"I'll be round in twenty minutes."

She put down the phone and made automatically for the
bathroom to get changed and ready, as if his six-month absence
had not occurred. The previous two years of visits had trained
her well. Halfway down the hall she stopped. The hell with it.
She went back into the living room where she sat waiting in her
old jeans and tee shirt. She was completely unsurprised at
Joshua's return. She had known he would come back and here
he was. Good, she shrugged, wondering what the detention
centre was like and how Pete was after a week on the streets.

When Joshua arrived she greeted him with slightly raised
eyebrows and a small nod of her head. He looked tired, less
complete than usual, as he followed her up the stairs. The
clothes weren't different but somehow dishevelled. As they sat
opposite each other in Rachel's living room a silence began to
elongate until Rachel broke it.

"You're looking decidedly raddled this evening."

He inclined his head in acknowledgement. "Busy day. Get
some glasses."

Rachel provided two glasses as Joshua pulled two half bottles
of Moet et Chandon from his plastic carrier bag.

"I thought we'd sit on opposite sides of the room with a bottle

each to cuddle," he said, as he popped both corks. Rachel sank
into the chair as Joshua sat back on the sofa.

"Lot of style," Rachel commented, smiling a little. "What are
you going to do for an encore?" She propped her bottle against
her crotch in the gap made by her Buddha-crossed legs and
sipped from her glass.

"You'll have to be punished you know. Little girls who can't
be discreet have to be punished."

"I'm sorry, you've lost me. Could you elaborate?"

"We had a deal. You weren't to discuss my visits with anyone.
You got sloppy, Rachel. Word got around that I was seeing you,
so I stopped coming, and I won't come again unless you give
your word of honour that you won't tell anyone. And I mean
anyone."

Rachel laughed. "What are you talking about? We don't have
any friends in common except for Molly and I've not been in
contact with her since I met you. No one else I know knows you
and anyway no one knows your name."

"I can't say any more about it. I simply require your promise
that you won't tell a soul—or I shan't come again." Joshua
looked deadly serious, very severe. Rachel laughed again.

"What on earth makes you think that I'd keep such a promise? Especially since you haven't given me a good reason," she
inquired, wide-eyed.

"You keep your promises, surely? We are both people who
keep our word. I can't give you reasons, you'll just have to do as I
say. If you tell anyone at all, I'll know about it, I assure you. You
wouldn't make a promise and not keep it, would you?"

"Certainly I would, particularly if it made no sense. I've
never been much of a boy scout, but it's interesting to see you
suddenly revealed as one. A man of honour!" she raised her
glass to him and wondered as she downed the champagne if he
were actually stupid or just plain and simply crazy.

"Come over here," he demanded, putting his glass on the
table beside the sofa. Rachel got up and walked across the room.
She stood in front of him, their knees almost touching as he sat
watching her from the sofa.

"Take off your jeans," he ordered coldly. It was the tone of
voice, the command which fired her suddenly. Excitement and

desire shimmered inside her; she wanted more instructions and forgot for the time being the absurd conversation they'd just had and the contemptuous reception she had given it. She didn't unzip her jeans, but stood there waiting for the command to be repeated.

"I said take off your jeans," Joshua barked at her, eyes flashing anger.

She unzipped them slowly, and stepped out of them and her pants, keeping her eyes on his face all the time, looking every bit as angry as he. She stood facing him where he sat on the sofa, her tee shirt just skimming the top of her thighs.

"Open your legs and stroke yourself."

She did as she was told slowly, awkwardly, as she felt herself observed, and he began to run his hands over her thighs and buttocks.

"Did you think about me these past six months?" he whispered, a small smile at the corner of his mouth. "Did you imagine me fucking you when you touched yourself?"

"Sometimes." Liar. Mealy-mouthed woman. All the time.

"What did I do to you, tell me?"

She bit her teeth together and stared at him coldly.

"Mostly you beat the shit out of me." She tried to look detached, ironic, but her eyes and cunt were wet. She couldn't win at this game, not without losing; if she was going to play the fantasy she had to have wanted only him for the past six months, have found no one else to touch her and beat her the way he did. She couldn't retain her dignity by pretending she had better things to do and stay inside the game—and she wanted to go where the game was leading. Boxed in, back against the wall—no alternative but to relinquish power; nice to want something so badly that she couldn't push it away. Nice to be demolished.

"I touched myself and thought of you touching me, stroking my cunt, beating me," she said, undetached, unironic.

"What did I beat you with? A strap or a cane?" His voice hoarse.

She thought quickly; he'd used a strap on her already.

"A cane."

He began to smack her and then pulled her down onto his lap. She sat astride him and moved against him, feeling the roughness of his trousers against her nakedness as he smacked harder and harder.

"This," he explained softly between smacks, "is to remind you to behave in future."

"Please . . ." she murmured.

"Please what? What do you want?" he whispered into her ear.

"Please, please fuck me," she begged.

He undid his trousers and lifting her, pulled them down. She manoeuvred his penis into her and then very slowly, very gently rose and fell on him as she tightened the muscles in her vagina so that he was totally inside her, then, as she lifted herself, he was almost out of her with just the tip of his penis in contact. As she rode in slow motion along the length of his cock Joshua shut his eyes and his mouth set in a grimace somewhere between pleasure and pain.

"Please," she whispered as she began to come.

"What? Tell me what you want." Joshua's eyes opened and looked into hers.

"I can't . . . I don't know . . . please, please," as she trembled into orgasm. And then there was a war on.

Joshua demanded fiercely, "What? What? What do you want to say?"

She looked at him pleadingly, then angrily. "No. No, I won't. I won't!"

"Say it," he snapped. He was moving now, thrusting into her, one hand circling her throat tight enough to threaten, not too tight. "Say it?"

She said, "I love you. Christ, I love you," knowing that that wasn't really what she couldn't say, but hoping he would settle for it; it came hard enough.

Joshua started to come, repeating, "What? What? What?" as he shuddered his semen into her.

She squatted on him, her head on his shoulder, wondering what it was she couldn't ask him for. She thought she had asked for everything but knew there was something left, something not only unsayable but unthinkable, too. Something she couldn't ask him for; that Joshua wanted her to ask for, not because he wanted to give it, she was sure of that, but because it represented a final capitulation. It was beyond giving and re-

ceiving orgasm, beyond the defeat of telling him she loved him
—it was something so remote, so unattainable that it couldn't be
consciously acknowledged even to herself.

"I'd like some bread and butter," Joshua informed the back of
her head.

"Why not?" she answered, and immediately lifted herself off
him, closing her legs and taking a deep breath against the
abruptness of the separation.

"You know," Joshua said from the sofa as she sliced the bread,
"two hundred years ago they would have burnt you alive."

"They only burned heretics alive," she replied, without looking around. "Witches were strangled first. You aren't accusing
me of heresy I take it?"

"I'll have to think about that. I'm not as up in the field as you
seem to be. What was it Cromwell said as he put his hand in the
flame . . . ?"

"Cranmer," Rachel interrupted briskly.

"Such erudition."

"Mmm. Sometimes I think I'm wasted on the sort of people
who make no distinction between heresy and witchcraft and
don't know their Cranmers from their Cromwells," she said, as
she offered him the plate of buttered bread.

"I don't think your real talents are being wasted," Joshua
grinned. "Tea. I want tea. Please."

"You know where the kettle is," Rachel hissed before turning
on her heels and switching it on as she stage-whispered, "Fuck,
shit, men!"

"Come on, that's not worthy of a woman of your intellect. I
did say please. If we had another girl with us she could make tea
for both of us. As it is I'll make it next time—assuming of course
there is a next time. You haven't promised yet."

Rachel came into the living room with two cups of tea.

"God, you're ridiculous. I'm not going to promise anything."

"Then there won't be a next time. What a waste," Joshua said
calmly.

Rachel sat sipping her tea. "Perhaps you'll conclude it's too
good to waste over a pointless promise."

"Wrong. I have boundless self-control in sexual matters. It'll
be a pity, but there it is."

They stared at each other, rock-solid stubborn.

Joshua said, "This isn't a power game, you know. It's purely practical."

"Balls!" Rachel replied, although he looked as if he meant it. She wondered for the second time that evening if he were always conscious of the games he played, but again couldn't believe he wasn't quite aware of what he was up to. Was it just that she needed him to be so very clever, so consciously manipulative? To promise not to tell anyone at all that he had come back was to isolate her; normal people told their friends who was coming and going in their lives even if they left out the details. If he became her secret then she was also cut off from the outside world. There would be no chance to measure the relationship and assess how far the two of them moved from what anyone else considered normal. Joshua's power would be complete, he would come and go, she would wait by the phone, they would act out fantasies while he continued to behave as if nothing out of the ordinary was happening. Already she found it hard to judge; maybe everyone carried on like this in the privacy of their own affairs. Cool, calm, terribly normal, Joshua managed to make leather straps and canes and sodomy seem like the most commonplace of practices. But what confused her most was Joshua's apparent belief that she wouldn't see the implications of his demand for silence. She found it so hard to believe that he imagined she wouldn't see something so obvious that she began to wonder whether it was there to be seen at all. Perhaps it was a straightforward request: there *was* someone who shouldn't know about them, whom she shouldn't know about. Perhaps she was the only Machiavelli around, imagining conspiracies and plots where there were none. Sweet Joshua, just fucking around and not wanting things to get complicated. At which point she decided that she had just followed exactly the route that he had laid out and mined. When it comes to power, confusion is everything. Get the woman tied up in the knots of her own thought processes and she'll never escape to the clear blue light of day. For the professional manipulator the creation of paranoia is a priority. Bastard.

Rachel sat curled up on the sofa next to Joshua, drinking tea and pulling corners of the slices of bread on his plate. She saw them both from a far corner of the room, a picture of post-coital domesticity, tired and happy lovers, eating and drinking after having eaten and drunk each other. She laughed aloud.

"What?" Joshua asked, smiling.

"Nothing," Rachel replied.

"Had any serious affairs while I've been away?" he inquired casually.

"I don't have *serious* affairs, you know that."

"One-night stands?"

"Some."

"Never saw anyone more than once, hmm."

"Well, actually there was someone I saw twice—would that count as more than a one-night stand?"

"Consecutive nights?"

"Certainly not! Twice in two nights smacks of commitment, domestic bliss. I thought you knew me better than that."

Joshua grinned at her. She had regained a little of the ground lost by her earlier importuning. When the sex was over she bounced back like a well-fleshed arm released from pressure. Her dispossession was circumstantial, she felt a small cut above the wimps. You can have my body, she thought, my head I keep to myself. Except when you're alone, the voice whispered, waiting for the phone to ring, recollecting and reliving his touch, his voice, imagining humiliations he hasn't even come up with. Yet. Joshua was back; there would be more.

"Let's go and lie down," said Joshua.

They got into bed, Rachel naked, Joshua with only his shirt on. He had hardly ever stripped completely naked in the two years she'd known him. He put his arm under her head and she curled herself up against him, slipping her arm beneath his open shirt, feeling his warm fleshy skin, wanting to stroke and kiss and suck on it. Forbidden. Too gentle, too affectionate, too sensual. He was, she had long since concluded, the least sensual man she had ever been with. Sex was specific and genital. What they did to each other was to arouse particular organs of desire; there was almost no generalized touching and minimal body contact. Sometimes she ached just to lie close and naked with him and catch his smell and taste the sweat on his skin. It almost never happened; tonight was a rare event and she hardly dared breathe, let alone touch and stroke, for fear of him recoiling suddenly from the warmth. Her arm lay over his large belly while only her fingers pressed gently on the flesh of his back and made small circles around his spine, seeming to doodle, to act without erotic intention. Her mouth against his chest sucked in his taste and smell in tiny surreptitious breaths as he lay with his arm around her, seeming to sleep. Thinking him asleep, or not thinking at all, Rachel's tongue delicately flicked against his nipple then she took it into her mouth and played her tongue around it, just toying and pleasuring herself. Joshua's free arm slipped from her shoulder and began gently to stroke her thigh and buttock as she continued to suck, and her hand moved down his spine to mirror his caress. She scarcely breathed. It was as if she had a wild creature in her arms which would only allow her to touch it for as long as it was hypnotized by pleasure. At any moment it would come to itself and see the danger it was in, that the pleasure was being given by the enemy. Then it would leap away and stare fiercely at her, cold-eyed, fur erect, an angry alien thing almost captivated, almost captured, almost lost. She moved down his body, kissing and licking the soft, rolling flesh like a downy pillow but smelling of man, sharp, salt, sour, and took his penis into her mouth, sucking and tasting and feeling it grow larger and stronger as Joshua lay on his back breathing long, slow breaths, his exhalations becoming sighs and then groans as he held her head between his hands pressing tighter and tighter until finally he released her, his hands falling back to lie splayed on the pillow on either side of his head, and his pelvis jerked spasms of semen into her mouth. She had always hated the taste; this she swallowed, ignoring its acrid flavour, took it into her like some life-giving liquid, sucked him dry as she heard him sobbing convulsively, loose, wet, helpless cries she had never heard from him before. Panicking because she had never seen him lose control so visibly, audibly, she released his penis and lifted herself up, holding him tightly in both arms, her cheek pressed against his.

"Shh, shh, don't, don't. It's all right," she whispered, holding him, stroking his hair, calming him. She was scared, she didn't want him like this, and was relieved when at last his sobs died down and he lay quiet and asleep.

An hour later he woke and looked at his watch.

"Christ, it's half past three. I've got to go. I've got a meeting at seven." He sat up and looked at Rachel, pulled back the duvet and kissed her briskly on the navel.

"No one has a meeting at seven," she said, "but you'll have to go anyway. I never get to sleep with strangers in my bed." She smiled at him.

"*I* have a meeting at seven," he insisted as he dressed.

"Why bother?" she asked. "I don't need it."

He looked at her briefly as he shrugged on his jacket. "Well, are you going to promise?"

"I told you. No. It's silly."

"Well, you know the consequences," he said from the door of the bedroom.

"So this is goodbye forever? Well, it's been a pleasure knowing you," she responded, tough and cynical. She didn't think for one moment that he was bluffing, but she had reached her emotional wall. She couldn't bring herself to utter such a nonsensical and dangerous promise. Perhaps if he had incorporated it into the sex; there seemed, after all, very little she wouldn't do under those circumstances, but in the cold light of dawn it was impossible to play out such foolishness.

"A pleasure for me too," Joshua smiled. "I'm only sorry that it can't go on. Think about it. You can always let me know if you change your mind. 'Night 'night."

Foiled! The opportunity to change her mind was fatal; his absence would make the promise more and more possible. She was determined now not to make it, but she knew in a few days she would cave in. They grinned at each other as Joshua saluted farewell, and she settled down under the cover to breathe in his scent on the sheets and consider the possibility that she would never see him again by her own choice. She knew she wasn't up to it. She remembered all the ways she had given herself pain in the past, all the things she had wanted but rejected because the cost of losing independence was too high. That Rachel was still there in essence, she could still hold out—for a time. But Rachel, beguiled and besotted, was too manifest now, stronger, if strength could describe it, than the person who wanted only

rational, equal relationships. There was no doubt really who
would triumph.

She woke in the morning inside a dark cloud. Hardly woke
because she had barely slept. Carrie slipped into her bed at half
past six and snuggled herself around Rachel, entwining her
limbs like a rampant creeper around Rachel's body. Rachel
groaned, and pulled the covers over her head. Carrie followed
her into the darkness.

"This morning, my darling, is not a good morning. Let's take
it slowly and calmly. I feel very bad-tempered," she croaked,
giving her daughter a hug.

"Why do you get bad-tempered in the morning?" Carrie
asked.

"Low blood sugar. Life. Come on, let's get it together, kid."

Carrie dressed herself and washed while Rachel lay in bed,
fighting the need to sink back into sleep.

"Come on. Up, you lazy woman," Carrie demanded from the
hallway.

"Yes, I am, I will. You're absolutely right," Rachel muttered,
heaving herself out of bed.

She pulled on clothes lying on the bedroom chair, discarded
the night before, and sloped down to the bathroom where she
dowsed her head under the shower. She felt wetter but unim-
proved. Tea.

Carrie ate cereal unenthusiastically. Cereals were for mornings like this—eggs, bacon, porridge demanded powers of concentration that were presently unavailable.

"Got what you need for school?"

"Yes. Swimming stuff. Can I put on a record?"

Good timing.

"No."

"Shall I practise my violin?"

"No!"

"No one cares about me; no one loves me." Margaret Sullivan
to the life. How had she learned such pathos? Wide rolling eyes,
deep sighs. Must come with the kit.

"Yuk. You're loved. You're loved. But I still don't want you to
play the violin."

Plans for the day. She would go and visit Pete at the detention centre, shop for food, phone Donald to see about getting another pupil. Don't think about Joshua. Yes, think about Joshua—phone Becky as soon as she had dropped Carrie at school and tell her that he was back. Lay the ghost, tell someone, don't let the poison even begin to work. No wondering whom he knew among her friends: was he fucking Becky, a girlfriend of Michael's? Don't. Make the promise or not but whatever, tell someone. How was it possible to be so aware of the implications of what he was doing and yet still be locked inside the game? Did intelligence ever stop anyone being a victim? Not if they are intent on it, she supposed. But she wasn't a total victim. She dropped Carrie and got home fast.

"Becky? Guess who turned up last night?"

"Dawn raider? Demon lover? Right?"

"Right."

"Only part of me is pleased for you. Will he come back?"

"I don't know, it seems to depend on promising never to tell anyone he's around."

"Well, you've just told me. Does that mean you're not going to promise?"

"Not necessarily. It means if I do I'll be lying."

"Well that's a start. How was it?"

"Good. Apart from the secrecy craziness he was almost human. I think he was glad to be back."

"So he bloody well should be. Let's hope he starts to treat you better."

"I don't think I'd like that at all."

"God, you're such a pervert!"

"I am! I am!" Rachel nodded, mainly into the telephone.

"I think what you need is more inhibition. Bloody Sigmund did us all a great disservice. What I say is 'repress it!' Everyone should get back into their closets fast and start behaving themselves properly. Like I do."

"How's William?" Rachel asked.

"Boring. And there's nothing wrong with that. It's true he doesn't beat me or bugger me. If it comes to that he doesn't do anything at all to me at the moment, but at least he's there *and* we go out together, unlike you and your weird friend."

"You mean you bore each other in restaurants as well as at home?" Rachel suggested.

"Listen, we all have our own routes to nirvana. Mine's ecstatic tedium. I love it. Cosy, safe and familiar, that's all I ask for. Excitement's too . . . exciting for me," Becky ended wanly.

"Becky, you're so adjusted. What you need is ten years of analysis to make you see that *really* you're deeply angry and frustrated. It's really sick to be as contented as you are."

"Well I'm sorry. You see I had a terribly undeprived childhood and I'm not gay, black or a single parent. I can't help it."

"You should try harder," Rachel laughed. "You must be a minority of some kind."

"I am. I'm in the minority of perfectly happy people. We're the most disregarded group in the country. Want to join my movement?"

"Shit no. I'm deeply prejudiced against the happy. They're liable to start marrying our men and turning them contented, to say nothing of seeding the population with millions of sweet-natured offspring. I won't stand for it."

Becky snorted, "There's not much chance of a population boom in my neck of the woods, I'm afraid. I may not be deeply angry, but I am frustrated. William's completely uninterested in me at the moment."

"But that comes and goes, doesn't it?"

"I suppose so. I'm trying very hard not to think what you're thinking."

"Is it likely?" Rachel asked worriedly.

"Don't know. There are a lot of publishers' parties. Don't want to think about it." Becky's voice was clipped.

"OK. I'll be here if you want to drop round any time, or phone, or anything."

"Thanks. I am glad your bloke is back."

Rachel put the phone down, thinking that if she wasn't all that happy being who she was there certainly wasn't anyone else she would rather be. It seemed to her that Becky's way had as inevitable and painful an end as her own. If life was about avoiding pain then the human race hadn't got very far, but then perhaps that wasn't what life was about. Nor, she reminded herself, was it about embracing pain. Pain was just a side effect, a kind of tax on human relationships—or lack of them. Pleasure then; was pleasure the centre? Joshua said once that people got stuck on other people out of gratitude for pleasure received. She didn't believe in gratitude as a first principle, greed more likely. I like that so I want more, I'll stick with you so I can get more, and I'll call it love. What about those of us who stick with people who won't give us more? she wondered. That's easy; if we don't get what we want we don't have to risk not wanting it when we've got it. A fail-safe security system.

Rachel pulled on her jacket and slung her bag over her shoulder. She drove broodily to the detention centre. She was dreading seeing Pete, imagining him dark and withdrawn, locked up in the lock up. On the way she stopped and bought forty cigarettes and six Mars Bars to go with the copy of *The Big Sleep* she had brought for him. The detention centre was a large, modern brick building set back from the main road. She parked in the driveway and walked through the asphalted exercise area to the door marked Visitors. The whole place was surrounded by a twenty-foot wall. She rang the bell and waited while she heard keys being turned in a lock, then a face appeared in the six-inch window of the steel door and after a moment's scrutiny another key turned and the door opened. A brisk looking woman said uninvitingly and unsmilingly, "Yes?"

"I've come to visit Pete Drummond. I believe his social worker has been in touch with you to say it's OK. My name is Rachel Kee."

"What are you?" the woman asked suspiciously.

Bloody good question.

"I'm a friend of Pete's. I'd like to visit him. I'm a friend," Rachel insisted, tensely.

This was clearly a meaningless statement to the woman whose keys hung—the archetypal jailor—from a chain at her waist.

"What is your official capacity?" she asked again, her question not, as far as she was concerned, having been answered.

Don't fight it, Rachel, she thought, give the woman something she can relate to. She took a deep breath.

"I was his teacher."

"Wait a moment, please." The woman shut the door in

Rachel's face, locked it, locked the inner door and disappeared for a few moments. Then the unlocking again, and Rachel was admitted, each door being locked once more as she passed through into the office.

"I've had Pete sent for. He should be down in a few moments. Have you brought anything for him?" the woman asked as she sat at her desk. Rachel put the two sealed packets of cigarettes on the table along with the Mars Bars and book.

"We'll keep the cigarettes for him," the woman said, handing her the rest of the things. "We only allow them five a day. The rest have to be earned with acceptable behaviour."

"I see. How is he?"

"Very well. He's cooperative, but I'm afraid he's refusing to see his social worker. He's angry."

"Yes, I know. I suppose that's why he's here. Is St Stephen's still on the cards?" Rachel asked.

"We're in the middle of doing assessments for the court. I must say that so far no one's very enthusiastic about St Stephen's, but Social Services are pushing very hard for it. They're likely to be listened to by the Magistrates."

"What's the objection here to the hospital?"

"Well, Pete definitely needs some kind of structure, but on the whole the staff here feel that boys like him are too easily institutionalized and that St Stephens is excessively rigid. But as I say, that's an unofficial opinion at the moment." The woman was very much more relaxed inside her office than she had been at the door. She also needed some kind of structure, apparently. Another door was unlocked and Pete appeared in the reception area, accompanied by a man whose size and musculature made even Pete seem dwarfed.

"Here he is," the man said. "You're honoured. You're the first visitor he's agreed to see."

"Well, I am honoured," Rachel smiled. "Hello Pete. You OK?"

If outward appearance meant anything he was more OK than she had ever seen him. He was squeaky clean and glowing, pink-cheeked with exercise and fleshed out with food. His hair had grown about an inch so that he had lost his old cadaverous look, and he was dressed in a neat red tee shirt, new clean Levis and a pair of sporty-looking trainers. He grinned at her.

"You can talk in here," the man said, showing them to a small room which had been partitioned off from the reception area. It had three chairs in it and a small table; two of the three walls were glazed so that what went on in there could be seen from any part of the office or reception room. Rachel sat down and handed Pete the chocolates and book.

"I brought you some fags, but they said they'd dish them out I'm afraid. I'll have to smuggle them in next time."

Pete smiled. "Ta," he said.

"You look incredible. How is it here?"

Pete shrugged. "It's all right. The food's shit, but the people are OK. I've been playing a lot of football, and doing woodwork. I made you a plant holder, but it's being varnished so I can't give it to you yet."

"How nice. Thanks. You don't mind it here then?" Rachel asked.

"Not really. There's too many rules and that, but it's all right. Better than Wentworth. The other kids are all right. You know what? There's a kid here being done for murder. He killed his brother with a kitchen knife when they were having a fight. He's got a terrible temper, but he's been good as gold here. If you don't behave they lock you in your room for a day and bring your meals in to you. They did that to me on the second day because I had a bit of a ruck with one of the staff. It's all right. I don't mind being in my room."

"When are you due back in court?"

"In a month. They're doing an assessment. I don't mind being here but I'm not bleeding going to that hospital. There's a kid here who's been there and he says they drug you up and lock you in a padded cell if you don't behave yourself. And you only get fed Complan if you don't score enough points for behaving right. I ain't going. I'd rather go to prison. I'd rather be fucking dead."

"Well, dead is a last resort. What *do* you want?"

Pete sat spruce in his chair, his long legs splayed in front of him.

"I want to look after myself," he said. "Live in a bedsitter and get a job."

"Living alone is quite difficult if you haven't had any practice."

"Yeah, well I'll get practice by doing it, won't I?"

True and not true. Kids with a family leave home but have parents and friends around, and in any case have spent most of their lives watching how it's done. Pete had none of that, just some disturbed, glue-sniffing mates who spent their lives in and out of prison and borstals. They chatted on for a while: Rachel told him of Carrie's doings, things she had seen on the television; visiting talk. When she left, after Pete had been escorted upstairs by the giant, she stopped first at the office.

"By the way," she asked the woman, "how has Pete's encopresis been?"

The woman looked up from the desk. "His what? Oh that—no sign of it. Will you visit again?"

Rachel said she would come later that week, as the doors were unlocked and clanged behind her. Driving home, she considered how well Pete responded to institutional life. He would have been quite happy to stay there, kept out of trouble, safe and contained. If he lived on his own it would only be a matter of time before he did something that took him back there or to prison. The institution could straighten him out, make him clean, healthy and unanxious, but it couldn't make him want to succeed without it, it couldn't make him want freedom and independence. Actually did anyone? Initially it was always a matter of taking a deep breath and jumping; the institutions, schools, borstals, families, had a double aspect: safety and containment but with the knowledge that the individual would have to leave. In fact, when you thought about it, very few people really leave; they rejoin institutions as fast as they can. Maybe, she thought, Pete could become a residential care worker for Social Services; but he was too delinquent, the system would be flexible enough to offer him that route: it wanted him to go to St Stephen's to "socialize" him with drugs and threats into a society he had never been a part of. Don't ask why, just do it. Although if he were going to reinvent his past like everyone else does then trouble with the law, being in prison, represented the only path he could take. Why shouldn't

Pete be different, though? Maybe he wouldn't have to do what everyone else did; why shouldn't he find a new way for himself? Fairytale time again.

Back at home the thoughts about Pete extended to the others in her life—all of them just doing what they were supposed to do. Becky trying for marital bliss, respectable married love; Isobel solitary, successful, living in her work, dismissing life and messy emotions; Joshua enticing and destructive but also alone, Mr Nice Guy to some, whipmaster to others but never really known, so never really loved, by anyone. Everyone just treading the path set for them; no one really beyond their conditioning, no surprises. And Rachel? No surprises. It was such a treadmill, everything known before anything happened, scripts written, so dreary, so bloody predictable. How did anyone ever get outside it? Disaster probably does it; catastrophes that turn expectations inside out and leave you with nothing but imagination and freedom. A painful void where anything and, most terrifying, nothing is possible. A painful business breaking free; who would do it voluntarily?

Suddenly the memory of last night flashed into her mind, the brief moment when she had loved Joshua gently and he had responded; she felt a contraction in her uterus as she recalled it and whispered to herself: I want to love someone. After a pause she added: I think.

She went to the kitchen drawer where she kept a small collection of postcards and flicked through them until she came across one that seemed appropriate; it was a late-nineteenth-century photograph of two rocks weathered into fifty-foot plinths in a wilderness in Wisconsin; their flat tops were separated by eight feet of nothing, just a deadly drop to the ground. The photographer had caught a man frozen in mid-air between the two rocks; you couldn't be quite certain he was going to make it to the other side. It was entitled "Leaping the Chasm;" Rachel smiled with satisfaction and took the card to her desk. On the reverse she wrote:

"All right. You have my word—and on paper too. Mind you, so was the Munich Agreement. Love R."

She addressed and stamped the card and took it to the postbox on the corner. Nothing, she thought as she slipped it through the slot, if not equivocal. He'll just have to take it or leave it. She guessed he would take it.

The following evening he called and came round, no mention of the card. They sat for a long time, sipping the wine he brought, talking. Not of themselves, they never discussed each other. They talked and argued about "people," not Joshua and Rachel.

"It's obvious that men should be fetishistic," Joshua declared apropos of nothing. "We see things as their component parts and fix on this or that bit as the object of desire. Women don't do that, they see totalities, it fits with their need for protection, keeps them attached to individuals."

"Whereas you people fix on disparate bits to achieve diversity?" Rachel continued.

"Exactly. Women need the protection of men, the security of a regular man to take care of their needs while they're bringing up babies."

"Oh shit! You've been reading to much sociobiology. Social economics. The old cost/benefit routine. Women have a major investment in expensive time-and-energy-consuming eggs and child-rearing; men have vast quantities of low-cost sperm so the more babies they make with the more people the greater the chances of reproducing themselves effectively. Women on the other hand are limited in their possibilities of reproducing themselves so they must put a large investment in a few off-spring. Women have to care; men just have to make babies."

"Right. So women need to make families to ensure that their babies will grow up."

"If you're right that women are biologically determined to seek security, then logically the last people they should seek it from are men. It would be the worst possible strategy. Men are biologically determined to piss off; women ought to protect their investment by fucking men to get their babies and making families with other women. If it's efficiency you're on about, that's the way to do it."

"Yes, but men stay free to go off and get food, and fight off intruders, while women are hampered with young children," Joshua argued.

"That's true, but only useful if they can be relied on to stay.

The optimum arrangement would be groups of women of different ages, in different stages of reproduction, protecting each other, and receiving men to seed them. If your argument holds then men are simply reproduction machines; women are social beings who can rear babies, forage, farm, do anything if they organize themselves. However we are not, you may have noticed, in a state of nature. Most of us fuck each other most of the time for reasons other than reproduction and these days social groups serve more than sheer survival. If you reduce everything to its origin you're going to miss an awful lot of what's going on. Also, my fetishistic friend, if I were you I'd think twice or twenty times before using myself as a template for male sexuality."

Rachel smiled charmingly at him as he flashed a sudden gleam of white incisors.

"Careful," he warned.

"Always careful," she retorted, as she refilled his glass.

Afterwards, when they had finished with each other's bodies, Rachel said, "Tell me something, just to further my education you understand, what happens to you once you've come?"

Joshua lay on the floor beside her, Rachel naked, he in shirt and pullover. He raised himself up on one elbow, head in his hand, and looked at her.

"Total mind change," he replied. "No desire, no sexuality."

Rachel rolled on to her side and looked up at him.

"But what about the woman you're with? Seconds after you've fucked her?"

"Depends on the woman. If it's someone I fucked because there was just one particular bit I fancied, I feel completely disgusted and leave as fast as I can. If she's small or very young I feel protective, paternal. But never sexual."

"Oh." Rachel blinked with the effort of not wincing. "Well, that's very interesting, thank you."

"You're welcome," Joshua smiled, stroking her gently from waist to thigh. Without desire, evidently; still, she supposed she was thin enough, if not young enough, to warrant his protection. She made a mental note to lay off the pasta, just in case.

Joshua turned up twice in the following month; it was business as usual, nothing changed. She visited Pete twice a week and found him well and reasonably contented, although still determined not to be sent to St Stephen's. He had his ups and downs with the staff, testing them, but not too far. He was one of the more cooperative inmates, she was told, and he stayed clean. She smuggled in cigarettes, giving in one packet to the woman in the office, slipping the other to Pete beneath the table in the goldfish-bowl visiting room, and brought chocolate and Marvel Comics. Pete gave her the plant holder and made her a wooden bowl on the lathe of which he was immensely proud, and rightly. They talked about his future, about living alone in London, although always with the threat of the hospital in the background and that made it impossible for him to acknowledge the problems he would have to face living alone in the bedsitter. It had become a dream quite inaccessible to reality. He had, after all, nothing else on offer. She felt sometimes like a solution that refused to present itself. Why didn't she whisk him out of his impasse, like Isobel had done for her? Why didn't she pass her good fortune on? It wouldn't have been sensible to offer something that was unlikely, given the difficulties, to work. Of course it hadn't been sensible of Isobel either to give her a home when she had nowhere else to go. She knew that Isobel had been warned against the foolhardy enterprise of taking an unknown and disturbed girl into her home. Nice thought, but could have disastrous consequences in practice. But here she was, alive if not kicking, not institutionalized, not a junkie, not dead. Isobel had survived too; they were both scarred to a degree, but human relations make wounds; they weren't fatal necessarily.

Still, she didn't offer Pete more than friendship and he took it because, immature and disturbed as he was, he also had a survivor in him that was in touch with reality and took what was on offer if there was nothing better. Up to a point. The war in Pete was in abeyance for the time being while the detention centre held him firm without squeezing too tight. He was breathing easy so long as he didn't think too hard about the future.

"I'm making you a bookcase next," Pete told her on the last visit. "You need one with all them bleeding books."

"Too true. It sounds like a major enterprise. Have you

thought about getting a training in carpentry? You seem pretty good at it."

"Nah, they're all right the things I make because the bloke gives me a lot of help. He doesn't get riled when you make a mistake."

"Yes, but that's what training is. Someone to teach you how to do it, let you practise till you get the knack."

"I don't know. Maybe. I could work for myself after I'd learned, couldn't I?" he asked.

"Yes. It seems like a good idea to me. Why don't I check out the possibilities?" Rachel said, feeling suddenly enthusiastic; a small chink of light, perhaps he could find a way for himself after all.

"All right."

As she left the woman in the office told her that Pete's hearing was due the following day. Mary was coming to take him to court.

Two days later Pete was dead.

Mary phoned to tell Rachel the news, gasping and stuttering through her sobs. The Magistrates had made an order for him to go to St Stephen's. He was completely silent in the car as Mary drove him back to the Detention Centre. She tried to get him to talk, tried to explain, but he just sat there, dark and glowering at the road ahead in complete silence. Mary, terrified that he was about to explode, drove as if the road were made of glass, waiting all the time for him to grab the wheel, hit out at her, something. But he held on to it all, and remained mute as they arrived and he was escorted through the locked doors to his room. He was to be taken to St Stephen's the following day.

During the night the fire alarm sounded; staff ran about, unlocking the doors, yelling as they went for the boys to assemble in the courtyard. Pete was ready as the key turned in his lock, standing in his jeans and training shoes, naked from the waist up. He pushed past the warden and raced his long legs to the fire escape, but when he reached it ran up instead of down. He clattered up four flights of metal stairs to the roof of the building while the warden tried to beat out the smouldering bedsheets that lay piled directly beneath the smoke detector in Pete's room. In the courtyard boys and staff milled about until someone yelled, "Look!" and pointed to the tall bleak figure poised on the edge of the roof, colourless in the grey dawn. For a few moments there was silence as everyone stared up at Pete, their necks strained back, eyes narrowed with the effort of keeping him in focus as if just holding him in sight were force enough to prevent his fall. Pete stood half naked in the cold morning, four storeys up, watching the paralysed figures below, and yelled down at them. "You fuckers! I don't care—I want to be dead. I'm going to jump, cunts, none of you can stop me!"

He pulled off one of his shoes, raised it above his head and flung it down with all his force on to the group below which scattered as it fell. Then the next shoe. "I hate you! You bastards! I don't care!"

Some of the staff started to call up to him, reasoning, calming. Someone began to climb the fire escape, someone else went to call the police. Pete stood barefoot in his jeans, sobbing as male voices shouted up common sense and hope; if he came down they could talk about it, they would sort something out. Pete sobbed and listened, wanting to believe but too angry, too hopeless. Someone saw him wipe his tears with the back of his hand and shake them off as if he were throwing them down too, like his shoes; heavy dangerous tears liable to crush anyone they fell on. Then there was nothing else to do with his rage, nothing else to throw, except himself. He flung himself off the edge and hurtled towards the ground, following the shoes and the tears, throwing himself away, launching his body as the last weapon he had, a missile that would blow the world to pieces.

"Bastards!" he screamed as he jumped, and then they heard his skull crack against the asphalt and he lay face-down, smashed and dead in the appalled silence.

A boy began to sob and two of the warders ran forward to check pointlessly for a pulse. For a few moments the boys and staff stood gazing blankly at the mess that lay at their feet.

Mary sobbed into the telephone while Rachel listened in silence, her fingers pressed against her lips as if to keep control of the dangerous sounds inside her. The words poured into her ear and she pressed the earpiece hard against her to stop those sounds from seeping out. She took it all in, let Mary tell the story, and when there was silence whispered,

"Thank you for letting me know."

Rachel's need now was to think. Or rather not to think but to allow herself to float aimlessly about in the space left by Pete, like a foetus suspended in amniotic fluid. She wanted to lie in bed and live what she had known of Pete, to be in it or go through it, come to some understanding of what his life and death meant for her. It was a desire to wallow, but so strong that she had to keep bringing herself back into the living room as she found herself edging towards the bed.

After a while she began to recognize her state. She had thought of it once as Joshua's Syndrome, or as the space reserved in her for sexual obsession and activated by Joshua, when she lay hour upon hour fantasizing and recollecting. Now it seemed it was a more generalized condition, the symptoms were indications of obsession per se, her sexual need for Joshua being just one form it took. There was the same dreadful weight, the heaviness that made her body ache to be horizontal. The desire to be in bed was so strong that she couldn't do anything physical with ease. Her body stubbornly demanded to be rested while her brain longed to put all other concerns aside and concentrate profoundly on the single theme of Pete. She felt her mind as quite separate from her will, needing not to analyse but determine to relive, remember all the moments and events of her relationship with Pete. It wanted to swill experience about like a wine-tasting, re-experiencing not thinking, as if this were the only way in which sense could emerge. There wasn't any conscious need to understand, just the feeling that there would only be understanding through such a process. Pete and Joshua were not to be thought out. Wherever it was in her brain that solved problems by logic had switched off. Still, there was something battling inside her to keep out of bed and out of the condition she wanted so badly to be in. She pushed her heavy limbs about the flat, hoovering carpets that had been cleaned only a day before, scouring sinks that already shone well enough—anything to be busy and above what she per-

ceived as an abyss. She forced herself not to go down into it,
knowing she was putting it off rather than winning the battle.

She became very cold, very angry, and went about the normal business of the next day or two with her face set, her being
geared to pursue what had to be done, all icy calm and reason.
She phoned Isobel and Becky and told them what had happened in a voice that refused them the right to gasp or say the
usual comforting words. With Isobel it was easy; they had had
such conversations before about other tragedies.

"Oh dear, what a pity. You must be feeling terrible. Well,
that's life. Perhaps he made the right choice," Isobel suggested
sensibly.

"Yes. I don't think he had any other choice available to him,"
Rachel replied, grateful for the cool tones. Pointless death,
pointless life needed Isobel's common sense.

"Will you go to the funeral?"

"No, there aren't any loving relatives to be comforted. It was
Pete I cared about and he won't be there."

"You don't think you'd feel better if you went? Ceremonies
are useful sometimes."

"I don't think a communal weep with the powers-that-be in
Social Services is going to improve my mood much. I'm all right,
really. It's just, as you say, a pity."

"Well, let me know if there's anything I can do. Not that there
is anything one can do," Isobel said, sighing at yet another
instance of life's impossibility.

Rachel put the phone down feeling slightly irritated. She
hadn't wanted an emotional response, that was why she had
phoned Isobel first, but it grated that for Isobel all individual
sorrow conflated into the Human Condition so that all private
pain became nothing more than a minor proof of how she knew
things were anyway. Not that it wasn't true, only it seemed to
deny people the right to feel the hurt they had.

Becky put Rachel into reverse.

"Oh Rachel! Oh no!" She was immediately close to tears.

Rachel said crossly, "Well, it's hardly very surprising. Another
of life's sad stories."

"Stop it," Becky sniffed. "You don't have to pretend you don't
care."

"I do care but there's nothing I can do about it. Tears won't help."

"They might help you."

Rachel prickled with resentment. Becky's tears angered her. They had come so easily as if they had been gathering for days waiting for an opportunity to overflow. They were tears, not tears for Pete. But why not? Why shouldn't sorrow be available for whatever need arose? Who was Rachel to deny Becky the right to cry over someone she didn't know? And if tears mean anything to the dead why shouldn't Pete have some? Maybe Becky's tears were more efficacious than her own. Rachel, of course, hadn't cried. She offered Pete's memory her thoughts instead. What was the difference?

"I'm sorry. It's just that I feel a bit grim. I don't see much point in wallowing in it. It's strange but very few people in my life have died. A lot have disappeared, but not died. It's different."

"It's such a waste," Becky said.

"Not exactly a waste. Not more of a waste than Pete spending a long life in and out of prison or drugging or drinking himself to death. I'm not sure if there's much to choose between them," Rachel suggested.

"But if he'd lived he would have had a choice at least."

"I don't know. His chances were so slim. It's only that I'm so sorry he's dead. I wish he wasn't dead." Rachel squeezed her eyes tight shut against the tears that suddenly welled painfully against her lids. She was *not* going to cry. There was no point in crying. She was scared to death of crying.

Becky said, "You should go to the funeral. It'll make you feel better."

"Going to a funeral to make myself feel better will probably make me feel worse. I think ritual only works if you don't know that it's supposed to. Anyway, why should I feel better?"

"I don't think I really meant feel *better*, I think I meant feel anything. Feel." Becky, practical, perceptive and concerned, made Rachel want to scream."

"Oh for God's sake, Becky."

"Sorry, I'm probably talking about myself. It's not much compared to Pete killing himself but things are really bad between

William and me. I'm so scared I can't really think about it." The
tears began to flow again.

"Is there someone else?" Rachel asked.

"Think so. I know this is crazy, but I don't think I can live
without William. It just hadn't occurred to me that I wasn't
going to have him for the rest of my life. I know you must think
I'm incredibly naïve, it's not that I don't know most marriages
break up, don't last forever . . . but not us."

Rachel tried to put herself in Becky's place and couldn't. So
William was having an affair after five years of monogamy; it
seemed so normal, so like everyone else. She did think Becky
naïve. How was it possible she could have imagined that they
would be different? How could she have thought that they
would both go on with equal intensity, wanting each other
forever? It was beyond Rachel's powers of imagination. Habit
was the answer. Becky's belief that *they* were different was
retrospective; she probably hadn't thought about it at all. But
she had got used to living with William and now he was irreplaceable, not because he *was* irreplaceable but because she
was in the habit of him. How could William be the single perfect
match for Becky? How could anyone? By chance in the small
world we each inhabit we meet a few people who suit us; that
was accident, not destiny, in a world teeming with people who
would never, by sheer numerical improbability, meet each
other. No Mr Rights, just Mr That'll-do's who become necessity
from force of habit. But Rachel and Becky had pain in common
if not belief, and Rachel could empathize with that at least.

"Come round this evening," she suggested. "I could use the
company."

"Thanks, I will. I could use your cool view of life right now."

Rachel grunted. "So could I. You're a little out of date. Rachel
the Invulnerable seems to have sunk without trace, but I might
be able to dredge her up just for you."

She would, of course. That Rachel was still there, especially
for other people, still there for herself too when she could get
feeling to subside.

Pete and Joshua. She was in mourning for the ghosts of both of them, for the lost potential of both corpses. One death was not more serious than the other merely because it was more corporeal. She was, although she didn't acknowledge it, primarily in mourning for herself.

FIVE

Becky arrived looking awful. All the usual surface effort had been neglected so that although she looked like herself she also didn't, like the suddenly strange face of a friend who for a moment takes off the glasses they habitually wear. The raw material was there, the precisely cut hair, wide clear eyes, well-defined bone structure, but she hadn't washed her hair so that it hung limp and thin around her face, and her unmade-up eyes were bloodshot and swollen from too many tears. Both women wore faded jeans, though their basic difference in style remained: Becky with her neat silk shirt that outlined breasts moulded into shape by the brassiere beneath, Rachel's loose unstructured tee shirt draping over the naked nipples beneath. Rachel made coffee and they sat on stools at the kitchen table, picking at slices of salami and breaking off bits of cheese.

"Have you asked William what he's up to?" Rachel asked.

"No. No one says anything much. It's just that he's so absent, even when he's there he isn't. I think he might leave me," she said, looking up suddenly, eyes wide and scared as if at a totally new thought. "How do you manage to live alone?"

"I've told you, it's just habit. I'm not *able* to live with anyone. I don't know how people live alone when they're not used to it."

"What about the Demon? What if he wanted to live with you?"

"He won't. That's the point, I suppose. There's not the slightest chance that he's going to want any more than there is now.

That's my security. And why I'm so trapped. If he made himself even a little more available I'd lose interest in him like I always do. I only want more of the bastard because I want to stop wanting him. It's true. Hoist, as they say, on my own petard—whatever that is. But that's no help to you, except to say that you wouldn't be any better off if you were like me instead of like you."

"That's a comfort."

"Not to me, it's not," Rachel muttered gloomily.

"Well, at least we're in the same boat."

"Except that I deserve it and you don't. Probably. I've been playing games with my fantasies. Sometimes I think I've invented the man. It's as if he'd stepped out of my head, me taken to a logical conclusion, and of course the one person I can't cope with is another me who's even better at it than I am. He'll always defeat me because he knows exactly what I want." Rachel got up and opened a bottle of wine.

"What do you want?" Becky asked.

"To be made vulnerable. Not to be allowed to be tough and cynical. It's only partly the sex, that's where it's most obvious, but the real pleasure is being made needy and pathetic. It's like being released, it's such a relief to lose and not to care that I'm losing. Oh shit, it's awful isn't it?" Rachel covered her face with her hand and gave a grim laugh. "And in the meantime," she added, looking up, "Pete's killed himself and your marriage is in a mess. But I don't seem to be able to think about anything except bloody Joshua. I'm sorry. You know what really scares me? This thing will end sooner or later, but I don't think I'm ever going to want anyone else, nothing else will ever do. I feel like I've been condemned." She cradled her wine glass in both hands and stared into it, seeing nothing in there but a long bleak life of aching. That, of course, was exactly how Becky was feeling, she thought. Bleakness and forever. There was so much time to get through. And Pete too. As he stood on the roof that was what he must have felt beneath the anger. If you were standing on the edge four storeys up and feeling like that, just hopeless, it wouldn't be hard to take a step off into space. The alternative, going back down the stairs, would be more difficult. There would be nothing to go down for except more nothing.

"But you know how to be alone. Rachel I can't . . . I can't do it."

Becky suddenly let the last remnants of composure go and seemed to crumple in on herself as tears flowed freely through the fingers she clasped against her face. She sobbed, shuddering and heaving, releasing the misery untidily as Rachel watched and felt herself firm up from the inside, everything tightening, organizing itself to deal with the situation. Yes, it's good for Becky to cry; she needs to be comforted and touched; tears are functional, they release waste proteins; people need holding when they lose control so that they feel safe. Rachel watched Becky for a moment, dry-eyed and calm, permitting her to do what was necessary, then she took a deep breath and stretched her arm across the table.

"Poor Becky, I'm sorry, love," she murmured, as she took one of Becky's hands from her face and held on to it tightly. The sobbing deepened into a lamentation, a grieving. Rachel got up, still holding Becky's hand, still staying in touch, and moved close, taking Becky's head against her torso and stroking the lank, damp hair.

"It's all right. It's all right," she whispered over and over as she rocked her gently, rhythmically against the tempo of the cries.

"I can't bear it," Becky sobbed. "What can I do?"

Rachel, all brisk and efficient on the inside, gentled Becky from the table onto the sofa where she held her in her arms and stroked the smooth silk of her shirt. She felt perfectly cool, prepared to respond in any way that was necessary. What did Becky need now? Comfort and permission. She was like a sensitive instrument, gauging the atmosphere and setting appropriate reactions in motion, feeling nothing, simply alert. She held and caressed and gradually Becky subsided, hiccupping from time to time as her body readjusted. Then she was quiet and lay breathing slowly against Rachel's breast, one arm resting on Rachel's shoulder. Rachel continued to stroke hypnotically down Becky's back as she whispered, "Are you all right?"

Becky lifted her head so that her face was just a few inches from Rachel's and looked red-eyed and swollen up at her. She wants me to kiss her, Rachel thought. Does she want me to make love to her, she wondered. Will it help or make things worse? Is it the right thing to do? She didn't think, do I want to? But she did want to, or at any rate was intrigued with the idea, with this woman in her arms, of slipping from consolation to eroticism, though her main conscious concern was to do whatever was best and most appropriate in the circumstances of Becky's distress.

Becky wasn't thinking about anything at all; she brushed her lips gently against Rachel's mouth and then softly probed with her tongue between the lips already opening to receive it. They kissed each other for a long time, familiarizing themselves with the contours of their lips, running tongues along teeth, sipping and pushing gently into each other. They undressed, investigated each other curiously and a little shyly, getting to know the soft curves of breasts, unfamiliar nipples, silky rounded thighs and damp vulvas. Rachel took Becky's broad dark nipple into her mouth and sucked gently on it, feeling a shiver of pleasure run through her as she touched and tasted the body whose owner she knew so well. Becky as friend had had no body, or at least one that only related to others, a body Rachel knew only through conversation. It had never occurred to her to connect the friend and the flesh in her affection. And as she stroked and touched and felt her own body being caressed, she became enchanted by the confusion. She was Alice at the moment when the looking glass dissolved, kneeling on the mantelpiece, pressing her palms against the glass and feeling the reflection of her own flesh, touching another, touching herself, familiar but quite different, creating a third neither one nor the other, making love in a glass that became a liquid refracting pool, not you, not me, strange and strangely known.

They lay naked together on the floor, sleepy and satisfied, holding each other and kissing from time to time to keep the throb alive between them. Rachel looked at Becky and was thrilled at how lovely she was; her eyes feasted on the lines and curves as she remembered the feel of them under her hand, how they had become taut as Becky climaxed, climaxed because Rachel had made her, how fluid and soft they were now in the dim light. She was aware too of her own body as beautiful and mobile, small and angular to Becky's roundness, and she

saw them both as if from above, shockingly naked, shockingly
women together, female form wrapped around itself. She
touched her lips against Becky's and stroked her hair as she
smiled sleepily.

"Rachel," Becky whispered, as she kissed her back.

"Becky," said Rachel, smiling too.

Rachel drifted into sleep and dreamed mysteriously of architraves, intricate white mouldings delicately carved. But it's the
door, she told herself in the dream, it's no good concentrating
on architraves when there are doors to be dealt with. But no
matter how she tried she couldn't tear herself away from the
forms around the door, hypnotic angles, curves and shadows
demanding her attention. She woke with an image of a solid
white door imprinted on her mind, the door she should have
attended to in her dream but couldn't. She blinked the image
away and turned her head to look at Becky asleep beside her.
She felt chilled and saw Becky's skin goose pimpled by the cold.
It was late and the heating had switched itself off. She sat up
feeling icy. All the sensuality, all the warmth had gone. She was
hard and tight inside, like a diamond, sharp glistening edges,
smooth cold facets. She looked coldly at Becky still sleeping and
wanted her gone, wanted only to be alone in her flat. She
wanted to shake her awake, hand her her clothes in silence and
have her go while Rachel shut herself away in the bedroom.
Damn, another mess, something else to be handled, dealt with.
Why did she let that happen when really she wanted things
simple, wanted only to be let alone? She remembered that she
had enjoyed making love with Becky, but that was then, while it
was happening; she didn't want an aftermath. She didn't want a
continuation, and she didn't want to explain, she wanted only to
be *left alone.* Being alone was what kept Rachel safe and being
safe was the major guideline of her life. Her flat and a few not-
too-close friends were safety, the rest of the world different
degrees of anxiety. In the most harmless of social events there
was always a reserved area of Rachel that ached to be back in
her flat on her own. Relationships were brought to a swift conclusion or never started because solitude was always preferable
to the unease she felt with others, with the threat they presented. Even with Carrie sometimes there was a feeling that

she was making polite conversation while waiting for her to go to school or to bed and allow Rachel once more to be on her own. Joshua was safe because he was guaranteed to go away and because although he broke her reserve sexually he would never go so far as to endanger his own reserve. The limits on what she could want were set by him and kept both of them secure. She told herself now that what she had to do was learn to be even more alone than she already was. She had to do without safety nets which turned inexorably into traps—like Becky lying there sleeping peacefully on the floor. Like Pete, she was never going to get what she had never had, but, unlike him, she knew that. It was her advantage. She had only to come to terms with it and stop getting involved at all.

She suddenly had the wrenched feeling she remembered having as a child. She would lie in bed at night and find herself floating off away into space. She tortured herself with the idea of infinity, of infinite emptiness. Later they made movies of her recurring waking nightmare. As she lay in bed she lost the walls of her room, her parents sleeping or fighting, the solid structure of the building, and drifted into black empty space, floating completely alone up there where there was nothing; no edges, no boundaries, not the slightest hope of rescue, just alone in the blackness forever. Years after, when she watched the same image on the cinema screen, she had had to fight off the empty terror it produced in her. The astronaut drifting beside his ship has his lifeline cut and spins off, a minute object in vastness rolling away forever towards more and more nothing.

Becky woke smiling, still wrapped in sexuality, and put her hand out to touch Rachel. Rachel snapped to her feet.

"It's cold," she said. "You'd better get dressed."

Becky's hand retreated and she looked puzzled. "Are you all right?" she asked.

"Fine," Rachel replied, very short, as she pulled on her jeans and tee shirt.

Becky got up and dressed slowly as Rachel busied about collecting empty glasses and putting them in the sink with the coffee cups. She clattered about in the silence for as long as she could, holding the talk at bay until Becky said, "Let's have some coffee."

"It's very late. Won't William be wondering where you are?"

"He knows where I am. What's wrong?"

"Nothing. I'm tired."

She started to make coffee, thinking the quicker it was made the sooner Becky would leave. Becky finished dressing and sat at the kitchen table.

"It was wonderful. It was so good," she said, as Rachel put the coffee cups on the table. Rachel could feel her aching to be touched, reassured, and turned her back immediately to fiddle unnecessarily with the coffee machine.

"Rachel, what is it?" Becky insisted.

I want you away, out of here, she thought; I want you to stop being so pathetic, so fucking warm, so loving.

"Look," she said, with immense effort, still with her back to Becky, "you were upset, we were a bit drunk. It was fine. I just don't want . . . to get involved. It happened: that's OK, but that's it."

Tough, hard as hell. Total mind change.

Becky looked as if Rachel had thrown the coffee at her instead of just putting it on the table as she spoke.

"Of course. If that's what you want. It just seemed right, though. You were so loving and gentle to me when I was crying. I'd never seen you like that before . . ."

"I was just doing what was necessary," Rachel interrupted, correcting her.

"I don't care. You *were* loving, and you were loving when we touched each other. You can't pretend it didn't happen and that it didn't mean anything to you."

"You're in love with William, remember? I'm not pretending anything. It was sex and I like sex, but there's no need to complicate it. We were just comforting each other."

"Rachel, I love you. You're my friend. I loved you before tonight; we've taken it further but that doesn't change our friendship. It's only that I loved your body tonight as well."

"You love William. I can't replace him. I don't want to. Friendship and sex don't mix as far as I'm concerned." Rachel poured more coffee into her cup.

"All right, if you don't want it to happen again we won't do it. But we'll go on being friends, won't we?" Becky searched for

Rachel's hand resting on the table, as Rachel pulled it away and turned her head to gaze out of the window.

"Yes, I expect so," she said, in a voice a million miles distant, a voice that meant, "I doubt it very much."

"Rachel, please. We're friends." Becky's eyes filled with tears, her hand was still outstretched on the table.

Rachel stared ahead of her for a moment. She felt completely hollow, as if there was nothing inside her but empty space. She didn't want to lose Becky. All she wanted, impossibly, was for tonight never to have happened. She heard herself being cold and angry and knew exactly how much pain she was giving Becky just by the tone of her voice. She could imagine exactly how she would feel if she were on the receiving end. She didn't have to imagine, she could remember. So she was paying Becky back, punishing her for Joshua, for everyone who hadn't loved her? Not consciously. She didn't want to hurt Becky, but she couldn't feel or be any different. She had shut down, there wasn't an ounce of kindness or warmth in her. Being what she was, she was being what she was, and couldn't help it. She was simply terrified of getting any further involved, and panicked as she felt Becky's emotions close in on her. Everything in her screamed, *leave me alone!*

But the situation had to be handled.

"Look Becky, I'm sorry. We *are* friends. You know I can't cope with involvement. We've talked about it often enough—did you think I was making it up? I'm sorry, I shouldn't have let it happen. It's my fault. I want us to go on being friends, but we'll have to leave sex out of it. In any case, we're both hooked on men. We'd never be able to make up to each other for what we really want. We'd just be comforting ourselves And I know," she added before Becky could say it, "there's nothing wrong with comfort, but it wouldn't be enough."

"I didn't make love to you because I can't have William," Becky protested. "It was because I wanted to, it was a natural thing to do."

"Nothing's a natural thing to do," Rachel snapped back.

"Well, it is for me. I didn't use you. It won't happen again, but please let's stay friends." Becky got up from the table. "I'd better get home," she said flatly.

Rachel followed her out to the hall.

"I'll ring you tomorrow," Becky said at the door. She leaned forward to kiss Rachel who turned her head slightly so that Becky's lips merely brushed her cheek.

"Bye. See you," Rachel said casually as she shut the door.

Left alone Rachel ran a bath, pouring in twice as much scented oil as necessary, pulled off her clothes and stepped with relief into the pungent water. She lay there, soaking in the steam, wondering when it was all going to stop and if it did stop what would be left. She was even more empty than before, a vacated shell that circumstance did things to. Things happened and she was a body in the way. Joshua, Pete and Becky. Complications. Circumstances. Nothing to do with her, not really. They were all pursuing their needs, reacting to their lives; she just happened to be there. She had no sense at all that *she* happened to anyone or reacted to anything. Not so—she reacted to anything by withdrawing, disappearing. But she didn't feel that she was the cause of anything. Pete was dead and she suspected that she had just lost an old friend. There was only Joshua now and it couldn't be said that she "had" Joshua. A mess. What a mess everything was. Chaos descended like a great dark cloud, like a mist that spoiled and dampened everything, wrecking the order she tried to create by holding still. She really couldn't function out there in the real world, it was too untidy, too disturbing. Was it really not possible to keep still, do nothing, see no one, just potter about the flat, teach for a couple of hours, be Carrie's mother, keep it all confined, stop life spilling over the edges? And what about sex? Abolish it. Can't. If I were a man I'd buy it, she thought and wondered if there were any brothels for women. Now there's a gap in the market: a service centre for women who want fuss-free sex.

She woke at five, losing a long struggle to remain asleep. A massive black cast-iron vise sat on her chest, so heavy it made her ribs ache. This mustn't happen, she thought, knowing that it was happening, recognizing it instantly. It'll go away if I sleep again, in the morning the weight will be gone. Finally she did sleep, but dreadfully. She wept in her dream, sobs that wrenched and convulsed her body; there was no reason, no narrative, just the weeping and the knowledge that at all cost she mustn't wake herself with her dream-cries, not allow them to become real. But of course the moment this thought came to her she was already in the process of waking, and sensing the danger fought down consciousness, but rose inevitably to it and to the real wet tears that she had been shedding as she slept. She buried her face in the pillow and cried as she hadn't done for years—perhaps ever; not a few tears squeezing out of her tight, defiant face, but a deluge, a tide of tears she had no power to control, that threatened to go on without end. She sobbed for an hour or so and then lay limp and exhausted, damp-haired in the soaking bedclothes. God, don't let this happen, she whispered to whoever it was that probably wasn't listening. When the alarm sounded she couldn't move. She lay on her stomach, watching the figures change on the clock, intending with each new number to call Carrie and make the day begin. In the end Carrie came down herself.

"Don't get into bed, it's late. We've got to get up."

Rachel's voice was strangely toneless, uncharacteristically calm. Carrie looked at her sharply. Where was her bad-tempered morning mother? Why was she just getting dressed and not nagging? Carrie knew trouble when she saw it and she didn't like this quiet, passive woman. She went on the attack in an attempt to smoke out the real life person she was used to living with, but ambled about the flat naked except for one sock for a full ten minutes without provoking anything. She lay on the living room floor, waving the socked foot in the air, and tried harder.

"I think boys are cleverer than girls."

But got only "Please get dressed, love," for her pains, too quiet, barely audible. Rachel went through the motions of preparing breakfast without even suggesting that Carrie feed the cat.

"I don't have anything to wear, Mum."

"I'll go and fetch something from your room," Rachel said absently. This was unthinkable; choosing her clothes and feeding the cat were Carrie's jobs, definitely non-negotiable.

"Rachel, do you love me, darling?" The word "darling" was guaranteed to get a rise, something about using words that don't mean anything, copied words.

"Yes."

Nothing.

Carrie walked into the kitchen and stood looking up at Rachel, her hands behind her back.

"If I wasn't your daughter and I was someone else and you had another child would you wish you had me?"

Rachel stopped in mid-movement, cornflake packet poised, and stared blankly at Carrie.

"What?" she asked in disbelief.

"I *said*, suppose I wasn't me or your daughter, although I was *me* and you had a daughter who wasn't me, would you wish you had me for your little girl instead of the one you had?"

Rachel sat down heavily on the kitchen stool. Her long puzzled stare gave way suddenly to a burst of laughter as she clasped her hand to her shaking head.

"Probably. I think," she laughed, and then noticed the clock on the table. "Caroline Kee, if you don't get washed and dressed *immediately* I'm going to start yelling."

"You *are* yelling," Carrie grinned happily; and as Rachel took a deep breath in preparation for the next volley, "All right, all right, I'm doing it," skidding on her sock across the kitchen floor, delighted that the day had started properly after all.

Dressed, washed and breakfasting, Carrie demanded, "What's the worst thing you've ever done in your whole life?"

Fucked Becky and then rejected her. Begged Joshua to beat and sodomize her. Not given Pete a home. Not loved her mother. Loved her father. Loathed everyone.

"Something really wicked," Carrie insisted.

Nothing really wicked meant giving gratuitous pain. She couldn't come up with anything she'd done, any unkindness that was completely without reason, wasn't at some level understandable. There were causes for her actions or lack of them and as long as she could see causes in her own or anyone else's behaviour she couldn't use the word "wicked" without qualification. Behaviour was just that: behaviour. We all dance around each other in devious and difficult patterns, but there are patterns, everyone responding to something. Everyone? Was Joshua wicked? She would have loved to think so. She wanted, above all, to feel rage against him; but if she could forgive, or at least understand, her behaviour last night to Becky then she couldn't avoid understanding Joshua's pain-giving as a response to pain received.

"Well?" Carrie demanded.

"I'm thinking about it. I don't think I've done anything that was just wicked."

Then she remembered. Six-year-old Rachel had done the only thing in her whole life that she could never justify, that would, when the time came, cause the gates of heaven to clang shut finally and forever.

"Yes, there was something I did once that I'm really ashamed of."

Carrie wriggled with pleasure at the prospect of a good bad story about her mother.

"What? What? Tell me."

"All right, but finish your toast. I was about six at my first school and we had this system where new kids were looked after by someone in the class who had been there a while. They were called Shadows and you were supposed to stick with the new pupil and show them around and sit with them in class and at lunch, all that sort of thing. I'd never been a Shadow until one day a new girl arrived and the class teacher put me in charge of her. And I really didn't want to. I didn't want to be in charge of anyone. The girl arrived and I hated her."

"Why?" Carrie asked, munching on her toast, wide-eyed.

"That's the point. For no reason at all. She was a perfectly nice, quite ordinary girl. She was fat and ordinary and sort of . . . happy. Well, that was why I hated her, for being fat and ordinary and happy I suppose. Really because I didn't want to look after her. Anyway I hated her, and I don't think I thought too much about why at the time. I made her life a complete misery. I used to drop rubbers and pencils on the floor so that I could crawl under the desk and pinch her leg, or I bit her or twanged her legs with a ruler. Oh God," Rachel covered her eyes in shame at the memory.

Carrie was loving it. "Didn't she tell on you?"

"No, I must have frightened her so much she didn't dare. This is a terrible story, isn't it?"

"Go on," Carrie begged, worried she'd never hear the end of

this wonderful tale, that it would be turned off like an unsuitable film on the television. "Go on."

"All right. I did get my comeuppance so I suppose it counts as a suitable story," Rachel muttered half to herself.

"But it is true, isn't it?"

"I'm afraid it is. Well, I don't remember how long it went on for but one day I arrived at school and was told to go into the headmaster's office. I'd never been in real trouble before so I wasn't particularly worried. He stood up and looked incredibly serious when I went in, and he told me that the girl's mother had been to see him the day before and told him what had been happening."

"What was the girl's name?" Carrie interrupted.

"I don't remember. I remember what she looked like but not her name."

"Well, can't you just make one up?" Carrie liked her stories to be stories.

"No. Do you want to hear the rest of it or not."

Carrie nodded fiercely and held her tongue.

"It turned out that she'd been so upset that she started having nightmares about me and waking in the middle of the night crying. And in the morning she cried because she didn't want to go to school, until finally her mother got the whole story out of her."

"Rachel!" Carrie breathed.

"Well, you wanted something really wicked. This is it. So the headmaster was, as you can imagine, very angry. In the corner of his office he had this long cane. I kept looking at it out of the corner of my eye. I was sure I was about to get caned but he said he wouldn't cane me because I was a girl."

"That's not fair," Carrie protested.

"No, I suppose not. He said I should be ashamed of myself and that he was going to tell the whole school what a horrid little girl I was, and marched me into assembly and suddenly lifted me up and stood me on his desk so that everyone could see me. Hundreds of people. All the children and the teachers, and he told everyone what I'd done and that I was very wicked."

"Poor Mummy. What did you do?"

"I had a friend I called Mouse. I don't know why she was

called that. Anyway she told me later that I'd looked really brave and as if I didn't care at all. I remember standing there absolutely determined not to cry. I bit the inside of my cheeks, and clamped my jaws together and dug my nails into my hands. I was not going to cry. And I kept hearing the headmaster behind me telling everyone how awful I was and it suddenly occurred to me that he could see up my skirt. Somehow I was almost as bothered by him seeing my knickers as being shamed in front of everyone."

Carrie burst out laughing.

"Then he told everyone that nobody was allowed to talk to me for two weeks, not even to ask to borrow a pencil, and I was to spend every lunch and playtime standing in a corner. And that's what happened. Except for my friend, Mouse, who was wonderful and kind, which was certainly more than I deserved. When I was sent back to my row she secretly took my hand and squeezed it to comfort me. And she used to sneak me a sweet when I was standing in the corner. She was very nice."

"Then what happened?"

"That's it. End of story. I don't know what happened to the girl. I think she stayed on at school and it blew over."

Carrie thought for a moment. "But that doesn't sound like you. You're not horrible like that. Why did you do it?"

"Honestly Carrie, I don't know. I suppose I wasn't very happy at home. My parents argued a lot. I suppose I felt very thin and miserable and couldn't stand the idea of this fat and happy girl following me around. Perhaps I was jealous of her. But I don't think there's any excuse for making anyone that unhappy."

"Oh, it makes me feel so sad for you, Mum," Carrie said.

"I think maybe it's the other girl who deserves your sympathy more. But thanks, you're as good a pal as Mouse. Anyway, that's it, that's the only very wicked thing I've done, the thing I'm really sorry for."

"That was a good story," said Carrie, as she got up from the table and put on her jacket.

In the car Carrie hummed her way through her repertoire of Assembly songs while Rachel drove thoughtfully. It occurred to her that the girl was a woman of her own age getting on with life somewhere. Did she carry an image of little Rachel around in her head? She saw herself enshrined forever, cruel and vicious, something against which the girl-turned-woman measured the unpleasantness of life. Someone's first persecutor. The angry, hateful part of Rachel was locked away, forever six, unable to change or understand or develop—something the other Rachel could do nothing about, couldn't connect with because she belonged to someone else as a frozen memory, used perhaps to explain and justify the confusions of life. Perhaps when you hurt other people you give a part of yourself away thinking all the time that you are keeping safe and separate. And if that were true she also had received others as the gifts of pain. If she loved Joshua that was because she had part of him inside her, he had made her a present part of himself with every act of aggression, unkindness, coldness. No wonder, then, that she wanted more; she stole Joshua bit by bit like a bird carrying away twigs to build itself a nest. Or a prison. Neither Rachel nor Joshua in the real world felt themselves to be simply the cold, alienated creatures that were locked irretrievably and unchangeably away in someone else's awareness. Rachel's Joshua was irredeemably her own thing, he could never get it back, never alter that slice of himself that she had imprisoned.

Rachel hugged Carrie goodbye at the school gate and set off in the direction of the café. Newspapers, hot coffee, sense of privacy that only public places give. She skimmed the paper, reading only the beginnings of paragraphs, and slipped to where she really wanted to be, in a reverie. Gazing out of the window she saw movement and pattern but no detail. She experienced herself as a dangerously unstable structure, a form held together more with glue and bits of string than nuts and bolts, that any kind of stress threatened to bend and warp, bring the whole edifice crashing down in a disordered, unrecognizable heap. Not even stress, though; merely life, anything that happened and impinged on her felt dangerous. This vision of herself was terrifying because it seemed to have overleaped fifteen or twenty years of imagining herself strong and capable. Adaptable. Now suddenly all that time was wiped out and she was back to the flailing, confused adolescent as if nothing had changed, no development had occurred, and the last twenty years represented mere self-deception. She felt ashamed, and the more so because she knew that there was nothing much wrong with her life. Fed, clothed, well housed, a charming daughter: privileged. No need to detail the misery most of the world lived and died with. Unlikable Rachel, moaning about— what? Nothing. Absolutely nothing was wrong, and all the while that awful weight inside her, physically painful, making her breathing shallow and cautious, made her protestations that nothing was wrong a nonsense. It was, that pain, itself an accusation. She felt so bad but *nothing was wrong*. She hadn't the right to that degree of pain. She couldn't justify the misery or herself. She felt tears pool behind her eyes and hurriedly searched her purse for a coin to pay for the coffee, hoping desperately she had one because she knew the tears couldn't be controlled through the process of offering a note and waiting for change. Finding a 50p piece she set it on the table beside her half-empty cup and made for the door.

Outside she stopped, desperate in her need to be at home, in her flat, *now*. The short walk to the car, the drive, even the pause of unlocking her front door seemed unmanageable, a series of insuperable obstacles. She thought for a moment "I can't move," and then knowing there was no alternative and that the longer she stood there the harder movement would become, she unstuck her feet from the pavement and made them walk in the direction of the car, arranging her face in what she hoped but couldn't be certain was a normal expression. She observed, or thought she did, people glancing at her as they passed by and checked from time to time that she wasn't spilling fountains of tears or gasping in air in the effort to keep going. It seemed like a long walk.

The car, when she got to it, was a halfway house. She sat in it for a moment, gathering the energy to drive. It's all right, she told herself, nearly there, only a few minutes and you'll be home. Just drive, be calm, you *will* get home. On the way it began to rain, a downpour that turned the road ahead to a watery haze. She flicked on the windscreen wipers which screeched dryly across the glass and did nothing to improve visibility. She blinked and glanced up at the cloudless sky, feeling at the same time a wetness on her cheeks. No rain; she was crying it seemed. She sniffed back the tears and pressed her lips together to achieve some semblance of determination. As she got out of the car she organized herself so that once inside the door there would be nothing else practical required of her. Glasses off, key in the right hand, cigarettes and lighter in the other, she had only to shrug off her coat, place the cigarettes beside the bed and then she was free. To do what? Never mind, free to do nothing, to be obliged to do nothing. Except that once inside the flat Shamus bounded up, mewing for food. No good ignoring him, it had to be done. Deep breath. The effort of getting the tin of cat food from the fridge and spooning some into his bowl was ridiculous. Every movement, every second an impossible demand on her resources. Inside her head she screamed, I've got to stop, I can't do this, it's not tolerable, but finally done, it was an achievement, and a great sense of relief spread over her. Nothing else. Nothing. She pulled off her boots, closed the bedroom curtains and lay on the bed.

Here it was again. Unmistakably It. She remembered depression through her fear of it, felt it lurking, knew it had happened before and could happen again, but when it came, when it felt so precisely as it felt, she was always taken by surprise. It was like malaria, like a fever. Sometimes when you have a cold you wonder if you don't have flu, but when you have flu you don't wonder at all. Depression was as specific as that, an instantly recognizable condition as if a switch had been turned. A physical pain in her diaphragm, a weight as if she had been filled with lead, the absurd difficulty of doing anything—automatic actions having to be thought out to be achieved: how do you get across the room, make the legs move, keep breathing, think carefully about it all. An hour, two hours, all day spent trying to get the energy and will to perform some simple task, feed the cat, take a pee. The unreasonable difficulty of everything made more unreasonable, more difficult knowing that nothing physical was wrong. And the deep shocking despair inside her head.

It was impossible to remember or describe the hopelessness, the absolute blackness that descended: the blackness was infinite, she was hopeless because there was *nothing* to hope for. It was a shift in perspective; it wasn't that she felt bad so that life seemed miserable, it was the falling away of a distorting rosy curtain that made life, most of the time, seem livable. In fact, it was not. When she was depressed she saw what there was to see, and knew with complete certainty that what she saw was reality. She knew the gauzes had to be there in order to stay alive but the times when they blew aside were when she was seeing things as they were. Depression was an excess of reality: intolerable and unlivable.

Rachel lay on her bed in the dark room and felt it happening. She was still only partially inside it, still watching to some degree. She kept trying to push away the blackness thinking, it's all right, I've done it before, it goes away. But how long before it went, and could she survive it? What if this time it didn't go? And Carrie? She hadn't been in this state for years. Before Carrie, when the depressions were more frequent, she had found a way of living through them. She had let go of the fear and allowed herself to feel the whole thing, let it happen to her while she sat alone in her flat and attempted nothing but staying alive through it. She lay on the floor, sometimes listened to music, but the trick was to accept it like a hurricane blowing through her life. Isobel helped once she realized what was happening; she came round with food that required no effort, that could be just left around and picked at from time to time, and she sat with Rachel sometimes without needing any talk. Having another human being in the same room seemed in some way to warm Rachel, locked away and inhuman, as if sheer body heat could infiltrate a little. But that was years ago, and Carrie hadn't been born, wasn't to be considered. Sometimes it had taken weeks, eight, ten weeks to get through it and gradually to realize that it had passed and it was time to get on with being alive. There was no way of letting the fear go with Carrie on her mind. She had to keep control, somehow stop the process, but here she was lying on her bed, exhausted with the effort of getting there, knowing she had no idea how to control it.

Today was Friday. Michael would pick Carrie up the next morning so that Rachel had a clear weekend in front of her. He would bring her back on Sunday night; all Rachel had to do was pick Carrie up from school and get through the evening until Carrie went to bed and then deal with the morning. Rachel laughed grimly, it sounded like a five-year plan; she imagined herself alone in a vast horizonless field picking ears of corn one by one. "And when you've finished that," boomed the Commandant in her head, "there are the other fields to be harvested. And you'd better hurry because there's not much time." Panic, terror and shame. Picking up her daughter and giving her supper could not be counted along with the unsupportable burdens that humanity had suffered; it was, nonetheless, unimaginable. She looked at the clock. If she left now she could get down to the doctor's surgery before it closed. Why? What could he do? Don't think about it, someone's got to do something. She put on her coat and went to the car, saw her face in the reversing mirror and went back into the flat for sunglasses to hide her dead, swollen eyes.

The surgery was crammed with sniffing, coughing humanity. People who were really ill. Kids crying with pains in their ears, old men wheezing. People suffering but waiting patiently for their turn. There were twenty-five people crowded into the small waiting room. Children sat uncomfortably on their mother's knees to make room for their elders, young men stood, acknowledging that their youth gave them an edge in spite of their ailments. The air wasn't air but a mingling of human breath, damp and heavy with contagion. It was probably possible to contract a dozen different diseases just by staying alive in that room. But no one complained, they were all in the same boat, everyone felt lousy and soon, well, fairly soon, a doctor would see them and give them sensible advice and medicine. All these people had something wrong with them, unlike Rachel who was quite well, no cough, no cold, no virus to explain and excuse how she felt. She stood at the receptionist's window and turned her coat collar up against the gaze of the bored and curious.

"Can I see Dr Stone, please?" she asked quietly. Too quietly, she had to repeat it. It was very difficult to talk, each word needed so much effort and at the same time she was fighting against the tears that pushed their way into her eyes.

"He's got a long list this morning. It'll be quite a wait." The receptionist didn't look up from her list. Rachel thought, go home, back to bed. I can't wait. But she had to because if she left there would be nothing else to be done.

"I'll wait outside. How long, do you think?"

"At least an hour."

This was very difficult. Ridiculous to make life so difficult for herself, to stand around in the street for an hour waiting to see a doctor to say what? To ask for what? But since she was here she had inertia on her side: it was now more difficult to go home than to stand still and wait.

She sat on the wall outside the surgery for an hour and then waited for half an hour more inside until finally her name was called, and she walked into Dr Stone's consulting room with no idea what she wanted, except that she was desperate. Dr Stone knew her mainly through Carrie's illnesses and a couple of bouts of flu. He glanced up from her medical notes as she walked in.

"What can I do for you?" he asked, young, friendly and more relaxed than most of the other doctors she had known.

"I'm not feeling very good," Rachel muttered, embarrassed as the tears immediately sprang into her eyes. "I get depressed, not for a long time, but it's bad now. I can't cope and I have to—Carrie . . ."

The tears rolled down her cheeks as the words came out tight and controlled through her gritted teeth.

"I've been looking through your notes," he said quietly. "I'm not surprised you get depressed. Life's been pretty complicated for you, hasn't it?"

"There's nothing wrong with my life. There's no reason for me to feel like this now, nothing's happened. There are people with three kids, full-time jobs, problems. I just can't bear it. I can hardly move."

The control went and she began to weep openly.

"I'm sorry. I don't know what to do. I can't go through this, I just can't."

"Are you suicidal?" Dr Stone inquired calmly.

"I don't see any point in being alive. There isn't anything ahead."

"What about Carrie?" A question she thought about.

"I don't think it's better in the long run for Carrie to have a depressed mother than a dead mother. I wouldn't have been worse off if my mother had killed herself. Look, I don't really care—about anything or anyone. I don't feel anything except that I've got to get out."

"What do you want me to do for you?" he asked.

Good question. She didn't want anti-depressants, she had tried them fifteen years before, they hadn't helped, only made her groggy for a couple of weeks until she adjusted to them. She couldn't look after Carrie, drive her to and from school feeling like that. In any case, it was a hit and miss business. She had known people who had spent years chopping and changing pills until it seemed to her to become an activity in itself, a way of transforming depression into busyness without really touching the misery. She had seen people disappear behind a pharmaco-poeia of avoidance and seem to become mere shadows. It didn't seem a viable way of staying alive, especially when staying alive didn't count for much.

She said this to Dr Stone.

"But your feeling that you don't want to be alive is a function of your depression." he said.

"My feelings now are *not* unreal," she said, determined that he should understand. "I feel like this most of the time, only now I can't dismiss it so easily. I'm a sort of empty space. A mistake. There just isn't any real reason for going on except sheer survival, and I don't see the point of that. I know you're committed to keeping people alive but sometimes it's better for everyone if they don't. I could live for another thirty or forty years, for nothing, just wasting space and probably damaging people. It's the only thing I can do. It's . . . logical." She spoke fiercely through her tears, angry that they, not her reasoning, might influence him.

"Well, what do you want me to do?" he asked again, and she was at a loss.

"I don't know. There's nothing you can do. I don't know why I came."

"Yes, but you did come."

"I want someone to deal with it. I don't know what to do."

"All right. Who can look after your daughter?"

"No one. I can't ask anyone to take Carrie over. Michael's working, and there isn't anyone else."

"If you can't cope for a while then your ex-husband will have to cope. He's her father. What about this woman, Isobel Raine? she's the woman who adopted you, isn't she?"

"I can't ask her to take on Carrie. She's busy. Anyway, I don't want anyone to know. Michael's having Carrie for the weekend, it'll give me a couple of days . . ."

"What about spending a few days in hospital? As a kind of refuge?"

"No. I can't do that. I was in hospital fifteen years ago. It would be such a defeat."

"Right," said Dr Stone briskly, "you will have to tell someone and get Carrie looked after. You are not in any condition to cope. Go home and phone Michael. Have you got any sleeping pills?"

Rachel nodded. "I've got a dozen Temazepam left, but they don't seem to get me to sleep. They're very mild."

"Yes, they are. Take them over the weekend, you can take three to get some sleep, they won't hurt, and then phone me on Monday and let me know if you're feeling any better. If you're not we'll think about finding somewhere for you to go for a few days, a hospital, just to relieve the pressure on you."

Rachel left feeling worse than before for having made it so real. Had she wanted Dr Stone to tell her there was nothing wrong and to pull herself together? He wasn't surprised that she felt like this, thought she should be in hospital, acknowledged that she was feeling as desperate as she thought. There was some relief in that but also terror. It wasn't a fantasy that someone would blow away. This *was* how it was.

She got home and phoned Michael.

"I've got flu. Can you pick Carrie up from school, please?"

Michael said he would, and that she sounded as if she had a sore throat. It was quite impossible to tell him what was really going on. He found it very difficult to deal with other people's depression. It scared him in her especially; and more than that, she simply didn't want to acknowledge it, make it public. He would tell Isobel, she would come round, the whole thing would become real, out there. Isobel *was* busy and she would be disappointed. Rachel was supposed to have overcome all that. Guilt. Keep it to herself. If she couldn't stop feeling like this at least she didn't have to tell anyone, ask anyone for help. It did occur to her to wonder why it was all right to ask Michael to help her through flu, but it was obvious; flu wasn't her fault, depression was. A virus gave permission to opt out and make demands on people.

She had cleared her way through to Sunday evening, the impossible burden of Carrie was dealt with. She undressed and took three pills, took the phone off the hook and went to bed. She woke at four in the afternoon and took three more pills which kept her asleep until nine that evening. Then she got up and sat on the sofa in the living room, curled up in the dark, wrapped in an old cotton dressing gown. She sat there till dawn began to break, staring out at the grey room and whispering over and over again, "Help me. Please help me. Somebody help me," but always with the knowledge clear in one part of her mind that there wasn't any help she could imagine.

Then she began to think very practically about suicide. She was calm, very sensible, there were only details to be sorted out. She sat on the sofa chain-smoking with the look of someone who, though quite sure of her next move, had yet to sort out the best way of achieving it. She had always been at her best when problem-solving. The problem was essentially Carrie. It had to be done in the least damaging way and that excluded anything messy or bloody. In any case, the more violent methods of ending a life were for those who were angry and wanted to punish. She was not angry and had no desire to punish anyone including herself. She didn't want pain, not hers nor anyone else's. Blood-letting was out, car crashes were out, other people would be involved. A pity she didn't have some terminal illness, that of course would be ideal. Her death would then be inevitable and Carrie could be helped to come to terms with that. However, she was healthy and that was that. Which left an overdose, efficient and clean, but a little difficult to manage these days. Fifteen years before she had wandered around with lethal quantities of barbiturates in her pocket, prescribed by her doctor for sleep. At twenty, in just such a cool and logical state of mind, she had swallowed thirty seconal and quietly put herself to bed thinking she had forty-eight hours before anyone could be expected to find her. In fact a boyfriend who was supposed to be away for the weekend had turned up with his own key. This time she had two days and a lock on her front door. She would have to put a note on the door to her flat stopping Michael from coming in on Sunday evening. That was simple enough. Should she write something for Carrie? Something that might help when she was older even if she wouldn't understand it immediately? She couldn't decide on that. Perhaps better to leave it to the people who could better deal with it, see what was required. She began to feel that dealing with a future she planned not to be part of was more than she could handle, and perhaps more than she had a right to interfere in. She also began to feel that there was something more than a little barmy in her sensible, down-to-earth plans for ending her own life. You always take things so seriously, she told herself. She imagined herself sitting very solemn on the sofa and swallowing pills; sips of water then a few pills, very intense. Ludicrous. Then it struck her: it doesn't have to be so difficult, so po-faced. Pills and booze; the booze first; get a little tight, *then* take the pills. Simple and obvious. This moment of clarity hit her; it's not the end of the world, she chuckled to herself, enjoy yourself. She got up and washed her face, dressed in a comfortable pair of jeans and sweat shirt and looked at the clock. It was ten: time to go shopping. She drove to the nearest supermarket which was already filling up with Saturday-morning shoppers and bought a bottle of whisky and a king-size economy bottle of aspirin. She wasn't happy about the aspirin, she didn't know the effective dose and didn't want to make a mess of it, but anything really efficient would have to be on prescription and that was out of the question. Surely two hundred aspirin washed down with a bottle of whisky would do it. She didn't want to think about it out in the open for too long, feeling so transparent, made of glass, as if anyone looking at her would see her thoughts tickertaping around her brain. Being careful she picked a packet of chocolate biscuits from the shelf to confuse any onlooker. People about to kill themselves didn't buy chocolate biscuits. It would render the other purchases harmless, she hoped.

At home she leaned against the door like one who had reached sanctuary after a flight from man-eaters, and, safe again, panting from the strain of seeming just like everyone else, she took her brown paper bag upstairs and unloaded it on the kitchen table. The aspirin tablets looked incredibly chalky. Her saliva dried up as she looked at them. She prized a couple of ice cubes from the tray in the freezer and poured a third of a tumbler full of whisky over them. She planned to get tight in style. No reason why she had to gulp down luke-warm alcohol from the bottle. In any case she didn't really like whisky and needed the ice as anaesthetic. She planned to drink a third or so of the bottle before she began swallowing the pills, fancying a light-hearted exit.

But Rachel was not a drinker. The theory was fine for anyone whose body was well-adjusted to alcohol but the bottle of wine she shared with Joshua on his occasional visits represented her actual intake. For a couple of glasses everything was fine. She played a Mozart quartet and sipped at the icy liquid as she sat on the floor and watched the tree outside her window bristle its leaves in the light summer breeze. The music was lovely and the sunshine pleasing; she watched the light play on the dark green gloss of the philodendron and felt for the first time in many weeks a sense of peace and pleasure in being just with herself because, for the first time in what seemed now like many weeks, she hadn't to consider any future, any time to be "got through." What time was left was to be short and of her choosing. Decisions were very comforting. If life could be like this she might have made it through; no people, no requirements. But that was just to reiterate her failure, her inability to be part of life, to be in it. It reinforced her judgement and confirmed her decision. There was actually no question about it in her mind.

By the end of the third glass it occurred to her that she had to write the note for Michael and tape it to the door before she was too drunk. She should also, she thought, attempt the letter to Carrie. Suddenly there was life making demands again. She had to let go of the music and sunshine in order to do the right thing. She pulled several sheets of notepaper from her desk drawer and an envelope.

"DON'T COME IN. I'VE KILLED MYSELF," she printed on a sheet of paper, then squinted at it.

"Oh my God!" she groaned as she crumpled the note into a tight ball and flung it across the room. What was the unmelodra-

matic way of saying it? "Hello Michael, just a note to say I've
Od'ed. See you around, maybe." Or, "Just stepped out for the
rest of my life. Love to Carrie." Or, "Don't be upset about this
but . . ." Three more glasses of whisky later Rachel was lying
in a giggling heap on the carpet while Shamus played feline
football with the dozen or so paper balls that lay scattered
around the floor. She heaved herself up into sitting position and
eyed the half-empty bottle over on the kitchen table. Now I've
done it, she muttered to herself; this is a classic. Tiny drunken
Alice was too far from the bottle labelled "Drink Me." Never
mind the bloody note, how was she supposed to get to the bottle
and the other bottle? Willpower, that did it every time. She
rolled on to her hands and knees and prepared for the short
impossible crawl into the kitchen through a landscape that spun
furiously. Stupid, inefficient woman, she bellowed at herself
before collapsing on the floor in a howl of laughter, you silly
cow, you can't even reach the aspirin never mind swallow two
hundred of them. You've outfoxed yourself Kee. The penalty for
treachery is death or, in this case, life. *And* you haven't put a
note on the door.

She lay curled up on the floor like a hedgehog, her head
tucked into her knees, her arms covering the top of her head
protectively. Everything now was impossible, living, dying,
writing letters, opening aspirin bottles, moving; it was all out of
the question, all too complicated, too many problems, no solutions, just complexity on complexity, like a terrible spider web
that grew new and dreadfully intricate strands wherever she
tried to break through. Each thought connected with a dozen
others that led in turn to more so that it was impossible to
conclude anything, or to think at all. Ideas whizzed down neu-
rons and leapt across synapses and lost themselves in memories,
language and images. Her brain was a crazy house of devious
corridors where walls, floors and ceiling moved of their own
accord, buffeting thought through circuitous alleyways. There
were no straight lines, just everything trying madly to connect
itself to everything else; no sense, just fleeting associations that
led inexorably away from the original problem. There were
propositions and ramifications, but the ramifications had ramifications and confused and complexified any reasonable, simple

questions such as: how do I get across the room and what am I going to do? In a moment of stupendous concentration she finally came to the thought: *I need help,* and she hung on to it like a shipwrecked sailor finding the bit of flotsam that proclaimed the name of his sunken vessel. She made no attempt to define what she meant by help, didn't wonder whether she needed it for the purpose of life or death; *help* was the thing, it was a thing in itself. It was simple and revelatory.

She rolled onto her back and lay flat out on the carpet, watching the ceiling spin madly as hot tears ran down the sides of her face.

"I need help," she sobbed, "I . . . Need . . . Help."

She repeated this a few times, initially curious at hearing these words coming from her mouth, and then feeling that having made this momentous and remarkable demand something ought to happen. They were words, coming from her, with power; she incanted them as an "open sesame," waiting for the magic to work.

Nothing.

The tears stopped as suddenly as they had started and for a while she lay on the floor staring up at the ceiling. All right, she thought, switching suddenly into a logical mode, there's nothing basically wrong with yelling for help, but you have to do it within earshot to get results. There wasn't anyone to hear. Well, possibly there was God, but she suspected that God might not consider her predicament a priority, especially since she didn't have a very clear idea of what exactly her predicament was. Call it despair, futurelessness, her predicament was that she simply did not want to be alive any more but the details of achieving that seemed beyond her organizing abilities. She wanted someone there who would listen to her reasoned desolation and command her cool logic. She wanted someone who would assist her suicide, take over the detailed planning and provide her with the appropriate means. What she really wanted was for someone to hand her a bottle of pills and dictate the note—or something like that. Still, Rachel, drunk and desperate though she was, couldn't help but see that this was an unattainable goal. Neither the best of friends nor the worst of enemies was likely to take that burden on their shoulders.

Death was the thing you did alone, the only thing apart from being born.

Well then, what she wanted that perhaps she *could* have was someone there, but it had to be someone who wouldn't be scared of how she was, who wouldn't panic or take it too seriously; she didn't want it to *matter* that she felt like she did. Even Dr Stone had given her the impression that it mattered. There was only one person: Joshua. Joshua could handle this because he really didn't care, he was as objective another body as she could imagine. She wanted Joshua to sit through it with her and be that unemotional Watcher that she usually was for herself but which seemed at the moment buried under the seeping lava of her depression. It was a couple of weeks since he had called and in the meantime Pete had died and she and Becky had been lovers briefly, but so far as he was concerned nothing had happened, because she knew that she only existed for him when he was there. He didn't care, and that, at the moment, was precious, perhaps that was what had been precious all along. She badly wanted that cold, unresponsive man who wouldn't take her seriously, wouldn't worry. Isobel would worry and panic quietly, Becky would be loving and soft and scared, and Michael would run for his life; none of that was what she wanted. But Joshua would be cold and rational, would see her sense of pointlessness as a fact, and a small fact at that, and would not try to re-align her vision. He was the only person with whom she could unapologetically be herself, who wouldn't be hurt or scared. A man who didn't care for a woman who didn't care.

So. Problem solved, she knew who she wanted. Next problem: how to get him there. Joshua was hardly biddable; if she had never asked him to come to her it was because she knew quite well that he wouldn't—most especially not if requested. But now she had nothing to lose, she wouldn't be risking the relationship because as far as she was concerned there wasn't anything beyond now. She wouldn't be losing future visits when Joshua heard her needy voice and ran for his life because there wasn't any future that she could conceive. The rules were obsolete, having been designed for an ongoing game.

Finding Joshua's number in the phone book and dialling it

presented enormous difficulty. After three misdials she got
through and heard him telling her that he was a machine and
not there—all true.

"It's me. Can you call me, please," her voice thick and damp
in spite of an attempt at normality.

No good. He wasn't there, wouldn't come anyway even if he
picked up the message. She wasn't going to get what she
wanted—not very surprising really, considering who she
wanted it from—but having made the effort to know what she
wanted she felt doubly desolate. It wasn't going to happen and
she was alone. She sat on the floor and hugged her knees tightly
in some attempt to hold herself together. Never mind Joshua,
she couldn't go on being alone. She couldn't face more time—
minutes, hours, years—filled with certain nothing.

She reached for the phone again and called Becky. This number she knew by heart and didn't have to deal with the dancing
print of the telephone directory as she had when phoning
Joshua. But she still couldn't get the numbers right. A French
woman answered. " 'Allo? 'Allo?"

"Becky?" Rachel croaked, knowing it wasn't.

The voice asked her what number she was calling as Rachel
put the phone down and tried again, beaming concentration on
to the dial. Again she got, " 'Allo?" but crosser this time.

The third time she got through.

"Becky?"

"Rachel? Are you all right?"

"No." The sound of Becky's voice and her concern released a
flood of tears as she spoke. "Please . . . come round."

"I'll be there in a few minutes."

Rachel put the phone back on the hook and, still shaking with
her sobs, got up and lurched into the kitchen. She poured more
Scotch into a glass and gulped it down and then heaved herself
over to the sink and vomited massively. When she had finished
she sat at the kitchen table whimpering. What good was it going
to do to have Becky there? None, except that she had to have
someone. After a few moments she pulled herself up and went
shakily downstairs to open the door so that Becky could let
herself in. Back in the living room she sat on the sofa with her

knees hugged to her chest, her arms wrapped around her, holding on tight.

Becky arrived upstairs to see Rachel wound in her tight, space-saving ball, shaking all over, teeth chattering, tears running down her cheeks.

"Whatever's the matter?" Becky asked, horrified, from the door.

Rachel looked up and saw only a blur of human shape through her tears but the presence of another person in the room ran through her like an electric current. Someone else was there. Thank God.

Becky sat down and put her arms round Rachel. "What is it? Tell me what's wrong?"

Rachel collapsed into her embrace. Suddenly the room felt warmer and even the colours seemed to have changed, as if a painter had washed the misty grey background with delicate orange and reds.

"I don't know," she sobbed on Becky's shoulder, "I need help. I can't bear any more of this . . ." Rachel wept. "It isn't anything that's happened. I just don't want any more."

"Oh Rachel, what can I do? How can I help?" Becky asked, sounding frightened. Rachel's tears and loss of control were terrifying, quite different from other friends who cried on her shoulder occasionally when life got to be too much. This was more serious, more final somehow.

"Nothing. There's nothing to do. I'm sorry," Rachel sobbed.

Then Becky began to cry. "I don't know what to do for you, how to help. I can't stand to see you like this." In a moment Becky was weeping unrestrainedly. Hearing her through her own sobs Rachel stiffened and pulled away to look at her.

"Stop it," she snapped. "Stop crying. It's not a fucking tragedy. I just want someone here to sit with me. Don't, for Christ sake." She half-begged, half-ordered as she tried to get a hold on her own tears. She didn't want to share her misery or weep with anyone. She needed someone solid and tough there, not someone to commiserate and suffer with her. Becky sniffed back her tears as Rachel put her hands over her face and moaned, "I want Joshua," and then wailed hopelessly, "I want Joshua."

Becky got up and went to the bathroom. She came back with a wet flannel and gently washed Rachel's face.

"It's all right," Becky said with careful calm. "I'm all right now. I'm not upset. I'm going to make some coffee. You tell me what happened."

"Nothing happened. Really. It's just that I don't want to be alive any more. I got some whisky and aspirin only I got too drunk to take the aspirin and I needed someone around. I don't know what to do. It's all such a mess. Forever and ever a mess." She sat up straight and tried to pull herself together as Becky made coffee.

"Was it Pete? Or me? That brought it on?"

"No, it wasn't. I got depressed suddenly. It's like being in another country. There aren't any reasons that would explain feeling like this. Things have been . . . difficult, but nothing that's actually happened seems to be of any importance now. I don't care about any of it. That's the point—I simply don't care. That's what's unbearable, the fact that I couldn't care less about anything. I don't want to be alive because there's no point in being alive. No substance." Rachel spoke now in a monotone, though the tears still ran down her face.

"Rachel, that's not true. Of course you care. You care about Carrie, and me, and Pete, and Joshua. You care about everything. I know you do."

"You're wrong," Rachel said coldly, "I don't. I know I should. I should want to stay alive because I love Carrie. But I don't, I want to be out of it. I'm not interested in what's going to happen. Everything will go on well enough without me. People would be upset, obviously, for a while but then life would just go on. People survive other people's deaths. It's not important. Only I don't seem to be able just to get on with it and do it. I don't understand that. Becky, I couldn't give a toss about the entire human race. They are all starving and dying, all the time, everywhere. It's a dreadful place. Why does anyone want to stay alive? I don't understand. I'm appalled by this place, but I don't *care* about it. I have no real feeling, no compassion; there isn't anything at all inside me. The world will go on being its miserable self with me or without me. I don't want any more."

"Rachel, you do matter," Becky said seriously, sitting in the chair across the room. "People care about you and you care too, whether you can see that at the moment or not. You're in a depression, you know that. You aren't seeing things in the same way you'd see them if you weren't depressed."

"Rubbish. I'm seeing things completely clearly and what's more it's how I always see things, only usually it's possible to avoid noticing it all the time. Being depressed is just seeing things how they really are and not being able to look away. Who are you to say that this isn't real and the other is? I don't want to keep myself alive by never telling myself the truth, and that's the only way I can justify going on."

Becky was at a loss against Rachel's rationale. She couldn't argue against it, she simply knew it was wrong.

"Look, *I* don't want you to be dead."

"You'll get over it," Rachel muttered as the phone rang and Becky moved towards it. "Leave it, I can't talk to anyone."

"I'll get it. Hello," she said a little shakily.

"What do you want?" said a jovial voice, and then, realizing that it wasn't Rachel's voice, continued: "Who is that?"

Becky's huge eyes widened and her jaw dropped.

"Oh, I'm a friend of Rachel. She isn't feeling very well."

"She phoned me, left a message for me to ring her. What's the matter with her?"

Becky clamped her hand over the mouthpiece and mouthed "Joshua" at Rachel, who made frantic signals to Becky not to say anything more. "NO! NO!" she mouthed. This was a disaster. She could imagine Joshua's irritation at having to discuss her with someone he didn't know over the phone. At having to discuss her at all. He would be furious at being drawn in like this. Becky looked panic-stricken as she held the phone, then turned firmly away from Rachel as she said in a voice bordering on hysteria, "Rachel's suffering from a severe bout of pointlessness. Look, if you're a friend of hers you'd better come over, she needs a friend."

Rachel gasped.

"NO!" she screamed and collapsed sideways on to the sofa, "NO! Don't, don't . . ." Becky didn't turn around.

"Is she very bad?" Joshua asked.

"I think so. Yes, she is," Becky replied.

"I'll be round. I was planning to come anyway," Joshua said, as he put down the phone.

"You stupid cow. How could you?" Rachel yelled, staring in disbelief at Becky who stood looking at her apologetically.

"I'm sorry," Becky said, on the edge of tears again. "I didn't know what to say when I heard it was him. I was so worried it just came out."

Rachel began to laugh. She put her head in her hands and shook with laughter.

"Becky, if I spent the next thirty years searching for one phrase that would be guaranteed to send Joshua heading for the hills as fast as his legs could carry him I don't think I could have come up with anything better. 'You're a friend and Rachel needs you.' That's it. You've just solved the Joshua problem in one fell swoop."

"I'm sorry. But he didn't seem upset. He said he was coming over. He sounded really concerned."

"Of course he did. He doesn't want to seem like a shit, even to an anonymous voice over the phone. Well, he won't come. 'Rachel needs a friend' " she muttered to herself, imagining Joshua hearing the words. "You hit on the magic combination; you've put the dragon to flight. One day they'll name a public festival after you."

"Oh, Rachel, I'm sorry. Are you sure he won't come?"

"Absolutely. Never mind, it doesn't really matter, does it? I can't even care about that much. And it has given me my first laugh for days. Congratulations. Where's that coffee and where's the Scotch?" she demanded as she got up shakily.

Becky went back into the kitchen and poured black coffee into a large cup while Rachel stood in the doorway, leaning against the wall.

"You shouldn't have any more to drink. You've had two-thirds of a bottle already."

"Yes I should. I feel dreadfully sober and it's not better than being drunk."

"You don't look sober," said Becky doubtfully, eyeing Rachel propped against the wall. She had started to shiver again and her face was tight and pale, emphasizing the red and swollen eyes that stared glassily with exhaustion. She looked about ten years old, a child woken from a nightmare but still inside it, barefoot in skintight jeans and grubby sweat shirt, her wild hair awry, frizzing around the thin bleak face. Becky felt she wanted to hold her, wrap her up in a soft blanket and comfort her, but saw the wall surrounding her and knew she wouldn't be able to get inside the sharp protection to the vulnerability. She poured a little whisky into a glass and carried it and the coffee into the living room. "Where?" she asked.

"There." Rachel pointed to the living room table.

Rachel sipped whisky and coffee and stared out of the window as Becky sat opposite her at the table and wondered what to say. Something awful was happening for Rachel, she could see that, but still she remained prickly and distant. Asking Becky to come round seemed to be as far as she could go in showing any need. Becky's inclination to reach out and touch Rachel, to offer warmth and comfort, was stillborn. Rachel's power to keep people at bay was quite as awesome when she was depressed as in her normal condition. Becky decided that perhaps just being there might be helpful, it was all she could do anyway; maybe it was enough, or at least as much as Rachel could take. They sat in silence for a while as Rachel stared grimly through the window, at nothing. From time to time tears spilled from her eyes but nothing else about her face changed; she seemed not even to notice them.

"Isn't there anything . . . ?" Becky tried.

"Nothing. Thank you."

Very polite, very formal. Nothing much happening, no old friendship to lean on. Once when she was quite small Rachel had been taken by her parents to visit some cousins—way back when the visiting was still possible. There had been a sudden terrible row between her mother and father in front of the two children of the house; they had screamed abuse at each other, spat their loathing across the neat suburban front room of their hosts as Rachel stood frozen with the shame of it. The other children, older than Rachel, had giggled their embarrassment at the filth and hatred that came from the grown-ups. Rachel stared icily at them, her jaws clamped tight, and began a conversation—about school, about what happened at her last birthday. Formal teatime conversation demanding an equivalent response from the two other children, who tried but couldn't help the laughter that bubbled hysterically inside them from showing occasionally. Rachel kept up the patter as if the shouting and violence in the room were merely a television programme she wasn't watching, daring the others to do less. Nothing was happening, just polite conversation with distant relatives. Anyway, she wouldn't ever have to see them again.

Here was something similar: grown-up Rachel had got drunk and yelled for help, wept and didn't care, behaved, as Becky perceived it, not very differently from the way everyone else behaves from time to time. Rachel however was not so tolerant, at least, not the cold-eyed other Rachel who had begun to re-establish herself. Pretend that nothing has happened, the icy voice told her, ignore the occasional tear, it's only your body doing it; ignore the pain, it's just physical; if you can't do anything about it, and I'm afraid, Rachel, that that is the case on current showing, then pretend it isn't happening. We are not, the voice told her severely, the sort of person that yells for help or asks for comfort. You might try to bypass me with alcohol or Joshua, but what for? To become abject, a wailing neurotic, an object for sympathy? Face it, your value to your friends is that you don't land on their doorsteps screaming for attention. And it was true, Rachel acknowledged, she didn't want to be that. Whatever depression was, it was against her will; the body, the chemicals or something in revolt, and if she couldn't do anything about that she could at least contain the pain, stop it from spilling out.

"I'm all right. A bit drunk. Sorry, I shouldn't have called. Really I'm fine," she assured Becky, who knew better but nonetheless felt something like relief at Rachel becoming Rachel again. She didn't know what to do with the other one, had no practice and honestly felt a little disappointed at the prospect of Rachel being needy like everyone else. Only disappointed? Perhaps there was a little satisfaction too, but Becky dismissed this thought fast, it wasn't her way to overanalyse.

Becky left with assurances that Rachel would be all right and would ring if she needed her and would not do anything silly, and although she was uneasy about it, it really did seem that Rachel wanted to be alone.

This was true, she desperately wanted Becky to leave. She couldn't explain and in any case what was the point? She wanted to feel better, not discuss her condition, and while it was true that having someone else in the room warmed her in some way, it was also the case that it confused the issue. With Becky there she was torn between the need to behave properly and the misery she felt.

Half an hour later she was back on the sofa staring at the window when Joshua walked into the room carrying a bottle of champagne.

"Someone left the door open," he said briskly to her surprised, tear-stained face. "Glasses. How long has this been going on?"

Rachel shrugged, remaining where she was, cross-legged on the sofa, as Joshua fetched two glasses from the kitchen.

"Don't know. The sun was shining when I rang you."

It was dusk now.

"Sunshine will do it every time," said Joshua, very light, jovial, popping the cork. "Here, you're already awash with alcohol," eyeing the almost empty whisky bottle on the table, "more won't make much difference. Then coffee. Eaten anything lately?"

"Yesterday . . . or maybe the day before. Doesn't matter, I'm not hungry." The champagne tasted disgusting and her head revolved furiously.

She had the impression that Joshua had his sleeves rolled. He was all efficiency, common sense, had arrived ready for action.

"Where's your friend?" he asked as he put the coffee machine on and cut bread.

"She left. I wanted to be on my own."

"Quite right."

"But now you're here. How come you came?"

"I was planning to come round anyway. You were on my schedule."

"Yes, but drunken, desperate women aren't your scene," she slurred.

"That's true, but everyone's allowed a drunken binge occasionally. Very occasionally," he warned as he sat next to her on the sofa, holding a plate of bread and butter and a cup of strong black coffee. "Here, have some bread and drink this."

She sipped the coffee from the cup which he held for her and took a bit from the slice of bread he handed her, then spat it out.

"No, I can't eat. I don't want it. I won't. I'm not hungry," she wailed.

"You should try and eat something. It'll soak up some of that alcohol."

"No!"

The phrase "drunken binge" had an almost magical effect on her, it sounded so normal, denied the despair and the fear and the encroaching chaos and turned what was happening into a minor episode, a piece of ordinary human foolishness. She knew somewhere that it wasn't as simple as that, that the despair was there and would be there when the alcohol had been metabolized, but for now it lightened everything—just a drunken binge, something everyone was entitled to from time to time. Thank God for Joshua, she had been so right to call him, he could manage this without taking it seriously. None of Becky's tears or the weight of Isobel's disappointment or Michael's fear, just a temporary falling off of Rachel's otherwise excellent self-command. How amazing that he had turned up; still, as he said, he'd been on his way, he would loathe a disruption to his timetable. I don't even have to feel guilty about him being here, she thought. Anyway, hummed her voice, let's face it, this is a real sadist's night out—a drunk, desperate woman all needy and pathetic. What fun!

Rachel got into a party mood. She became a grim, funny, recalcitrant five-year-old, teasing and irritating, a wicked grin on her face. She vaguely recognized the little girl she was being, sapping amusement and admiration and fury from the adults for her wit and cleverness. Death and desolation were stored away beneath the performance and Joshua played his role to the hilt, exasperated and entertained at the fast and funny patter. He humoured and she tested—up to a point. She wouldn't eat, she would drink, she wouldn't let him watch a play on the television without smartarse interruptions.

"Bloody John Mortimer, all fine prose and delicate middleclass perception. Bla bla bla . . ."

"Shut up and go to bed. Now." Very severe. Daddy's cross, but still, good point.

She went off and ran the bath and lay in the bubbly water, splashing and humming loudly. Smoke Gets In Your Eyes. I Get No Kick From Champagne. Let's Face the Music and Dance. Golden oldies. Back in the living room Joshua looked up from the television to see her dripping and naked in the doorway, looking wet, young, head perched quizzically to one side, small wicked grin on her face.

"Still trying to get a bit of culture, eh? It's for the birds, all that real life on the screen. It's the fantasy of day-to-day living that you've got to engage with, buster."

"Get a towel and dry yourself. You'll catch cold. Then go to bed . . . Do as you're told!"

Unmoved by her nakedness, by the firm, vulnerable, appealing little body, he was the strict father who knew her game and wasn't having any of her nonsense. But what a pleasure game to play; the nakedness and the vulnerability hadn't passed him by, the eyes narrowed and smiled a little. Small signals from the sexual Joshua to the sexual Rachel were sent and received at a low enough level to avoid interference with the other game they were playing. Rachel continued to stand where she was, her naked body quite unconsidered by either of them.

"I want to go for a drive. Now. Fast. Please?" she asked sweetly.

"Then will you go to bed?" he asked.

"Yeth. Will. I promise."

"Right. Put a coat on." He got up and switched off the television. A very patient, managing man.

She went into the bedroom and pulled a trenchcoat from her wardrobe.

"This do?" she asked, pulling it over her still-damp body.

"That'll do," he said calmly.

"Shoes."

"Shoes? That necessary?"

"Yes."

Bright pink ankle boots appeared and they were off. It was midnight now as they whizzed down the Edgware Road towards the motorway.

"Faster. You can do better than that," she urged.

"Drunken hussy. I *am* going faster. You're just too pissed to notice."

"Oh."

Somewhere along the journey reality started to reassert itself, the pain began to come back. By the time they were back at her flat she was quiet and grim-faced. She dropped her coat on the stairs, kicked off the boots and crawled straight into bed in silence. Joshua, also in silence, stripped off his clothes and got carefully into bed next to her, not too near. She lay curled foetally with her back to him as he rested his head on his arms and stared up at the ceiling.

"I'm scared about tomorrow," she whispered, half to herself, after a long silence.

"Why?"

"Tomorrow won't be funny. I don't think this is going to go away."

"Take some anti-depressants. Does this happen often?"

"Not for a while. I won't take anti-depressants, I won't live in a cloud. You take the pills and start to feel that the intolerable is tolerable. I'd rather see things as they are."

"And end up killing yourself?"

"If that's necessary. I don't want to be alive—not only now but fundamentally somewhere most of the time I don't want to be part of it. I really don't care about anything."

Then at least he would understand.

"I don't believe that," he said surprisingly. Apparently he thought alienation his private domain.

"As you like, but the fact remains."

There was a brief silence while he considered.

"If that's what you really feel like most of the time then you're right, life isn't worth living. You should kill yourself—only don't fuck about with aspirin and whisky, you'll only turn yourself into a vegetable. Do it efficiently."

Rachel shrugged. "As long as I don't know about it it doesn't matter if I do become a vegetable. I've enough sensible friends who would pull the plugs if that happened."

Two Rachels reacted to this conversation; the first, canny and devious, understood Joshua's agreement to her suicide as excel-

lent therapy, a manoeuvre designed to make her react against
what she said she wanted, a solid, hard wall he had backed her
up to, shocking her into climbing over it; the first Rachel
wanted to smile at his expertise. The other Rachel experienced
a rush of relief, the first for days. She was released suddenly,
listened to; here was someone who had heard what she said and
accepted it as plain fact. She didn't have to soften what she had
to say to protect his feelings since he had none that she could
hurt. He heard how it was with her without shock or embarrassment and made no attempt to dismiss it as the "mere" result of
depression. Joshua being Joshua took what she said at face value,
thought about it and agreed that her life was not so precious
that she shouldn't let go of it if it was unsatisfactory. This after
all was what she loved him for, if she loved him at all—telling
the truth. No social niceties, no reassurance, no apologies to be
made for saying uncomfortable things. And practical too. The
moment was to be cherished, an acknowledgement of who she
really was.

"Thank you," she whispered, curled up in the dark, feeling an
extraordinary sense of peace. The frantic and guilty need to die
she had felt earlier was transformed into calm decision, a cool
calculation, a promise she had made to herself.

There wasn't anyone else in the world who could have done
that for her. Now if he could get hold of some killing pills for her
. . . All right, so that wasn't reasonable, even Joshua would
baulk at doing the deed for her. Complicated business, sado-
masochism; truth and pain, pleasure and then the *real* pleasure,
wanting and giving and not-giving, loving and punishing and
gratitude and anger: when do you get to the end of it? Share my
suicide with me, Joshua—my present to you, yours to me. Let's
get to the bottom of this thing: kill me, Joshua. But their pantomime stopped short of what they really wanted, the line between fantasy and reality was well drawn, the hurt and pain had
no more after-effects than the odd bruise, just enough to feed
the fantasy, not enough to put one's real life on the line. That
was Joshua's skill, knowing one thing from the other, where the
line was. That was why she felt safer with him than any other
man (or woman) she'd ever known.

She rolled over to face him, still on his back, his arms behind his head.

"Fuck me," she said, as she climbed on to him and crouched astride his substantial belly.

He glanced at her. "Ask nicely."

"Fuck me . . . please," she whispered, as she settled herself over his penis and began, in fact, to fuck him.

He gave small indications of pleasure as she moved carefully up and down.

"What do you want me to do to you?" he demanded.

"Smack me."

"What?"

"Smack me, please."

He smacked her a half-dozen times, rhythmically and quite gently.

"Is that hard enough?"

"Harder. Smack me harder. Please," she begged as his hand came down with increasing force and she felt the pain on her arse and the pleasure of his cock inside her with equal intensity.

"Please, please, please," she wept. "Hurt me. Please hurt me," repeating herself over and over as she came and wept on his chest.

"What else do you want?" he asked after a moment, still inside her, her heart still racing.

"Bugger me. Please."

When they finished Joshua held her tightly in his arms and stroked her hair until the sobbing died down, then he slept a little.

Rachel lay awake and watched the dawn begin to break through a crack in the curtains. Tomorrow would come and the weight would be there; there would be no Joshua, no anyone. She had achieved a delay of the pain but it was still to be lived through and the chaos was already beginning to seep back: what to do about Carrie, how to appear to be functioning, how to get through the minutes. Fear. She was grateful to Joshua for the time off but that was over. Joshua woke and watched her for a moment, staring at the light, then he looked at his watch.

"It's four-thirty. I have to go."

"I know," she replied, without taking her eyes from the curtains. He saw the alarm in her eyes.

"I really have to go. Where are your sleepers? Take two, it'll be better in the morning."

"It is morning. It won't be better. Never mind, I know you have to go."

He didn't have to go. There was no one waiting for him. But she knew he had to go, there was no question. He found the bottle with the last two sleepers and handed them to her.

"I'm so scared," she whispered, as she swallowed them; perhaps he didn't have to go, if he just stayed until the day had started it might help.

"I really have to go," he repeated quite softly, dressed now and sitting on the edge of the bed as tears began to spill from Rachel's eyes. "Look, I'll ring you in the morning, come round maybe around midday for a coffee. We'll have a chat. Just sleep now—don't drink anymore, don't take anything. Wait for a bit. I'll call tomorrow."

Was this a way of making leaving more comfortable for himself? It was so unlike him, this gentle man who made promises about tomorrow. But the pills were beginning to work and the idea of Joshua ringing—someone being there tomorrow—made her feel more possible.

"All the women I know seem to be cracking up," Joshua said, as if he were beginning a bedtime story. "Women your age, without a man there all the time. Of course the ones with a man aren't happy but they aren't falling apart."

Rachel felt a dull fury beneath the alcohol and the sleeping pills.

"You can count me out of your generalizations," she said as sharply as she could manage. "It isn't the lack of a cohabiting man that's doing for me. I don't know about the other women you know but I suspect you underestimate my testosterone levels."

He glanced at her admiringly, partly impressed at her ability to get the word "testosterone" out in her condition—as indeed *she* was—partly wondering if what she said wasn't true.

"Perhaps I do," he said seriously as Rachel's rage at being boxed in with "Women" subsided beneath the sleeping drug.

Joshua left quietly as she drifted off to sleep. She dreamed she
was on a ship, cruising between islands that she took to be the
West Indies. What astonished her, even while she was dream-
ing, was the extraordinary colour, the vivid pure blue of the
cloudless sky, the clean white paintwork of the cruiser, the
sparkling turquoise of the sea, and in the distance on the island
they sailed towards the rich dark tropical green of plants and
trees. Rachel was searching for somewhere to settle and
climbed white metal staircases from deck to deck, all of which
were full of people pleasuring themselves, lying on loungers
taking in the sun, sitting at white tables chatting and drinking,
wandering in elegantly dressed groups of two or three, smiling
amiably. Perfectly ordinary people enjoying themselves in the
ways people do on ships in the sun. She moved from one deck to
another, finding nowhere she wanted to be. She didn't want to
be with people but there were people everywhere. She came
across a bar some three or four flights up and ordered a tequila
sunrise for its glowing orange colour, then wandered off, glass in
hand, still trying to find a place. She looked up and saw at the
very top of the ship a tiny deck enclosed by gleaming white
rails, just large enough for the two chairs that stood on it. One
chair was empty, on the other sat a man, his eyes shaded by the
brim of a white fedora, reading a book, very still and quiet,
immersed. She didn't know him, he was no one she recognized,
but *that* was where, at last, she wanted to be. Not to disturb the
man, not talk, but to sit and sip her drink on the other chair and
watch the colours of the sea and sky and oncoming island. She
ached to be in that place, but as she craned her neck she could
see no way of getting up there, no staircase, no access. Desperately disappointed she made her way down to the bottom of the
ship and found herself somehow beneath the bows from which
a small plank of wood extended, the size of a surfboard, just
large enough to hold her lying on her stomach. Her face was a
few inches above the rushing water and she could see the island
ahead of her and the sky too, if she twisted her neck to one side.
She tried to look up to see the man on the top deck but he was
out of her vision. She wasn't exactly where she wanted to be but
this was good and peaceful. It was all right. Then as the island
came closer and she could clearly make out the jetty she real-

ized that she was unable to move, her neck was trapped in some way between the plank and the bow of the ship. She was caught, held rigid, her face separated from the waves only by the thickness of the plank, and no one would hear her call for help down there. She saw the jetty approaching fast and knew that as the ship docked her head would be crushed between the two; ship and jetty would smash her skull like an egg held in a vice. She took in the still magical colours of sea, sky and foliage as she waited—heart-thumping, terrified, doomed, excited—for the inevitable.

Well, she thought as she woke and considered the dream, I may not have a subtle psyche but at least it tells it like it is. She was surprised though that the man was not Joshua; he hadn't looked or felt like him. It wasn't anyone she knew although he had had a very particular, definite sort of face. Well, no matter, it wasn't the point. The weight was there, bearing down on her diaphragm, as she knew it would. She got up and dressed, a slow, laboured process, and set herself again in the corner of the sofa, upright, straight-backed, legs curled neatly away beneath her. Waiting—or not waiting. Hours passed, occasionally the tears came without disrupting her pose, once she got up and fed the cat from the tin which thankfully was already open. For the rest she sat and stared at nothing in particular and breathed carefully.

Joshua did not ring. She thought she had known all along that he wouldn't but there was a dull surprise at his complete lack of curiosity. How strange. It wasn't his lack of caring that perplexed her but his capacity not to want to know what, if anything, happened next. She couldn't begin to understand that. Was he so sure that she wouldn't kill herself? No one could be that sure, entirely sure; she certainly wasn't. Or perhaps it simply made no difference to him if she were alive or dead? But it made some small practical difference if he ever fancied fucking her again. And he had said he would ring—his image of himself was of a man who kept his word. What happened to the boy scout? But the real point was curiosity—sheer curiosity would have had her on the phone the next day if the roles were reversed.

Well, what the hell, she thought, it wouldn't have made any

difference. One phone call more or less wouldn't have changed
anything. She didn't have the energy to care about Joshua. His
not ringing was a kind of blow but really not so very important.

Becky called and was told quietly that Rachel was all right
and would be sure to ring if she needed anything. "Really, I'm
fine."

Dusk fell and Rachel sat on in the darkening room until some
time in the evening when she heard the front door slam and
footsteps on the stairs. Isobel walked into the room carrying
several carrier bags.

"Michael phoned me. He said you were feeling bad. Are you
depressed? Silly question," she said, as she inspected Rachel
who still hadn't moved.

Rachel took a deep breath. "No, I'm fine," she croaked
through a knot in her throat.

"Rubbish. I've seen you like this before. Not for a long time
though. I've brought some stuff. I don't suppose you've eaten
anything for days, have you?"

She went into the kitchen and unpacked salad stuff, whole-
meal bread, butter and cat food, then washed lettuce and sliced
cucumber into a bowl before putting on the kettle and making a
cup of tea.

Isobel sat down heavily in the chair opposite the sofa in the
still unlit room.

"How long has this been going on?" she asked, with the slightest suggestion of a sigh. She looked tired, had spent the day
working on her lectures. Her clothes, neat, efficient, hung as
elegantly as ever, but on a body that sagged a little with the end
of the day.

"I don't know. A few days," Rachel answered dully.

"Why didn't you let me know?" Isobel asked a little crossly, a
bit hurt.

"I didn't . . . want it to become real. I feel such a failure."

"Nonsense. You can't be alone when you're like this. Good
God, after all these years you ought to be able to let me know if
you're feeling bad. Have you been alone all the time?"

"No, someone was here last night."

"Not that man? It was, wasn't it?" Rachel didn't answer. "He
didn't fuck you, did he?" she asked, building up to outrage:

what kind of monster would take advantage of a woman in such a condition?

"As a matter of fact I fucked him," Rachel answered firmly, trying to close the subject.

"Oh. I suppose he's the cause of this."

"No, he's not the cause of it. There isn't one. Since when have I needed a reason to get depressed?"

She really didn't want to talk, or explain. There was increasingly nothing to say, the deeper inside herself she got the less events or people seemed to have to do with it. A switch had been switched, it had nothing to do with anything.

Isobel was clearly unconvinced. "Maybe, but why now? It's years since you were like this. There must be a reason. "

Rachel didn't answer. She didn't know the answer, she didn't think she knew anything. It was good that Isobel was there, having her in the room woke her a little, but there was the talk and Isobel's evident tiredness and beneath that, beneath the briskness and practicality, her feeling of helplessness. Rachel wanted to tell her that just her presence helped, but felt that to do so would be to criticize, to be telling her to shut up, to stop worrying about food and reasons. Rachel remained silent, and then after a while began to feel that her silence was itself critical, too demanding. What was there to do between silence and talk? And why did she have to worry about it when all she wanted was to be left alone? Being alone seemed the only possibility.

"Thank you for the stuff. You look tired, why don't you go home? I'm all right. I just want to sit here. Don't worry, there's no need for you to be here."

Rejecting.

"It's perfectly all right. I'm not tired and you can't be left alone. I'll stay."

Dear God, a new nightmare, we're going to drive each other mad being nice to each other. Try saying exactly what she felt.

"Isobel, look, I'm feeling terrible but I'm going to be worse, guilty, about making you sit here with me when you're busy and exhausted. Please don't stay. It'll make me feel worse."

Isobel sat on in the dark. "I'm going to stay for a while. I'm

afraid you'll just have to put up with me," she said firmly, and
then closed her eyes for a second as she stifled a yawn.

Help. Help. Let me out, Rachel screamed silently. She was
over-alert, appallingly observant; she saw every movement, every nuance, seemed to see beneath Isobel's skin to her facial
muscles pulling themselves into the correctly bland expression
appropriate to the situation, but saw how they ached with the
effort. She observed the limp arms that lay heavily on the sides
of the chair and the depth of Isobel's breath that stopped just
short of building into a full-blown sigh, and each thing she
noticed added another small weight to the load that already
filled her. Then she felt guilty about that too.

After a while Isobel said, "Becky phoned me. She said you
sent her away. She's very upset and worried. You can't reject
people like that, you must let her come and see you, you're
being unkind."

This was insane; suddenly the world was full of people she had
to see so that *they* would feel better. If you can't behave badly
when you are feeling suicidal when can you? Never, apparently,
not Rachel, who depressed or not was supposed to know better,
to understand what was going on and therefore in some way
had an obligation to do the right thing. There was no time off for
bad behaviour.

SIX

Her mood over the next few weeks remained and deepened and she continued to sit in a corner of the sofa.
Isobel came twice a day, brought food and sat with her
for an hour or two. Sometimes they walked. Rachel came to feel
herself possessed, and they discussed this when Rachel could
talk at all. Rachel had listened hour after hour to her interior
monologue—hateful, worthless, stupid, boring, dangerous, destructive—on and on. There's no point in you being alive,
you're a waste of space . . . It was the voice that was always
there in the background but which had now grown strong and
taken possession entirely. She had no strength, no resources to
battle it. Only the Watcher was uninvolved and simply listened
and noted what was happening. She explained this to Isobel.

"It's like there's a demon inside me, a devil, hating me, wanting me dead. I know it's *my* devil, but it doesn't help knowing
that. It wants to kill me, and I can't do anything about it, it's
overwhelming. Drowning me."

Isobel understood this but was as baffled as Rachel to know
what was to be done. Three weeks had gone by without any
change. Rachel hardly ate, slept for two or three hours a night,
hadn't left the flat, and Isobel's sense of helplessness grew. She
was anxious and tired. Their first conversation kept repeating
itself. Rachel begged Isobel not to come, Isobel insisted that it
was perfectly all right, necessary. It wasn't perfectly all right,
guilt grew like a Russian vine, Rachel felt she had trapped them
both in an endless nightmare. So did Isobel but only said so with

her body language and suppressed sighs. Rachel heard the reassurance and saw the discomfort and became confused. Was she, wasn't she seeing what she thought she saw, hearing what she thought she heard? There was no way to go, no right thing to do. Die, her voice told her. And that really seemed the only move she had.

Becky arrived every couple of days and filled the uneasy silence with talk—about William and his affair, she still hadn't confronted him with it, was too afraid to disrupt the relationship, wasn't sure how she felt about him now that he wasn't, for her, the same William; about depression, she had been reading up on the subject, had actually gone to the Association for Mental Health and got booklets on the subject. There were two kinds, exogenous and endogenous, and different kinds of antidepressant for each type; also there was some suggestion that large doses of vitamin B complex was effective in some cases . . . Rachel listened in silence and felt more and more like a therapist, a seeing eye, a hearing eye, listening to her patient work through the chatter, the panic, to the heart of the matter. She wanted to ask Becky to stop—stop talking, stop coming— but couldn't because she knew it would upset her.

Michael took care of Carrie and assured her over the phone that everything was fine; he at least knew he couldn't stand Rachel's depression but did what was the most practically useful thing. Carrie was naturally worried but had been told that Rachel was ill. Mothers did after all get ill, Rachel reminded herself; she didn't want to see Carrie, didn't want to worry about her—but of course had to worry and knew that eventually, inevitably she would have to see her, have to take back the responsibility.

The anxiety peaked. She called Dr Stone.

"Please, can I go into hospital? Go somewhere? What you said about asylum," she sobbed.

"If that's what you want," he replied carefully.

"It's too difficult for everyone. I have to go away."

She was admitted to Friern Barnett hospital that afternoon. She drove herself there shakily, clutching the steering wheel so hard she got cramp in her fingers. She parked in the tarmac and flower-bedded driveway and found her way to the ward she had been allocated in the annexe for emergency admissions. As she walked into the nurses' office she saw her name chalked up on the blackboard—she was expected. When she announced herself a large black staff nurse asked her, "Who brought you?" looking around as if she expected someone else to walk through the door.

"I brought myself."

"You came on your own?" The nurse glanced at the duty doctor who sat opposite her. "By yourself?"

It hadn't occurred to Rachel to ask anyone to come with her, and even faced with their surprise now she didn't think that Isobel, for example, would have thought it necessary. Well, she was here, wasn't she?

The annexe was filled mostly with geriatric cases whose senility made it impossible for them to live without full-time nursing. The hospital, like its patients, was decrepit and neglected, scheduled for closure whenever someone could work out what to do with its able-bodied but broken-minded inmates. Rachel's bed was one of four in a tall square room painted a pallid green. The floor was covered with dark blue cracked lino, a large washbasin stood between two curtainless windows. She climbed on to the iron bed gratefully and sat crosslegged on the orange cotton counterpane as a nurse took her name, address, next of kin. The bed in the corner opposite was the only one occupied. A small body lay curled facing the wall; it could have been that of a child except for the mass of iron-grey hair that spread over the pillow.

"That's Rose," the nurse told her as she left. "She won't answer you if you speak to her. She likes to pretend she's asleep— but we all know better—don't we, Rose?"

Rose remained emphatically asleep and Rachel was relieved to know that she didn't have to make conversation. Left to herself she sat on the bed, taking in the dingy surroundings. She didn't mind at all; she had answered the questions quietly and was now being left, at least for the time being, to her own devices. As she sat there a weight seemed to lift from her; she was here in a place where she could just *be*, people were either paid to be here or too wrapped up in themselves, as she was, to care about her. Here, she was permitted to be depressed, to sit

and be silent; they were used to people not behaving themselves, and she didn't want to misbehave, just to be left alone
and not have to concern herself with anyone. They could handle that, she didn't have to worry about them. She had been
right to come here, should have done it sooner. She had asked
the nurse to call Isobel and tell her that she was all right.

"Please, could you tell her not to visit? It's very important—I
don't want anyone to visit."

The nurse amiably took the number and told her not to
worry, she would be sure and phone. Another weight gone,
someone else was going to deal with the world for her. Another
nurse popped her head round the door. "The duty doctor wants
to see you. Come with me, dear."

She led Rachel into a small room where a young woman
waited at a desk looking through notes in a file. She smiled as
Rachel came in.

"Hello, I'm Dr Newbold. I have to ask you some questions, it's
routine I'm afraid."

Rachel sat in an armchair beside the desk and smiled politely.

"Could you tell me the date?" Dr Newbold asked.

Rachel remembered this catechism from fifteen years ago—a
previous hospitalization, a previous depression—so she answered matter-of-factly; it was just something that had to be
done.

"Tuesday the 29th of July."

"Yes?" Dr Newbold encouraged.

"1983," Rachel offered patiently.

It was only later, lying awake in the ward that night, that she
remembered that it was actually the 30th; she had a momentary
impulse to call the night nurse and amend her answer—but
what the hell, she thought, I got two out of three.

Dr Newbold continued without comment.

"Could you tell me the name of the Queen's children, Rachel?"

Rachel dredged her reservoir of trivia; it was a pity she hadn't
asked who had starred in *It Happened One Night*, that she had
on the tip of her tongue.

"Um . . . Charles, Anne . . . Edward—there's another one
. . . Andrew."

Now what?

"Rachel," the doctor asked conversationally, "do you think there's any meaning in life?"

Rachel fought back a powerful desire to scream with laughter but then decided that it was, after all, a question she could answer.

"Well, yes, I do. I think that life is meaningful to other people, I think, even, that there is a Meaning, I think it's probably *for* something. But I don't think it needs me. Whatever or whoever it is that has a purpose for all this can achieve it without me. I don't think I have a place here."

Dr Newbold looked up sharply, clearly her answer revealed something—although it seemed not what was expected.

"God?" she asked.

"Whatever," Rachel replied. "It and I don't care enough about each other for it to be worth trying to define. It doesn't matter. It's nothing to do with me."

The doctor wrote something in her file.

"Please could I go back to the ward now?" Rachel asked.

Dr Newbold looked at her for a moment and then closed the file.

"Yes, we'll leave it at that for now. Dr Cloudsley will see you in the morning. Thank you, Rachel."

When she was back on her bed a nurse popped her head round the door.

"Dr Newbold asked me to tell you to get into your nightie and dressing gown, dear." She explained pleasantly, "We have to, you see, with patients who are a bit depressed. We don't want you running off or anything."

Rachel shrugged and said she would but sat on fully clothed. She didn't feel unhappy, just absent, empty—but this was somewhere she could just be; even if it hadn't the comfort and warmth of her flat, it really didn't matter. It was evening now. In a couple of hours the other patients would return to the ward and wait for the sedation trolley. They had had supper and were watching television in the dayroom or sitting over cups of tea in the small canteen, or wandering the corridor. No one bothered Rachel, it was quiet and peaceful.

Suddenly the silence was broken by a long dramatic groan

from the bed opposite as Rose swung her legs around and got herself upright beside her bed. Her tiny emaciated body was covered in a huge floral cotton dress, hospital issue for patients with no clothes of their own, which flapped about her skinny ancient legs as she began to walk across the room towards Rachel's bed. There was something distressingly wild and youthful about her loose grey hair. She moved purposefully toward Rachel without actually looking in her direction.

"Damn!" thought Rachel.

Rose, her face turned away from Rachel to gaze absently at the window, stopped six inches from the side of Rachel's bed and slowly, very deliberately, pulled up her skirt to the level of her baggy, hospital-stamped knickers, set her feet well apart and without any sign that her top half knew what her bottom half was doing, began to urinate on the floor. The liquid fell from her in a heavy stream like horses' piss, steaming slightly and splashing as it hit the cold lino. Then, her face still impassive, never acknowledging Rachel's existence, she started to walk, stiff-kneed, legs apart, around the room with the urine streaming and splashing as she went. She described the contours of the beds and the walls between; a nonchalant wanderer oblivious of the rushing waterfall between her legs. Rachel wanted to applaud; it was a magnificent performance. She was astounded at the quantity of liquid the minute body contained —by the time Rose got back to her own bed and settled comfily in her previous position the entire floor was covered in urine, pungent puddles and riverlets that flowed together and joined suddenly like mating amoebae. Rachel smiled silently and shrugged; she couldn't have cared less. The room filled with the warm, damp, sour scent of urine; the floor was awash. Rachel was trapped on her bed by a sea of piss. She didn't mind, the smell didn't bother her particularly and she didn't want to go anywhere. She went on sitting, not having reacted at all to the performance. That's not kind, she thought to herself. If I were a nice, kind person I'd scream blue murder, shock, horror, look what that disgusting old woman has done! Let me out of this madhouse! Poor Rose, I'd do it for you if I could, I just don't have the energy. Eventually one of the other occupants of the room came in and screamed satisfactorily, hurled abuse at the appar-

ently sleeping or possibly dead Rose and ran wailing for a nurse
to come and see what the filthy mad old cow in her room had
done. The nurse arrived with a mop and bucket and set to work.

"What *have* you done, Rose? You're a very naughty girl. Did
you see what happened?" she asked Rachel, who shrugged
lightly and smiled noncommittally. The shrug was clearly a
useful gesture here.

"I didn't do nothing," complained Rose, who had opened one
eye to check on Rachel's response. "I've been lying here on the
bed. Why don't you all leave me alone? I want to die; all I want
is to die and you scum won't let me. Let me be!" she moaned.

"You're very bad," the nurse scolded as she sopped up the
wetness. "There's nothing wrong with you, you're not inconti-
nent and I'm busy enough without having to do this."

Rachel closed her eyes. Her silence was not really collusion
with Rose, it was simply absence. She had no desire to make
allies, although she knew that not letting on was as likely to
make an enemy of Rose who wanted attention more than
friends. The other patient, a middle-aged woman, was too distressed to sleep in the ward that night and was given a side
room, so Rachel didn't have to meet or talk to anyone else. Rose,
having made her statement, remained silent for the rest of the
night and when the sedation trolley came round Rachel gratefully swallowed the pills she was handed and slept for a couple
of hours, then lay awake staring into the darkness until the day
staff came on duty at six. She was still not sorry to be where she
was; not until the nurse arrived and told her to get dressed and
go to the canteen for breakfast.

"I'd rather not," Rachel said politely. "Couldn't I just get a
cup of tea and drink it here?"

"You have to go to the canteen. Anyway, we lock the room at
eight-thirty. It's very bad for patients to lie on their beds all day.
You can sit in the day room and meet the other patients. Dr
Cloudsley will be making a ward round later in the morning and
he'll want to see you, so you can't go to occupational therapy
until this afternoon I'm afraid."

There was very little that Rachel wanted to do less than go to
occupational therapy at any time of the day, nor did she want to
be locked out of the room. She wanted, like Rose, to be left

alone. When she was admitted the doctor she saw had spoken of
"global depression" and suggested that antidepressants would
be the first line of attack; if they proved ineffective then "ECT
was often quite useful." Rachel had decided not to think about
it. She wanted asylum and felt that somehow she could avoid
the drugs and electrodes. Now it was becoming obvious that she
simply hadn't been thinking clearly. This was a hospital and as
far as they were concerned she was here for treatment, which
began with an enforced social life among the sad and desperate
characters in the canteen.

The day room was a bleak affair: high-backed plastic chairs
encircled the room against the pale green walls and a geranium
drooped dolefully on the window sill. Apart from that there was
a small plastic table in the centre of the room and a few left-
behind books lined up on a half-empty bookcase. Rachel sat
alone in the room on a blue chair—the others were red and
green—and smoked, putting out the stubs in an ash-scarred
wastepaper bin she found in one corner. The room was empty
for most of the two hours she sat there, but intermittently the
door would be flung open and a very overweight young man
would stand wild-eyed for a moment, glare into each corner
and then leave, muttering crossly to himself. Each time Rachel
got up and closed the door behind him, then went back to her
chair. There was no sign of Dr Cloudsley. Having refused the
canteen she had had nothing to eat or drink and was feeling
chilled and empty. She thought about her flat, warm and comfortable, where she could at least make herself a cup of tea if she
wanted one, where she could sit surrounded by her own things,
but then remembered why she came to the hospital—the people, the guilt. She would have been quite content on her bed in
the ward. Eventually she got up and walked down the corridor
to her room, tried the door which was indeed locked then
walked back up the corridor, passing en route several other
people who were shuffling up and down in carpet slippers. She
paced the length of the corridor two or three times, ignoring
the other walkers as they did her, and then noticed a linen
cupboard. It was a long, walk-in cupboard about three feet
wide, with shelving covering one wall and a window at the end.
The shelves were piled with hospital dressing gowns, nighties,

spare dresses like the one Rose wore, towels and the like. Rachel walked into it and stood at the window at the far end, looking out—it was the only one she had found with a view. It faced on to the main entrance of the hospital. The driveway had a neatly planted circular flowerbed in the centre and as she stood and watched, people came and went, cars arrived and doctors got out, or relatives come for a visit, there was no difficulty in telling them apart. A few patients emerged from the main entrance and headed for the shop across the road to buy chocolate, toothpaste, shampoo, cigarettes—small needs that provided an excuse for a brief outing. Rachel stood with her forehead pressed against the cold glass and watched the comings and goings, until a sudden voice behind her surprised her and she wheeled round to see a nurse looking at her curiously.

"What are you doing in here, Rachel?"

Rachel realized suddenly that her face was wet, that she had been standing at the window crying.

"Nothing. There's a window here, I was looking out of it."

She noticed the time on the nurse's watch pinned to her apron: it was twelve-thirty; she had been looking out of the window for two and a half hours. She thought, I've only been here one night and I'm standing in a linen closet gazing out of the window. This afternoon they'll put me on drugs and by tomorrow it will seem perfectly normal to be doing that, or shuffling up and down the corridor. I won't mind.

"I think I'd like to go home," she said quietly to the nurse. "Is there something I have to sign?"

The nurse looked surprised. "Why? You'd better come and talk to Staff Nurse."

Rachel followed her out to the office where she repeated her request. The Staff Nurse also looked surprised.

"You *can* discharge yourself but you'll have to wait to see the doctor. He'll be here very soon. Just go and wait in the day room —oh no, you can't, it's been cleared for the ward conference. Go and have a cup of tea in the canteen, there's a good girl. We'll call you when the doctor wants to see you."

Once you are in these places you have to do things by the book, Rachel realized. She said she'd wait and went back to the

linen closet. An hour later a nurse came to get her: the doctor
had arrived and would see her now.

"I really only want to discharge myself," she said, as she
followed the nurse to the door of the day room.

"In there, Dr Cloudsley's waiting for you," the nurse said, as
she knocked at the door for Rachel.

The first thing she saw as she walked into the day room was a
gold cardboard cake box on the centre table; she had seen a
man carry it out of his car when she was standing at the window
and had been surprised because the open-topped MG and his
natty three-piece suit had marked him as one of the doctors. She
had told herself at the time not to categorize people so rigidly,
the cake box made him a relative visiting a patient—perhaps it
was someone's birthday. But her first guess had been right: the
glossy golden box stood open and empty amid discarded plates
and teacups on the little table. The plastic chairs had been
drawn into a tighter circle than when she had sat alone in the
room, and were all, except one, occupied. There were perhaps
twenty or twenty-five people sitting in a circle watching her as
she stood flummoxed by the door. She had been expecting to
see a doctor, maybe two. Her eyes did a quick scan but took in
very little, more men than women, some nurses, several men in
natty three-piece suits who she supposed took it in turns to
bring in the cake for the conference—they probably didn't *all*
have MGs. She panicked. Her first thought was to turn and run,
her second was that she wanted to get out of here and this was
clearly the route since the ward was locked with her clothes and
car keys inside.

"Mrs Kee. Come in, take a seat," said the owner of a well-
groomed hand which gestured her, ordered her, to the empty
chair beside him. "I'm Dr Cloudsley. I'm the consultant. These
other people are members of my team. We'd like to have a chat
with you."

Well, you'd better not all talk at once, she thought as she
walked shakily across the room, now more like an arena. Dr
Cloudsley sat comfortably in his chair, one impeccably creased
trouser leg crossed casually over the other, a benign, faintly
superior smile on his face. Rachel sat rigid with anger as she felt
twenty pairs of professional eyes examine her unhurriedly.

What were the external indications of this specimen? The hair, dyed neon orange in parts was, of course, deliberately awry; wild, frizzing hair made wilder the better both to conceal and to attract attention; beneath it, behind it, a tired pale fierce face devoid of make-up. She wore an overall, fashionably baggy, body-concealing, dung-brown, the legs rolled to mid-calf, plimsols on unsocked feet—a commonplace this week Hampstead High Street, but in the context of an antique nineteenth-century asylum it was institution garb, shapeless, sloppy, a denial of body, sex and life. She saw herself as they saw her and sat waiting bolt upright, hands clutching the wooden arms of the chair.

"You seem angry, Mrs Kee," Dr Cloudsley invited.

"Yes, I am angry," she replied, icily polite, and turned to look at him. There was another part of her though that whispered in her ear, "Be very careful. You have to play this just right. Be very calm; don't *do* anything."

And yet another part, quite distant from her and the others in the room, conversing with someone outside the situation: "How can they do this? How can they be so stupid? What kind of experts are these? You don't do this to someone who has been depressed for weeks. You don't sit them in a room full of watching people and ask them questions. It will seem to them like an inquisition. Any fool would know that, would manage the situation better than that."

The anger and the panic welled in Rachel. She wanted to run, or throw things—she wanted very much to pick up those plates and cups and hurl them at the cool objective faces surrounding her, assessing, at Cloudsley's cue, just how close she was to violence.

"Careful," the voice whispered as she tightened her grip on the chair. She looked around trying to make contact with the eyes, feeling certain that someone in the room must know that this wasn't the right way to deal with her, but each glance she caught shifted too fast for her to see what kind of humanity might be behind it.

"Perhaps you could tell us why you are angry?" Cloudsley asked, smooth as silk.

She stared hard at the golden box and fought to stay cool and calm, very rational.

"Yes. I'm angry because I don't want to be in this room full of people. I had understood that I was going to see a doctor, not be the subject of a conference. I waited to see you because I was told I had to in order to discharge myself. Could you please give me whatever it is I have to sign and ask the nurse to unlock the wardroom door?"

"Why do you feel you want to discharge yourself?"

"I don't *feel* I want to discharge myself; I want to discharge myself. I would like to go home."

I want to discharge myself, you smooth bastard, because I'm sane enough not to want to stay in this place; and at home at least I can get a cup of tea. What better reason?

Dr Cloudsley opened the file on his lap and read through it in silence for several minutes, then he looked up.

"According to the admitting doctor you are in a severely depressed condition. He considers you suicidal and thinks that you need treatment as an inpatient to overcome your present feelings. I don't think I can allow you to discharge yourself."

Rachel stopped breathing.

"You can't stop me leaving. I'm a voluntary patient. I can leave when I like." Her voice rose several octaves.

"Whether you're a voluntary patient or not is for me to say, Mrs Kee. It's true that you came in voluntarily, but I have to consider the situation very carefully. I feel that you would be at risk if I permitted you to leave."

Rachel had experienced life-threatening terror in dreams, but this particular reality had all the hallmarks of her worst nightmares. Suddenly she wasn't free to leave, they could keep her here, put her on any treatment they thought fit: drugs, ECT, a bloody lobotomy if they wanted. She had put herself into another world and saw her right to choose, even her actual freedom, slipping away. She knew herself to be in immense danger and her body responded as it would to any threat from outside: a rush of adrenalin, racing pulse, absolutely alert, clear-headed, tuned for survival. Nonetheless liberal, middle-class, western Rachel couldn't quite believe this was happening. She was aware, however, of the rules—at least in general terms.

There was a section of the Mental Health Act that allowed a doctor to keep her there against her will if he deemed her a danger to herself or to others. Cloudsley was carefully implying that he could put her on a section, that she was a danger to herself, that it was his opinion that counted. She thought she remembered vaguely that she had to have done something to warrant that opinion, but she wasn't sure. She tried sounding informed.

"I am an informal patient," she said carefully, concentrating hard on the cake box. "You can't put me on a section unless there is some evidence that I might harm myself. I've done nothing to suggest I will. I don't think you have grounds to keep me here, and I want to leave, now."

There was a note of irritation in Cloudsley's voice as he answered, "The Act requires only that I and one other doctor believe you to be at risk. Why are you being so aggressive?"

Because you are threatening me, you self-important bastard!

He didn't sound as if there would be too much problem getting another doctor to sign and there were obviously a good few in the room that would scrawl their names on any document he produced. There were no heroes here. She knew that someone was bluffing and guessed it was probably her. The choice was to continue with the bluff or to appease the man in authority, evidently becoming irritated. How the hell had she got herself into this? The point was to get out at all cost and this man, she realized, would respond better with his authority intact.

"I'm not suicidal," she explained clearly and calmly. "I've been depressed but that's happened before. I want to sit through it, it will pass, and I think I'd be better if I were at home where things are more familiar."

Cloudsley seemed to relax a little.

"I think that you think that life is very bleak, Mrs Kee. I don't think you think life is worth living, do you?" he suggested, inviting her to share her innermost thoughts with them all, and, if she were stupid enough, to trap herself. This man, this healer of troubled minds wanted blood, wanted to hear about her pain, wanted a loss of control and an end to her hard-won self-possession. This was familiar: perhaps shrinks and sadists were bred in the same stable. He was requesting what he would call her cooperation: she should say, yes, I'm in trouble, I need help, do whatever you need to do, I'm not fit to judge, just help me please. Sir.

Fuck it.

"I don't have any opinion about Life. I assure you I am not going to commit suicide, you can have it in writing if you like. I want to leave," she stated firmly.

Dr Cloudsley re-crossed his legs and glanced impatiently around the room at his team. "I'm very loath to let you leave, Mrs Kee. I would be quite within my rights to detain you under a Section of the Mental Health Act, indeed it is my duty to do so if I feel you are at risk, but it would obviously be better if we could gain your cooperation."

Well yes, it's a terrible bore holding down unwilling patients while you inject them with sedatives.

Rachel said again, "I want to go home."

"Mrs Kee, do you think you are being fair to your friends? Do you have the right to demand that they worry about you and have to look after you? Have you thought of them?"

Got her! That was why she was here, wasn't it? Other people, making demands. Guilt. He was really onto something here, much more effective than a Section: just feed the guilt that was there already.

She couldn't answer that, there was no argument. She just held on tight as the panic and the memory of sitting in her flat, desperate when people were there, desperate when they weren't, flowed through her.

"I must go home," she answered with a long, straight stare into his untroubled eyes.

He looked at his watch.

"It's lunchtime now. You pop off to the canteen and have some lunch while I consider what to do. My registrar will come and see you later on and tell you what we have decided. Run along now."

She was dismissed.

Later this afternoon, or more likely this evening, the registrar would tell her that she might as well spend the night there and that he would come and see her the following morning. Inertia was a powerful weapon. If she fought them they would section her, if she cooperated they could put off her requests to leave until she stopped caring. She wasn't in any condition to care for very long—they had time and energy on their side. What she had was a still intact capacity to see what was going on and, curiously given her state of mind, a determination not to be drugged and institutionalized.

"It seemed to me," she told Laura a few days later in Cornwall, "a straight choice between killing myself and being drugged into not noticing or caring how I felt. Either way it was death. I couldn't see the point of staying alive just for the sake of it."

"Still, what you chose contained the chance of staying alive," Laura pointed out.

Rachel smiled. "Yes, I know, there's a small, stubborn survivor lurking inside me somewhere. I despise it, you know, I see it as a moron, an idiot child. It doesn't think, can't argue against my logic, it just sits in there quietly requiring my survival. When the crunch comes it renders me incapable of my own death. I hate it for its mindlessness."

"Well, I'd nurture it if I were you, it might grow up."

Rachel grinned again.

"Trouble with you is you've read too many books."

Rachel left the day room and stood for a moment outside the door. She had no plans to run along to the canteen and headed in the other direction to her ward. The door had been unlocked for lunchtime, so that patients could brush their teeth or something. She slipped into the room and pulled out her overnight bag, stuffing her clothes into it as fast as she could, slung the bag over her shoulder and walked as casually as she could manage down the corridor, past the day room where the doctors would still be discussing her case, past the nurses' office, a slow saunter so that they wouldn't look up from their newspapers, and to the stairs. Then she ran, two, three steps at a time and out into the driveway she had been watching from the linen-closet window. The car was waiting for her, animated by its familiarity. "Let's go, let's go," she whispered to it as she reversed out of the parking space and speed through the main gates, driving as fast as she dared through suburban north London with flickering images of Keystone Cop chases, *The Italian Job* and *The French*

Connection running around her head. It would surely be a
while before they noticed she had gone and anyway they would
hardly give chase. Would they? She thought not but wasn't
entirely sure and there seemed to be an unreasonable number
of police cars and ambulances rushing past her with sirens wailing during the twenty-minute journey. Each time one ap-
proached she studiously ignored it, feeling more and more like
a fugitive. She was obviously being paranoid—they had better
things to do than race after her—but then only a few minutes
before a man she had never previously met had threatened to
lock her up against her will and do whatever he thought necessary to change the state of her mind. It was as well to know
when one was being paranoid, but also as well to be careful.

When she got home and locked the door of her flat she made
herself a ceremonial and much-needed cup of tea and sat clasp-
ing the warmth of it in both hands. She realized suddenly that
she was shaking uncontrollably from head to foot. She had been
very frightened.

"Well, anyway, I escaped," she laughed a little hysterically to
Laura over the phone, "I escaped. Me and Steve McQueen and
Big John Wayne. We all escaped."

Laura, now running sheep and growing vegetables in Cornwall, had been a social worker and would know, Rachel decided, the legal set-up. She didn't think they could come and
get her, but she wanted to be sure.

"Not once you're out," Laura said uncertainly. "I think they
can only section you if you're in their care. It's a long time since
I read the Mental Health Act, though. I'm sure they won't.
Look, come and stay. I've got empty rooms and meadows. I
won't look after you, you can just lie around and relax for a
couple of weeks. We can meet over a cup of coffee at breakfast if
you like and then we'll both just get on with our lives. Why
not?"

Rachel agreed thankfully and arranged to meet Laura at the
station a couple of days later. It sounded like everything she
wanted and turned out to be so. She and Laura talked a little but

mostly she sat in her quiet wood-panelled room or lay in the long grass, waiting for the pain to go away, and gradually the pain turned to a kind of solitary peace, something almost positive, and she began to feel that she was recuperating, not dying.

SEVEN

J oshua turned up the night before she left for Cornwall, chatted, fucked her and left without asking her a single question about what had happened during the past few weeks. There was the slightest hesitancy, a certain caution for the first few minutes as he seemed to be checking her condition to find out whether they could proceed as normal, and she picked up his relief as he assessed her and apparently concluded she was all right. He'd come to check and decided that she would do. Not a word was mentioned about the last time he saw her, there was no suggestion that anything out of the ordinary had happened between then and now. A passing storm, nothing serious; so let's get on with it as if it never occurred.

Rachel did well enough; she beat him at Scrabble and snapped into her old sexuality when commanded. She didn't tell him anything he didn't want to know, didn't ask him what he didn't want to tell.

"I'm off to Cornwall for a couple of weeks, staying with an old friend."

"Man friend or woman friend?" he asked casually.

"Woman—and no, she wouldn't do for a threesome. Are you going anywhere?"

"Yes, I'm going to Scotland for a week at the end of August." She didn't ask him where exactly or who with.

He fucked her carefully, more or less conventionally, as if he didn't want to put her under too much pressure. He was helping her maintain composure since her act to anyone with as keen an eye as Joshua's was not entirely convincing. The show was back on the road but they both silently agreed it was as well to be careful. He left wishing her a good holiday; she returned the thought.

"See you when we're both back in London," he said, as he closed the bedroom door behind him.

On the train Rachel thought about Joshua, first with relief that he would go on turning up, then more speculatively as the rhythm of the train lulled her into reverie. Suppose she had met a Joshua untransformed by violence and cold anger. Suppose whatever life had done to him had made him gentler and more connected as, after all, it had some people. There was a recognition between them that she identified beyond their need to give and receive pain. Illusion perhaps, but she believed it was there and would have been whatever he had become. And her? What else could she have been? Could she have recognized Joshua without his hatred, was she responding to him because of it or because she would have responded to him in any way he presented himself? Perhaps after all the sadism was all there was really. She felt certain that wasn't so—but the "what-could-it-have-been" syndrome smacked of foolishness and romance. The realist was not going to permit such imaginings. What was the point? They were both what they were and that was that. Any other Joshua and Rachel coming together were phantoms. There was what there was, nothing else. His complete unconcern about what had become of her during the previous weeks said all that was to be said on the subject of their "relationship;" that was the cold fact to be held in her mind, she told herself as they pulled into the station, not some wistful notion of a deep link between them.

Now, back home, with the newspaper cutting in front of her, she was not exactly surprised at the possibility that Joshua was a rapist. Disturbed, distressed, but not surprised. Their particular brand of sexuality was under Joshua's tight control, thus far and no further. But it was hardly a new thought that controls snap, and that the tighter the control the greater the likelihood of it snapping. Implicit in Joshua's careful pantomimes of violence was loss of control. Why then should she be surprised if it had happened in some out of the way corner of the country? Snap.

Nothing more likely. Inevitable, the more you thought about it. One was always reading about men going out into the world assaulting, raping, killing—doing what they must for years have only fantasized. What impelled them when it came to it actually to go out and do it? Some button pressed, a moment of laziness when they lowered their guard and let fantasy slide mysteriously into reality. Joshua had gone a step further than fantasy with her and probably others; did that make him safer or more likely to act out there in the real world finally? She had no idea. She didn't feel that *she* could ever really blur the boundary between the fantasy and the real. Certainly their relationship confused her, understanding the necessity for coldness didn't stop her resentment of his emotional absence, her anger at his denial that they actually liked each other. But still she knew that they acted out games, roles, and didn't confuse them with her everydayness. And it seemed that when women snapped the havoc was generally internal, there wasn't the scope apparently for women to play out their destructiveness on the world as men could. She couldn't imagine how she might make her fantasies real, or more real than Joshua had made them for her.

She realized that she was sliding into an assumption that Joshua was guilty, and she couldn't know that. She imagined that she would know when she saw him and practically speaking he'd be on the run, a fugitive from justice. God, the melodrama! He couldn't have done it, it was too absurd. Still, he would either have left the country—Rio, Australia, she giggled a little to herself—or at least, it suddenly struck her, he would have to have shaved his beard: the photofit was too close for comfort. Well, there it was; if he turned up clean-shaven she'd know the answer. By now the silliness of her thoughts had more or less convinced her of his innocence; she was actually embarrassed now at ever having thought he'd done it. She imagined him finding the newscutting and realizing her suspicions; she felt very foolish. Of course he wouldn't do that. She crumpled the piece of paper and threw it in the wastepaper basket, then took it out and tore it into shreds before consigning it firmly to the dustbin. She was horrified as she remembered her call to the Inverness police—suppose she *had* given them his name? Enough, that's enough, she told herself, time to get on with your life—mother, teacher, part-time deviant. You want all that and excitement too?

She spent most of the next day at the Home Tuition centre, sorting out work for her pupil and shopping in preparation for Carrie's return from Italy. That night she was wrenched from sleep by the ringing of the phone. The clock by her bed said 1.00 am.

"Hello," she croaked sleepily into the mouthpiece.

"Are you alone?" Joshua demanded.

"Yes, do you know what the time is?" she said crossly.

"Lie on the sofa, take all your clothes off," Joshua instructed.

"I don't have any on. Joshua, it's very late . . ."

"Lie on the sofa," he repeated.

"All right, I'm lying on the bloody sofa."

"Good. Now stroke yourself very slowly until you come. I want to hear you come."

I don't have to do this, she thought, what's more he won't even know whether I'm doing it or not. What the hell is this?

"Are you stroking yourself?"

"No." She didn't have to tell him that.

"Then do it!" his voice cross, impatient.

And she did, telling herself that this was a new game.

"Imagine my cock inside you. Can you feel it? Can you?"

"Mmm," she moaned softly into the mouthpiece. "Want you . . ."

"Are you coming? Let me hear you come."

As she came she heard him whisper, "That's a good girl."

When she had finished and was lying limp with the receiver resting on her shoulder he said all brisk and businesslike, "I'll be seeing you in the next few days," and put the phone down.

First of all Rachel laughed; it *was* quite funny, or at any rate in the context of a normal relationship it would have been funny. Long-distance sex—a new kind of intimacy for an erotically charged couple who couldn't be together. That wasn't what they were about though, and there wasn't an ounce of humour in his voice. In the terms of their relationship she thought it more an act of contempt than anything; he didn't even need her physical presence for what he wanted. Sexual minimalism, post-modernist fucking, a relationship with narrative. She swung her legs off the sofa and made her way back to bed, trying to ignore another thought that was struggling for recognition; but it was too late, it had insinuated itself and was sitting full formed inside her head: it wasn't *she* who was not present but Joshua—a clean-shaven Joshua who didn't want to be asked questions? Absolutely not, she told herself, nonsense. She had already decided it was all nonsense. But what a coincidence, her voice whispered silkily, Joshua without a beard was a rapist— you decided, remember? Why the phone sex? Why now? It had never happened before. Rubbish, just coincidence. How many coincidences make an event? Check them all out. Joshua was in Scotland the week it had happened; what had been done to the girl had been a precise copy of his fantasies; the photofit had reminded her of Joshua before she had even read the report; why hadn't he turned up tonight?

The anxiety was back, full-blown. There didn't seem much reason not to suspect Joshua—that was the point. None of the coincidences would have meant anything if it didn't strike her as so likely and unless he was picked up by the police she realized there was no way she would ever know for sure whether her suspicions were real or not. It was the uncertainty as much as anything that bothered her. The fact that her own rationality was in question; she couldn't work out whether she was thinking straight or not, if this wasn't just a fantasy of her own. Right now, feeling very fragile after the past weeks, she didn't need this obsession, this confusion.

Carrie was coming back from Italy in two days, then she'd be back at school and Rachel would begin teaching again. She wished it could all happen faster, she wanted busyness in her life but could think of nothing to do in the meantime except take solitary walks, listen to music, sort out winter clothes: all activities that permitted a maximum of brooding about Joshua. Whenever she thought about the coincidences of his holiday in Scotland, it seemed a real possibility that Joshua had assaulted that girl. On the other hand it was impossible: there couldn't be anything in it. She couldn't allow herself to think in one direction without the opposite thought coming up and sneering at her. You think him innocent? Look at the evidence, kid, there's no doubt that that is what he wants to do. You've no reason other than sentiment and willing disbelief in someone *you* know doing that to doubt his guilt. You're convinced he's guilty? Vindictive bitch, you *want* him guilty. It excites you, it punishes him. You love the idea of him suddenly in a panic, on the defence, no longer in control, having to put himself outside the safety of fantasy. You want him sweating.

She thought, hell, this is a plot to send her crazy. Joshua arranged the whole thing, organized the newspaper report just to drive her into a frenzy of uncertainty. Now that *is* crazy, cooed her smarmy voice; Rachel, perhaps he has other things to think about than you, maybe he doesn't direct his entire thought-capacity towards manipulating you in craziness. He hardly needs to. Rachel, he doesn't know you exist when he's not actually in your company.

Thanks, Rachel directed at his voice, you're a pal, always to be relied on to cut me down to size whenever I seriously overestimate myself. What the hell would you do if I were suddenly discovered as a rare lost talent and the world bent its knee to me in admiration? What if some wise, witty and mature man took one look at me and thought, that's it, she's the one with all the qualities of an equal mate?

What would *you* do, the voice responded undaunted; you'd run a mile Rachel, very fast. Luckily neither of us will be presented with the problem, so we can just sit here in your head and argue enjoyably with one another. Better the devil . . . When are you going to accept what you are? You can be all sorts of things—clever, funny, even interesting, but you are not easily likeable and you are not lovable. That's that. People may admire you, they won't love you. It's a quality you've either got or you haven't. They'll want to talk to you, or fuck you, but they won't be drawn to you, they won't feel compelled to come back. Joshua is lovable. Foolish word, but accurate. Charismatic is near but it's only a way of avoiding the essential—lovableness. Joshua has that quality of making people love him, just as Pete had. It's not something you try for, it's there or not. Joshua perverts it and uses it to his advantage—without it he'd have very little going for him. He's an excellent lover, but no one would put up with his behaviour unless there was some compelling quality that allowed him to get away with it. The charmer.

He smiles and you say yes or you get in his car because you want
to get closer. Even when you discover that closeness is impossible you don't go away. There's something there you want, inde-
finable, and it keeps you on the hook. Joshua is fat and failed and
not as clever as he thinks, but even knowing that you want him.
I don't know, Rachel thought, I can't get him straight, I only
know a slice of him. I don't see the Joshua who functions out
there in the real world, who takes his kids to the park, or buys
groceries in the supermarket or chats to his friends—God, what
does he talk to his friends about? Not his sex life, I know that's
secret. People know Joshua as a nice, clever man, a bit solitary, a
bit reserved, but there's something about him that makes them
care for him, and invite him to dinner. People are concerned
about Joshua, they care about what happens to him and help
him out if he's in any kind of trouble. Of course, he may be
fucking their wives or seducing their daughters, but they'll
never know about that. Joshua inspired loyalty, people didn't
betray him.

Rachel brooded and questioned and analysed but succeeded
only in exhausting herself. There weren't going to be any answers. Once again she would have to wait for Joshua to arrive, if
he did, and if it told her anything at all. Life went on for a few
weeks. Carrie returned bronzed and full of energy, none the
worse for her exile though Rachel put a lot of effort into com-
pensating for her recent disappearance. There was a lot of
home cooking and classmates invited to tea after school. Carrie
asked Rachel if she was feeling better and Rachel said she was
and the subject seemed to be closed, and although Rachel
watched carefully for anxious glances there seemed to be none.
She began teaching her pupil, a girl who was more of a chore
than anything but at least kept her thinking about other things
for two hours a day. Three busy weeks went by without a word
from Joshua while Rachel's anxiety went underground, merely
rumbled darkly as the nights passed and the phone didn't ring.

Rachel didn't call Becky, nor hear from her, and wondered
what kind of loss that represented. She would miss laughing
with Becky at the absurdity of everything and miss her mysterious optimism. She didn't feel it or believe in it herself but it had
been good to know that it was out there somewhere. Becky had

in some way fed her, given her a sense that there were other options. Didn't matter though, Becky's feelings didn't save her from pain any more than Rachel's lack of them saved her. But still there was something to mourn in Becky's loss.

She brooded more often, though, on Joshua's silence and finally she just felt angry that he hadn't called; cross and used-up. Why should I, she thought, sit here waiting for the man to call me? Who else would put up with this crap? She let the anger work on her, a little amused at bottom at this rare rage. After three years she was objecting to the way he treated her? Well, enjoy it while it lasts.

One afternoon she called him, and remarkably it was the real Joshua who answered the phone, not the machine.

"I'm getting pissed off," she announced without preliminaries. "It's time to start pleasing me as well as yourself."

"You have a nice turn of phrase," he answered amiably after a brief pause.

"Right. Every word precisely placed. A polished, well-formed sentence. It took me ages to get it just right." It wasn't possible to maintain serious fury with this man; the tone, if not the meaning, became inevitably light.

"Well, it was worth the effort. Now tell me, what exactly are you accusing me of?"

"I'm not accusing you, I'm describing my condition," she answered.

Again there was silence, then, "When have I ever given you to believe that I was in any way interested in your pleasure? I'm only interested in my pleasure," he added pleasantly.

Rachel felt winded. The meaning of the first long sentence only became clear as he uttered the word "pleasure," right at the end; she heard the previous words coming through the phone as if they were jumbled letters that only fell into place with the final word. When they did it was as if she had been punched. Amazing that he could simply say that, and quite true of course. What right had she to complain about his treatment of her, he hadn't promised her anything at all. Any court of law would have given judgement to him.

"You haven't, that's my complaint. I'm calling to tell you that it's time to take *my* pleasure into account."

"But your pleasure is no concern of mine," he reminded her.

"Not so," she replied sweetly. "My pleasure is a necessary component of your own. You have to give me pleasure in order to get your own. That's basic sociobiology. Ain't no such thing as pure altruism. I see myself in relation to you as a resource."

"Yes," he agreed.

"Well, my message is that the resource is becoming exhausted —mined out. Through lack of attention."

This wasn't the simplest way to tell him she wanted to see him but simplicity was not among the qualities they brought out in each other.

He sounded thoughtful and amused as he answered. "Well, insofar as your pleasure is also my pleasure you are welcome to indicate what it is you want—assuming you have something more specific in mind than mere philosophy."

"Your presence would give me pleasure," she said, feeling she was entering dangerously demanding waters. "Anyway, it's a practical and necessary condition for any other pleasures which might follow."

"Mere presence isn't pleasure," he responded.

"You take pleasure in my company," Rachel said bravely, shutting her eyes against the blow that was about to come.

"Not necessarily. It's conditional on what we're doing."

Bastard.

"So if you have some particular pleasure in mind," he went on, "and always supposing that neither of us have anything more important to be doing, I suggest you let me know. In detail."

"And if it's my pleasure not to see you again?"

"Then you just phone and tell me that. I will make sure that that's what happens." Was there a small glimmer of light there, that he was still interested enough not to take her up on her threat and put it in the theoretical future—a phone call she had to make? Rachel was prepared to dig deep for very little consolation in this miserable dialogue.

"What about the loss of your resource?"

"I'd have to manage without it." She was pushing her luck. Nothing was going to be given away here.

"So I send in a list of my requests, is that it?" she enquired briskly.

"That's right. Look forward to hearing from you."

Rachel put the receiver down before he could. All she had achieved was an invitation to make a dirty phone call, to indicate her sexual requirements, once again to *say* what she wanted. Sexually. There was really no room now for any illusions about Joshua. But he did say it like it was and she still couldn't help but appreciate that, if a little grimly. He could take her or leave her, she remained a one-night stand regardless of the length of time they had been going on, but he was not averse to a bit of sexual input from her side—subject to contract of course. She had not been invited to suggest a long sensual meal at her favourite restaurant, or a weekend by a log fire somewhere remote; she was to submit her sexual requirements: do this to me or that, I want . . . What did she want? Was there anything—specific as he said—left to do? That she particularly wanted to do? It was probably a failure of imagination on her part but . . . She did begin to get intrigued by the idea of summoning him, of offering him something that excited him and made him respond. She began to like the idea of getting a response from him and of making real the subterranean power she felt she had in the relationship. Well, if he wanted fantasies he could have them—but on paper where she could construct them without interruption. She would write him a letter stating her requirements and he would get cold manipulation dressed up as desire.

Rachel took a notepad from her desk and settled herself on the sofa, using her knees to rest the paper on. She felt clinical. This was a project, a problem to be solved; she always enjoyed crosswords and the like, and started to relish this enterprise. Various situations had to be presented and organized in a way that elicited the correct response, it was a matter of recognizing the necessary components and then packaging them appropriately. But what about the tone, the context? Atmosphere was important, and this, after all, was a chance to play out sado-masochism without the paradox of the willing victim. A rape. That was it, she would invite him to a rape. Let him steal what

he had been getting for nothing for the past three years. She
started to write.

I had this dream recently. Listen. It was a Saturday and Carrie was with Michael for the weekend. [Practical instructions
as to when and where would have to be incorporated if they
were to play this out.] I spent most of the day pottering about
the flat, tidying up a little, reading, phoning friends. [Don't
skimp on domestic detail, it's important, this is a picture of a
woman happily alone.] In the evening I read for a while and
started to watch a movie on TV—it wasn't very good so I
switched it off halfway through and ran a bath, hot and very
scented, then lay in it for a long time with my eyes shut and
touched myself a little, stroked my clitoris slowly, imagining
someone there doing it for me. A woman, perhaps, who
sucked my nipples as she touched me. Nothing really frantic,
just quiet and private and peaceful. [Oh good, that's good,
sexy but calm. Maybe there's a career for you in soft porn,
Rachel.] I got out of the bath, dried myself and switched off all
the lights, then got into bed naked [naturally] and still warm,
smelling good. I felt good too as I stroked my skin, thighs and
arse, silky from the bath oil. I fell asleep with my hand between my legs. [Right that's enough, the scene's set.]
    Suddenly I woke feeling cold. The cover had been pulled
back. I was laying curled up on my side with my back to the
door and when I turned to pull the cover over me there was
the figure of a man standing in the doorway in the dark.
[Now, get on with it.] He held a leather strap in one hand and
stood for a moment watching. [How the hell did he get in?
This is clumsy, but I'll have to make the arrangements clear.]
I suppose he must have found the key I keep under the mat
for emergencies. [Well never mind. Onwards.] I was—what?
—very scared, very angry. I demanded to know what the hell
he was doing in my flat, told him to get out. [Yes, reported
speech is good, it leaves more room for imagination.] He was
quite unmoved by both my anger and my fear and told me
calmly to be quiet, that he was going to beat me and that if I
didn't cooperate he would tie me down. [Give him some rope
to play with.] He said he was going to hurt me and would

enjoy hearing me cry out with each stroke of the strap and that by the time he had finished doing what he planned to do I would be begging for more. I said the hell I would, that it didn't matter what he did I wouldn't respond. [It was an interesting challenge for both of us.] He ignored me, telling me to get out of bed and bend over. For a while I refused to move and his voice got harsher, more commanding. It is the tone of his voice that made me comply in the end more than the threat of violence; he sounded so confident that it dissolved any choice I may have had. He beat me with the strap, hard, many times. At first the pain was sharp and sudden, then there was a change and I was in a place where pain was the condition of existence and had no more meaning as *pain*. When he stopped I was weeping with humiliation and begging him for something—I didn't even know what, just repeated "please" over and over. [Who is this woman? I don't like her, why doesn't she fight him?] Then he came into me, into my arse. All the time he talked, told me what he was doing. He moved further and further inside me and it hurt terribly. It also felt incredibly good. I wanted him everywhere, didn't want to want him, but did. And I came profusely, protractedly. [Of course!] He got everything he wanted, heard everything he wanted to hear, did it all. And I groaned and came and begged for more. [I've had enough of this.]

Weird dream, huh? For a rational, thinking woman like me?

She read it over but didn't sign it, then addressed an envelope and put the letter inside. A present for you Joshua, she thought as she slipped it into her bag, a small gift from me to you. There was a little time before she had to pick Carrie up from school but she put her coat on and drove in that direction until she saw a postbox. As she slipped the letter through the slot she noticed the police station a few yards away, and instead of getting back into the car found herself walking towards it. Up the stone steps and through the glass doors into a lobby with a wooden counter running along the far end. The place was empty and she stood looking at the notices on the board. A child was missing; a man wanted for a robbery at a sub-post office whose description

fitted almost anyone who was black; the police wanted neighbours to watch out for one another; there was to be an open day,
everyone was welcome to come and see their local station and
meet their police.

"Can I help you?"

Rachel spun round to see a constable standing behind the
counter, smiling affably. He was a young man and seemed not
yet to have grown into his uniform; his face had a look of
guarded welcome, an expression that she felt had come with his
course on policemanship: how to look at the public before you
had ascertained the nature of their enquiry. She looked at him
for a moment without a thought in her head and wondered
what it was she was there for.

"Yes, madam?" he asked again.

She had to say something.

"I . . ." she started, blankly. "I want to report . . . there
seems to be someone watching my house." It spilled out suddenly. She was amazed, as she heard herself saying, "There's an
alleyway at the back of my house. It goes up to my garden wall,
then stops. There's been a man there, late at night, sometimes.
He stands looking at the house. Only at weekends, Friday and
Saturday, late at night, around midnight. I'm sorry, I don't want
to make a thing of it, but it's a bit worrying. He's been there for
the last three weekends."

The constable pulled a sheet of paper from under the counter
and took a pen from his jacket.

"Does he do anything? Have you challenged him?" His face
had settled into a look of one who was without opinions, an
information gatherer. But he spoke gently.

"No. He doesn't do anything. He doesn't expose himself or
anything. He just stands looking up. I haven't spoken to him. I
see him through the curtain as I'm going to bed. I don't think he
knows I've seen him."

"Let me take some details," the policeman said, settling over
the counter, his pen poised.

She gave him her address and a description of the man: about
six foot, grey hair, unshaven, quite big. Well dressed, not a wino
or a vagrant, rather respectable looking actually.

"Can you do anything?" she asked anxiously: the image of the man who stared up at her window late at night was clear in her head. Her sense of threat now quite strong. "It makes me very nervous. I live alone, you see, with my small daughter—though she's usually away at weekends."

"Is there access to your flat from the back of the house?"

"Yes. It's on the first floor, but there are steps leading up from the garden to the back door into my bathroom. It's locked but the top half is glass. I don't suppose it would be hard to break in."

"What about the front of the house?" the young man asked.

"That's secure. There's a good lock on the front door and the entrance to my flat has a Yale. But at the back I don't know. There are often parties, music, at weekends, I doubt that any-one would notice if someone broke the glass. Maybe it's noth-ing, just a harmless weirdo, perhaps I should ignore it."

"You were right to report it," the constable reassured her. "We don't want people hanging around like that. I'll write up a report and we'll have a couple of constables pass by on their beat at the weekend, just to keep an eye on things. Let us know if you see him again, Mrs Kee, and don't worry, the man proba-bly isn't dangerous, they usually aren't, but even so he can't go around frightening people."

Rachel felt much calmer as she left the station and drove to Carrie's school, sensing vaguely that something had been dealt with, a task that had been lying around was finally done. By the time she reached the school gates the entire episode had gone completely from her mind and she smiled sociably at the moth-ers of Carrie's classmates as they made arrangements with each other for their children to visit.

"Rachel, is Carrie free on Thursday this week?" Sandy's mum asked as she came through the gate.

"That's tomorrow, isn't it? Wait, let me see." Rachel rum-maged in her bag. "I only keep a diary for Carrie's social life, I can't keep up with it." They both laughed. "Yes, tomorrow's fine. I'll pick her up from you around six. Lovely."

Carrie wandered out into the playground looking, as always, much older than Rachel imagined. A solid, very real little girl after a hard day at school, trailing a plastic bag along the tarmac, chatting to her best friend, Sandy. One sock sagged movingly

around her ankle, the lace of the other shoe dragged. As she
bent to tie it Carrie glanced up and saw Rachel, gave her a
friendly smile and then continued her conversation with Sandy
as they both ambled towards the gate. Rachel loved these op-
portunities to watch Carrie from a distance and to be reminded
that her daughter had a separate, private existence. What went
on at school and in conversation with her friends was Carrie's
own world, barely glimpsed at by Rachel. She liked Carrie's
casual acknowledging smile to her and unhurried pace; they
had both spent the day going about their business and over tea
would talk and share whatever they chose with each other.

In the evening Becky phoned.

"How are you? I'm sorry I haven't been in touch since you got
back, I've been having a terrible time. Are you all right?" she
asked, concerned.

"Yes, I'm absolutely fine; all over. What's been happening
with you?"

"William," Becky groaned. "It all came to a head while you
were away. He confessed. About the affair he's been having. He
had to decide what to do."

"What?"

"I know. I had to decide too. All hell broke loose and I wept
and screamed. Typical wife. We've been fighting and crying for
days. When it came to it, Rachel, I couldn't face losing him and I
can't cope with the idea of being on my own. I ought to tell him
to piss off, I'm sure I should, but when it came to it I couldn't.
And I don't think he is really committed to this other woman.
Not particularly. Anyway, we decided to try and keep it going.
I've been asked to do some research for a tele-documentary—it
means six weeks floating about Europe. So I'm going to do it and
then he'll have time to sort it all out."

Rachel listened quietly and tried not to see the images of
Becky's future that kept flashing into her mind. Why should it
be worse to go on living with William than to be alone when she
didn't want to be or to start the whole business again with
someone else?

"It won't be the same between us obviously," Becky continued, "but nothing would be the same anyway. I think this is the

way marriages grow up; you have to make a commitment whatever."

"I'm sure you're right," Rachel agreed hurriedly. "It sounds
like you're doing the right thing. It's what you want, isn't it?"

"Yes, it must be," Becky said doubtfully. "We've decided to
make a baby as soon as I'm back in London. It'll be too late soon,
and anyway . . ." she trailed off.

And then another one, Rachel thought, next time, and had
William made a commitment whatever, I wonder? Oh well.

"How exciting," she said aloud. "Babies, travel. When are you
off?"

"In a week. Very soon. What about you, what's going on with
you? Is your bloke still around?"

"No, that's all over," Rachel said, noticing the leaves on the
tree outside the window were just beginning to turn; autumn
was finally here.

"Oh dear, was it my fault—that phone call?" Becky asked
anxiously.

"No, absolutely not. The thing was over anyway, petering
out. It just finished. I don't mind, it had come to its conclusion."

"Probably just as well as long as you don't feel bad about it."

"Not at all. You know me, I don't stay with things for long. I'll
miss you."

"Me too, but I'll write."

"Yes, do. Look, take care and luck and all that. Love you."

"Me too," sniffed Becky.

Rachel put the phone down feeling that Europe and Becky
making babies to keep things together was pretty remote, but
that if anyone could do it Becky could. She hoped so, anyway.

She dropped Carrie off at school the next morning and went
straight home. The phone began to ring as she turned the key in
the lock. It was Joshua.

"Thank you for your lovely letter."

Rachel smiled. You see, I *can* make you jump, so long as you
don't hear the sound of my fingers snapping. "My pleasure,
although I'm not sure 'lovely' is the adjective I'd have used."

"Leave the key under the doormat on Saturday night, then
go to bed early, before twelve."

Rachel smiled again. Through hoops.

"All right. By the way," she added, before he could put the phone down, "How was Scotland?"

Joshua chuckled.

"Exhausting! The kids ran me ragged. They must have raced up every mountain in Inverness with me panting along behind. I'm too old for that sort of thing. I was in bed by eight o'clock every night. Next time I take them away we go to Butlins, then I can just lie in bed all day and read." Then Joshua the Family Man switched off and the amusement left his voice. "Don't forget the key," he said, before he put the phone down.

Rachel blinked at the sound of the dialling tone buzzing in her ear. The tree outside had really turned, all the leaves were tinged now with a deep red so that the overall effect was almost of shot silk. It was happening so fast. She put the phone back on the hook and wondered what to give Carrie for supper that evening. There was some shopping to do and then the lessons to prepare for this afternoon and tomorrow. She hoped there would be a decent movie on the television tonight. She fancied an evening in front of the telly.

Michael picked Carrie up around midday on Saturday, and after she had waved them goodbye Rachel ran a bath, soaked in it for half an hour, washed her hair, then got out and shaved her legs. When she was dressed she sat for a moment on the bath-room stool thinking she really ought to go to the shops and get some food in for the rest of the weekend. She got up and un-locked the back door. Outside, the wooden steps down to the garden were covered in a film of white syringa petals from the tree next door. She kicked them into the semblance of a pile and picked up a trowel that was lying on the top step. Danger-ous that, someone might trip over it, she thought, as she smashed the glass in the top half of the door with the trowel's handle, stepped over the debris on the mat and shut but did not lock what remained of the door behind her, leaving the key sticking in the lock inside. She went off shopping, then pottered about the flat, cleaning and tidying for a while.

Saturday night television presupposed that everyone was out, as far as she could see from the programme guide. She turned the switch and sat watching, only just aware of what she was seeing until a half-hour variety show came on. It was compered by a popular comedian who was immensely fat and unprepossessing and made much of it; all his jokes, visual and verbal, were about fat, ugly people, mostly women, wives, mothers-in-law, fiancées, and he told them not with the usual spitting hatred but almost despairingly, as if he were purging himself. Rachel's attention was caught not by the content but the manner of the jokes, the evident necessity; they streamed out, these tales of ageing flesh and loathsome kin. And then, unbelievably, a chorus line of very fat, elderly ladies came on screen, arms on each other's shoulders, kicking their legs as high as they could manage, shaking mounds of slack flesh, naked thighs and upper arms dimpled and quivering with energy and movement as they danced an inefficient but good-humoured parody of Parisian Bluebell girls, grinning hugely and enjoying every second. The audience screamed with laughter as they watched the thick waists sway in spangled leotards and gigantic bottoms in frilly skating skirts wobble and heave. It ought to have been a disgrace, this parade of what is normally hidden from view for fear of contempt and disgust, but it wasn't somehow. It *was* outrageous but it seemed to Rachel finally to be a celebration. When they had finished and puffed and panted their way off camera the fat comedian did a sketch with a dwarf, the joke being that the fat man couldn't see the midget at all on account of his huge belly. Finally everyone was on screen, fat comedian, dwarf and wobbly chorus line and they all linked arms, kicked their legs and sang "When You're Smiling" along with the audience. Rachel sat with her mouth open, paralysed between laughter and tears. There were moments when she felt that the human race would be forgiven just because it *was* human. The news came on next and she snapped off the television.

Rachel was in bed by eleven-thirty, having put the key under the front doormat and turned off all the lights. She lay curled up in bed in the dark, with a small knot of excitement somewhere deep in her abdomen, but physically she felt exhausted, heavy with the need to sleep. She drifted into half-sleep like someone waiting for an alarm they knew would be going off soon. Her eyes stayed shut as she heard the front door click quietly and then the soft tread of careful footsteps on the stairs. She lay immobile, wanting to be asleep, not wanting the steps to reach her bedroom door, feeling that it was possible by doing nothing to stop the seconds that brought the event closer, to freeze time, to sleep for a hundred years, inhabit Never-Never land, to lie forever in a glass casket with a piece of poisoned apple stuck in her throat. The footsteps stopped and she heard the sound of breathing by the bed. She jerked into a sitting position. Joshua stood watching her, a strap and rope in one hand.

"Don't!" she said terrified, meaning it. Almost completely meaning it. "Don't."

"Be quiet," Joshua said coldly. "Be quiet and do as you are told."

She sat on the bed naked, tense as a rabbit, as Joshua began to stroke between her legs until she was wet.

"Now," he said, "what do you want? Tell me what you want?"

"Please," she whispered, "don't."

She meant don't do this, don't make me want, don't make me say, above all don't make me say.

"Say it" he ordered, still working on her.

"Please fuck me," she said.

He began to fuck her.

"I am fucking you," he whispered in her ear. "What do you want? Say it."

"I don't know," she whimpered.

"Yes, you do. Say it, you dirty little bitch."

"Beat me," she tried, "tie me and beat me, please."

That was enough, surely that was enough? He took the rope and tied her hands behind her back and had her lie on her stomach on the bed. He beat her hard with exact rhythmic strokes and then as she wept in pain and confusion he buggered her.

"What do you want?" he demanded as he felt her coming. "What?"

"Please . . ." she begged, "Please, please . . ."

"What?" he barked, pushing her beyond pain and orgasm with his insistence.

"Please . . . love me. Please love me. I want you to love me," she sobbed.

Joshua let out a single triumphant laugh as he tightened his grip around her and juddered into orgasm. She sobbed helplessly beneath him but was also aware of footsteps on the wooden stairs beyond the bedroom window.

"Bastard," she choked. "You bastard! Damn you, you bastard!"

"Mrs Kee, are you all right?"

ABOUT THE AUTHOR

Jenny Diski was born in London, attended University College, London, and then did two years toward an advanced degree but dropped it and wrote *Nothing Natural* instead. Ms. Diski lives in London and this is her first novel.